GOING HOME

CHARLES DEMARIS

1

Nathan Callahan hated funerals. He understood the necessity, that people needed the closure provided by public grieving, but he still was not fond of the whole charade. He was no stranger to funerals and no stranger to grief, but he thought the whole thing to be contrived and somewhat hypocritical. Yet for all that, he found himself sitting through one, and even struggling to hold back tears. He was doing better than Myrtle Callahan, his grandmother, who was sitting there next to him sobbing quietly. His grandfather's death had come as no surprise, the inevitable end of a two year battle with cancer.

Patrick Callahan had been a second father to Nathan since his own parents' tragic death in an automobile accident fourteen years earlier. Nathan heard the minister's voice drone on, but he was paying little attention. He knew by heart most of what he was saying, the same sort of drivel you heard at all funerals, words meant to provide comfort and little else. He knew the words were true in this case. Grandpa had served God faithfully his entire life, had been an example of integrity that anyone would do well to live up to. The last funeral he had attended was pretty much the same, the same scripture readings, the same songs, and most of the same sentiments. He had only been fourteen then, and that experience was much harder to take.

He could remember the day too well, though it was half his life ago. His parents had gone out to celebrate their anniversary and he had the house to himself. He had gone to bed, only to wake up at 2:00 am to the doorbell. He remembered the hangdog look on the police officer's face and the catch in his voice as he told Nathan that his parents had been killed by a drunk driver on the way home.

Fourteen years had passed since that night and the grief was still there just under the surface. The initial sadness had become manageable, and was eventually replaced by a profound regret. He loved his parents and he was a mostly obedient son, but he had never really told them how he felt about them, and now the chance was gone. The next few days were a blur, all the relatives arriving, all the hugs, the funeral in another church with another minister saying the same kinds of things in the same tone of voice, and then the overheard snippets of conversation, relatives discussing his fate as if he had no say in it. It was decided that he would move in with his grandparents, in Piscataway.

New Jersey? You have got to be kidding me, he had thought at the time. It was a hard adjustment at first, but he soon settled in. His grandparents did everything to make him feel at home, including giving him the space he needed. He had always been close to his grandparents, but now their bond was formed by a shared grief.

High school flew by. He was an inquisitive introvert, which made him popular with his teachers and kept his social circle small, a group of like minded nerds who spent all their time studying, playing video games, and fantasizing about girls, while having no clue how to actually approach one.

After graduating with honors, Nathan had a pick of college offers, settling on MIT, where he graduated near the top of his class four years later with a degree in software development. He had several job offers and accepted a position with an up and coming game developer in San Jose. That was six very good years ago. Tempest Games was now one of the top game developers in the country and Nathan had risen with them. He loved his work and he got paid quite well. At only 28, his life appeared to be on track.

Grandpa recognized early on that Nathan was not like him. Patrick had been an All American linebacker at Rutgers and then a mechanic. He was most at home working with his hands, the complete opposite of his grandson. To his credit, he saw where Nathan's talents lay and he encouraged him at every turn.

Myrtle Callahan was in a similar reflective mood, but she was paying better attention than her grandson. This was her husband after all, and she at least owed it to him to pay attention to what was being said about him, though she knew him far better than the minister did. The eulogy was true and it gave the people sitting there a picture of an honest and generous man who was now in a better place. Myrtle knew him far better than that. She remembered his faults, but also how he never wavered no matter the circumstances. He was her unshakeable rock.

He was an easy man to fall for, the very image of the man's man, tall and athletic, dark wavy hair, and eyes of a deep blue that she could get lost in. He was a kind man too, when he wasn't on the football field terrorizing opposing quarterbacks. She fell for him long before he even noticed her, but she waited for him to make the first move. That move finally came and everything moved fast after that, leading to their wedding a week after graduation.

That was in 1958. It seemed so long ago and at the same time it seemed like it was only yesterday. Patrick was by her side through the pain of two miscarriages and then the birth of their sons, Martin and Sean. Things were rough at first when he quit his corporate job to become a mechanic. He opened his own shop that eventually expanded to the six locations operating in New York and New Jersey. Then there was Martin's death 14 years ago. His death shook her to her core, but Patrick was her rock, and they made it through that trying time together. Having Nathan move in then helped more than they realized.

Now she had done it. She'd let her mind wander and the minister was wrapping up his remarks. There would be a hymn sung, then the procession to the cemetery, then the interminable reception afterwards, where she would have to be the dutiful widow and subject herself to all the well wishers who would smother her with sympathy and condolences, while all she really wanted to do was be alone to grieve in peace.

The drive to Resurrection Cemetery was made in companionable silence, passing by the golf course that Patrick had played every weekend for time immemorial. Nathan remembered accompanying Grandpa on a few of those occasions, and he remembered how he had tried unsuccessfully to get Nathan to share his passion for the game.

"He would love to be there today," mumbled Nathan.

"You say something, honey?"replied Myrtle

"The golf course we just passed. Perfect weather for it today. I'm sure he'd be there under different circumstances."

"Yes, you got that right. There were few things he enjoyed more on a day like this. He did try to teach you to play, didn't he?"

"Yeah, it didn't take. I wouldn't mind it now, if it meant spending another day with him."

When they arrived at the cemetery, Nathan helped his grandmother to her chair and joined the other pallbearers. He grabbed the handle and began to walk, his knees feeling weak and a solitary tear coursing down his cheek. His ears picked up the tat tat tat of a woodpecker not far off, and a robin in a nearby tree singing away without a care in the world. "Life goes on," he thought to himself. We are grieving here, but outside of our little bubble, the world just keeps on going.

He released his hold on the handle when they had set the casket down and took his place next to his grandma for the brief graveside service. By the time he was aware that the minister was speaking, he was done speaking, and all Nathan could think was that perhaps the Lord should forego the mansion and set Grandpa up with a small fishing cabin next to a lake and a golf course.

Nathan was taking his time on the drive back to the house, partly out of sensitivity to his grandma and partly due to an extreme reluc-

tance to deal with the crowd that would be gathered there. He knew
they meant well, but they could be smothering at times. The liability
of being an introvert in an Irish family, he thought.

"I can't keep it."

"What was that, Grandma?"

"I don't think I can stay in that house now. Too many memories,
and it's a bit big for just one old lady like me, and with you working
all the way out there in California..."

"What you going to do with the house?"

"Well, I figure I'll just sell the house and most of the furniture,
unless there's anything you want, and find a small place somewhere,
or maybe that assisted living place up in Raritan where my friend
Alice moved into. She's told me all sorts of good things about it."

"You can't move into a nursing home. You're still in decent health,
plus, you're not *that* old yet."

"It's an assisted living facility, not a nursing home. There is a
difference, and I'm 80 years old, just in case you forgot."

"Come on, Grandma. You don't look a day over 60."

"Flatter me all you want, Nate, but I'm selling the house, and
that's that."

"But you can't go to a home. Those places are depressing."

Five minutes later they turned onto Glenwood Dr and as Nathan
pulled into the driveway he said, "Ok, we're here. Let's head on in and
face the horde."

"Be nice, Nate, they're family."

It was this part of funerals that Nathan disliked more than the
service. He knew people meant well, but he felt that everyone was
reading from a script and never came off as completely genuine.

Then there were those who never struck a false chord, people like
his Aunt Lilian, who simply walked up to him and said, "You look like
you'd rather be anyplace else but here."

"You know I've never been one for parties."

"I wouldn't call this a party, Nate."

"You sure? The way the beer is disappearing..."

"Speaking of beer, you want one?"

"Nah, never was much for that stuff. Any Coke in the fridge?"

"I'll see. By the way, I heard your grandma talking about selling this place. Is she going to find an apartment or something?"

"She talked about some home up in Raritan."

"That assisted living facility up there? She has a friend who moved in there."

"Yeah, that's the place. I don't think she should do it. Those homes are for old people on their last legs. She still gets around pretty good, and she has enough family and friends around to check in on her."

"You ever thought she doesn't want to live alone?"

"You have a point. Never thought about that."

"Of course you wouldn't. You've always been a bit of a loner."

"You know, it's not so bad most of the time."

"Come on, Nate. You must have thought about finding someone."

"I think I'm going to scare up something to drink."

"Ok...well, I'll catch you later."

Nathan sipped his Coke and observed the room. His Aunt Lilian was deep in conversation with his grandmother and he could hear none of what was being said. His Uncle Sean was sitting on the end of the couch staring into his empty cup like he expected it to magically fill up again, which was the last thing he needed at this point. His cousin Margaret was sitting on the other end of the couch sipping a Sprite and texting away with...his cousin Jude who couldn't have been more than 15 feet away sitting in an armchair that afforded him an unobstructed view of the kitchen, which still held an ample amount of food. He was at that age where he was just starting to feel shame at overly obvious displays of gluttony, and he was wondering how many more times he could go back for another plate while keeping his dignity intact. Nathan was thinking of heading for another plate, and also contemplating how two people in the same room would be texting one another. Didn't people talk anymore?

Eventually, the guests made their excuses and departed, leaving Nathan, Lilian, Sean, and Myrtle sitting in a suddenly quiet living room. Lilian broke the silence.

"So, Myrtle, you're thinking of selling this place?"

"I think so. It's a bit too much house for an old lady like me."

"But you have so many memories here."

"No, the memories are here," she said as she pointed to her heart, "This is just a house now. Family with kids could use a house like this."

"So where will you go?" Sean asked.

"My friend Alice is staying up in Raritan. There's a nice assisted living facility up there, and they have all kinds of activities."

"Come on, Mom. We're not a family that dumps people in nursing homes."

"That's what I told her," said Nathan

"Guys," Myrtle said, "It's not a nursing home. It's an assisted living facility."

"Same difference," said Sean.

"There are decent apartments you could get, and there are people who can check in on you," Nathan replied.

Lilian said, "You guys ever think that maybe she doesn't want to live alone?"

"Nathan seems to enjoy it just fine," Sean said.

"I've never lived alone," Myrtle said softly, wiping a tear from her eye, "but I don't think I can stay here. Oh...I don't know..."

"You think we have room?" Lilian asked.

"With Chris moving back in," Sean replied, "Where would she sleep, the couch?"

"Well, there's no other family close. Maybe the place in Raritan isn't such a bad idea."

Nathan looked at his grandma, saw another tear run down her cheek, and his heart broke for her. He missed his grandpa, but Grandma had been married to him for almost 60 years. He had no idea how she must be feeling. An idea came to mind and he brushed it aside, but it only came back. He pondered for a moment and then said, "I've got plenty of space."

"What was that, Nate?" Sean said.

"I have plenty of space. I have a large apartment."

"But you're 2000 miles away."

"Actually, closer to 3000, but who's counting?"

"You think she should pack up and move all the way out to California?"

"You have any better ideas?"

There was an awkward silence for a moment until Lilian spoke up. "That's not a bad idea actually. She'd be staying with family."

"I'm right here guys," Myrtle said, "you're talking about me like I'm in the other room."

Nobody had a response to that and finally Myrtle spoke up again.

"That makes sense, but I'd hate to impose."

"It's hardly imposing if he offered," said Lilian.

"You got a nice church out there?"

"Sure, there are a few close to my place."

"Well...I suppose I can. I've never been out west. Lilian, dear, you think you can sell the house for me, and any furniture you don't want? I only want my bedroom stuff."

"Sure, I'll call my friend Susan. She's a realtor."

Nathan pulled out his phone and opened an app and Lilian asked him, "What are you doing on your phone? We're still talking."

"My return flight is tomorrow. How long will it take a mover to take her bedroom furniture out there? Four or five days at least. I'm going to have to cancel my flight and book us on a later one so we don't get there before her bed does. I don't have any extra beds. And I need to email my boss to let him know I'm going to be back a couple days later."

"Good thinking. Maybe you can find a moving truck while you're at it."

"Uh...guys," Myrtle interjected, "There's only one problem. Doctor says flying might not be such a good idea."

2

———

Two days later, Sean and Myrtle Callahan sat on the front porch, sipping coffee and talking. Sean had just finished packing her boxes and tearing down her bedroom furniture, and now they were waiting for Nathan to return with the rental car and trailer.

"Man, I miss Dad," Sean said wistfully.

Myrtle, lost in her own reflections, took a moment to reply, "Yeah, Lord knows how much I do."

"You know where he'd be on a day like this. Not here talking to us on the porch. He'd either have a golf club or a fishing pole in his hand right about now."

"Or some days both. You remember that day when you and Martin were still small. He and...what was that fellow's name who worked with him back then...Joe or John...hell, I can't remember. He moved to South Carolina a couple years later when his wife left him and...where was I. Oh, Joe Saunders, that was his name. Anyway, they had an early morning tee time, played so poorly they decided to stop and go fishing that afternoon and the fish weren't cooperating either. He came home thoroughly grumpy, mad at the golf clubs and blaming the fish for not biting."

"Mom, I think I was only about five at the time, so my recollection might be a bit hazy, but you've told the story so many times I could never forget it."

"Hmm, I might have told that one a couple times. Nathan seems to be taking a while."

"He needs to pick up a trailer after he gets the car. I think he was going to get the trailer from that U-Haul over on Stelton Rd."

"The one down from the Home Depot, at that storage lot or something?"

"Yeah, that's the one. Pretty big move, going all the way out there. If it weren't for Chris moving back in…"

"Yeah, that's why I never even thought of asking you. How many times does this make it now?"

"Third time. He was shacking up with some girl this time. Got kicked out."

"That's what he gets. All I hear about is young people shacking up. Any of them ever get married first?"

"Times are different, Mom."

"I suppose so, but that doesn't mean I have to like it. Sin is still sin, even if that word is out of style."

"Well, don't talk like that in front of Chris. He's touchy enough as it is."

"You guys are too soft on him. Boy needs to grow up. Anyway, enough about him. I hope Nathan gets here soon."

"You that anxious to get started?"

"I don't know. Thinking about it has helped. It's kind of exciting in a way, like going on an adventure."

"Some adventure it will be, cooped up in a car with a twenty something geek. What are you going to talk about all the way out there?"

Just then a Chevy Tahoe towing a 12' trailer backed into the driveway. Nathan put the vehicle in park, hopped out, and opened the trailer.

"You think you got a big enough vehicle? It's just you and Mom. Could have gotten something a little easier on gas."

"Only thing that had a hitch," Nathan said, pointing to the trailer as if it wasn't obvious enough already, "Smallest trailer I could get too. Doubt her stuff with take up all that space."

For the next few minutes Nathan and Sean loaded Myrtle's belongings in the trailer and wrapped everything in furniture blankets. Nathan secured everything, closed the trailer, and announced that all was ready.

Then a car approached rapidly and came to a quick stop on the street. Lilian jumped out of the car and ran up the driveway.

"You are not leaving without a proper goodbye, "she said breathlessly while handing Myrtle a small book, "Plus, you forgot this at church. You might want it. Oh, and Nate, you left this on my printer," handing Nathan a couple folded sheets of paper.

"Oh, thanks, wouldn't want to forget that," Nathan replied.

"No problem, you take care of her" and to Myrtle "I'll list the house and we'll give you a call when we have an offer. You take care. Love you."

"You take care too, and keep an eye on my son. Don't let him get out of line."

"You know I would never think of doing that," replied Sean. "Love you, Mom." He gave her a quick kiss and helped her into the passenger seat.

"Oh Lord, this is not going to be easy climbing in and out of this thing. Well, Nate, let's be off then."

Nathan put the Tahoe in gear and pulled out, glancing back once more at his aunt and uncle waving goodbye, and as he looked back he noticed a tear in his grandmother's eye.

"You ok, Grandma?"

"I'm fine."

"You sure."

"We lived in this house for almost thirty years. Lot of memories, is all. I'm ok."

"What's with the little book?"

"It's a journal. I write in it sometimes."

"What kind of things do you write in there?"

"Private things. You should try it. It's a wonderful way to sort out your thoughts and deal with things."

"Music does that for me."

They filled the gas tank before getting on I-287 and Nathan took that to I-78 and headed west. When they reached the thinner traffic farther from the city, Nathan set the cruise control and turned on the radio.

"It's kind of quiet in here, you want some music or something?" Nathan asked.

"Sure, as long as it's not that noise most people your age listen to."

"So what do you want to listen to?"

"Just pick something good."

"There's plenty good to pick from. This vehicle has satellite."

He scanned through the categories, landed at channel 32, and decided they could both find that agreeable since the music was mostly 60s and 70s tunes. He didn't think his grandmother was paying much attention to the music, other than sitting there staring out the window lost in thought, but when *Take the Long Way Home* came on the radio, she remarked, "That sounds like a good idea."

"What sounds like a good idea."

"What they're singing about."

"What who's singing...oh, the song on the radio. Of course it's a long way home, it's almost 3000 miles."

"No, taking the long way. There's so much to see between here and there, too much to just rush through."

"I do have to get back to work sometime."

"Look Nate, when you get to be my age, the only things you regret are not taking more time to stop and smell the roses. You go around hurrying from this important thing to that and then you realize you missed so much."

"I guess you have a point. What would you like to see on the way? I guess you've given it some thought."

"Well, to start with, maybe you should stop guessing so much and be sure of something. What would I like to see? For now, a restroom."

"Man, didn't you go before we left the house? We haven't even been gone that long."

"Wait until you hit 80 and we'll see how your bladder holds up."

"There's an exit up ahead for Bloomsbury. Looks like we can get off there."

He took the Bloomsbury exit and pulled into a TA truck stop, letting his grandmother off at the front door before parking the car. He found the place fascinating. He had no idea so many things were made for truckers. One thing caught his eye, a large cooler with a 12 volt plug, and he was buying it when his grandma came out of the restroom.

"For drinks and snacks," he said in reply to his grandmother's puzzled look. "We just plug it in and put it right behind the seats. No stopping every time we want a drink."

When they rejoined the highway, Myrtle blurted out, "Mt. Rushmore. I've always wanted to see Mt. Rushmore."

She then pulled out her journal and began to write. Nathan turned the radio up, took a sip of Coke, and thought about the route he would take that day. He would be on 78 for quite a while, all the way to Harrisburg before he would head south to pick up 68 down in Maryland, a bit farther going that way, but he didn't want to deal with the tolls on the Turnpike. Dad drove that way when they went to visit his grandparents years ago, and he remembered it being quite scenic.

Road trips with Dad. Now that brought back memories. Would his parents be proud of him? He thought they would. He had a good job with an up and coming company, and was one of the lead developers on one of the most successful video games released in the last decade. He was already making six figures and he wasn't even out of his 20s. Dad would probably still tease him about his lack of a dating life, if he were still around.

That was the only area of his life that wasn't successful, and probably the only area his dad wouldn't understand. Dad wasn't shy like he was. There had been the occasional dates, more casual than anything, but they were few and far between. He was painfully shy around women. Most women, even if interested, could only wait so long, so they ended up moving on to other guys, leaving Nathan beating himself up for being too slow.

Now he was afraid this scenario would be repeating itself again. Phoebe Imani started working at Tempest two years ago as an artist and Nathan was smitten from the first moment he saw her. He had never met a woman more beautiful yet unaware of her beauty. She had a smile to light up a room and a body like a gazelle, perfection in ebony. It wasn't her beauty that he found most attractive, though, but a grace and gentleness that he put down to coming from an immigrant family. She came from Tanzania with her parents at the age of two.

Myrtle chose the written form to sort out her thoughts and as the car was moving smoothly with the cruise control set, she took out her journal and wrote:

Why did I mention Mt. Rushmore? There are a dozen places out west I would love to visit on the way with no time to see them all. I would love to make this a long trip and see everything, at least the young woman inside of me wants that. That woman hasn't yet figured out that we're 80 years old. That's the thing with getting old. When you're young you think old age is something far away, something that you will eventually reach but not too soon. You think you have plenty of time, that life is long and that you have ample time to experience everything it has to offer. When you're 20 you look at 40 year olds and think them old, when you're 40 it's the 60 year olds who are getting up there, and when you're 80 you'd love to be as young as 40 again.

I look back and I've had a pretty good life for the most part, but it's been quick, way too quick. Where did it all go? Was it not only yesterday that I looked at that tall, handsome football player in my European History class and silently wished he would ask me out, only yesterday that he finally did? Was it not just the other day that we had our first date and we were both so nervous we hardly spoke to one another? It seems like no time has passed at all since that day I said yes to the most awkward proposal in the history of human romance, sitting in a boat under a blue sky with that evening's supper still flopping around.

Oh, Patrick, where did it all go? We had 58 years together and it was way too short. I know I said some harsh things to you at times and I could have been more forgiving, but you always were steady as a rock. Why did you have to go so soon? We were just really getting to know each other and I was just getting to fully appreciate the man you were and now you're gone. Why? Why did God, who is supposed to be loving and merciful, allow a good man like you to suffer so? And how did you go through it all without so much as one complaint? I could see the pain on your face, even though you tried to hide it from me. I knew what you were going through and I know now that you were trying to hide it because you wanted to spare me the pain of knowing how deep your pain was.

You would be proud of your grandson, but you already know what kind of boy he is. I'm going to live with him. I know it's sudden and all, but I couldn't bear to stay in our house without you there. It's not your home anymore. I figure you have a nicer home now and I so look forward to you showing me around when I get there. Who knows how long that will be? So you're up there no doubt sharing fishing stories with Peter and I'm sitting in a car somewhere in Pennsylvania with our grandson heading on one last adventure to live out my days in a place I've never been. It can't be any more traumatic than it was for him when he had to pack up and move in with us in a new place.

Yes, Nathan is a wonderful young man, but I do wonder about him. He does enjoy his work and he makes good money, really good money for someone his age, and he is always so kind and considerate, but he does seem so shy. Lilian asked him if he was seeing anyone and he changed the topic so fast your head would spin. I shouldn't have been listening in, but I couldn't help it. It might be a sore spot with him. We have a long drive ahead. Maybe there will be time to bring it up, but I must try not to wound him. You know how sensitive he can be.

Well Dear, I am glad you are free of pain now and I do so look forward to seeing you again. Why am I addressing him like this? It's not like he's here reading this, but it does take a load off in some way. Lord knows how much I miss that man and I'd give anything to have even one more day to tell him I love him again. I don't think I ever really let him know how much he meant to me. I just took it for granted what we had and now he's gone *and I still have so much to say to him, and we had so many things left to do together.*

If I keep going down this path, I'm going to start crying and Nate will ask me why, and I don't feel like talking right now.

She closed the journal and drifted off, smiling and thinking of her husband. Nathan noticed this and found himself smiling as well. He had no idea what she had been writing or why she was smiling, but it did him good to see it. Maybe there was something to her journaling. He might have to try it someday.

They were coming into Allentown, about an hour and a half from Harrisburg if all went well. Grandma would probably need to make a pit stop by then, so he searched in the GPS for gas stations near Harrisburg, found several truck stops listed near there, and selected one as a stop. He tried to lose himself in the music, but his mind kept going to his job and what to expect when he got back, and to a certain co worker. He though about his grandfather and wished he could ask his advice, but he knew what Grandpa would tell him, so he brushed that thought aside as well. Grandpa would tell him to just go for it, like he had done years ago. Good advice, but not easy, at least not for him. The ninety minutes went by fast as he pondered that advice, and wondered if he would ever be able to follow it.

3

As Nathan pulled out of the Flying J and headed south on I-81, his grandmother asked him, "How much farther are you planning on driving today?"

"Another eight hours, give or take, if we don't get held up by any road delays."

"So we'll be stopping by 8:00. Do we have a room yet? You haven't mentioned that detail."

"My friend Mark is expecting us. He has a couple extra bedrooms."

"Mark?"

"We went to grade school together, before I moved in with you and Grandpa. He has a house on the north side of Cincinnati. They don't have kids yet, so they have the extra space."

"So Mark's married."

"Yep, he married Evelyn. They've been dating since they were about 12 years old."

"How about you, Nate, is there a young lady I need to know about."

"I don't know."

"What do you mean you don't know. Either there is or there isn't."

"Well, I'm not sure."

"What do you mean you're not sure?"

"There's this girl at work. I'm interested, but you know how awkward I get around girls. I never know what to say."

"Tell me about her. Is she pretty?"

"Yeah, very, but it's more than that. It's the way she behaves, so respectful with everyone, please and thank you and sir and ma'am, all of that old fashioned stuff. But with her it doesn't seem old fashioned. She was born in another country, so that might explain it."

"What country is she from?"

"Tanzania. She came here with her parents when she was around two. It seems that people from there don't raise their kids the same. She just comes across as so proper and graceful and well mannered..."

"You're definitely interested. What are you going to do about it?"

"Yeah, I'm probably more than interested, and also frustrated. I hear other women talking about how some guy is coming on too fast and they don't like that, so I had this idea that I have to be the opposite, get to know someone really well and then see where it goes. Only problem is someone always beats me to the punch. So which way is it? Why do women complain about guys moving too fast, but they always end up with those guys? It's too confusing."

"Well, honey, let me let you in on a little secret. You're partly right and partly mistaken. As a woman, I might know a little thing or two. Pardon me for being a little crude, but we don't like the guy who is moving so fast because he just wants into your pants. You meet those kinds in the bars and clubs and he seems really interested and you can just tell the only thing he's thinking about is getting you home and into bed as fast as possible. We don't like that type, at least no respectable girl does, so when you hear your female friends complaining, that's the kind of guy they're complaining about. Let me tell you something else though. In my day, and it's probably not changed much since then, women are thinking long term. They aren't looking for the one night stand, at least not all of them, but a man they can think about going the distance with, and women have that ticking clock in the back of their minds. If a guy doesn't make a move in that direction fast enough, some other guy will. If you're interested in this girl, you have to throw your hat in the ring before some other young man does. Time's a wastin', dear."

"So I've been going about it all wrong?"

"What kind of results have you seen?"

"Uh..."

"Exactly. You're trying to get a hit without swinging the bat. Doesn't work that way. Anyway, what's the worst thing that can happen if you ask her out?"

"She'll say no?"

"Exactly, but how is that any different than where you are right now?"

"Yeah, good point. I just always figured a friendship would kind of grow to that point."

"You are one naive young man, let me tell you. When I met your grandfather, I knew right then and there this was the man I wanted. I thought he was interested in me, but he was a lot like you, shy to a fault. I waited for three months and he would never ask me out. Most girls would have moved on, and I had my chances. I had other suitors at that time, but I had my heart set on him."

"So what happened? I assume he eventually asked you out."

"I approached one of his teammates on the football team and told him I was interested. The word was passed and he asked me out a week later. Things moved rather fast after that."

"But I'm not even sure how to go about it, what to say or anything."

"Don't worry too much about that or how awkward you are. What matters is that you take the step. She might not be as patient as I was. You have to make the move."

"I guess you're right. I just wish it was easier. This radio station still good?"

"Sure, just don't change it as fast as you change the subject."

Myrtle opened her journal and began to write, and Nathan drove on, down 81, across 70 to 68, and up and down the picturesque mountains of Maryland and West Virginia. He found the miles going by rapidly as he contemplated what his grandmother had told him. Maybe she knew more about relationships than he did. Then again, most people did.

He thought he knew his grandma. He had lived with her for four years, but they had never really spent this much time in conversation. Of course, Grandpa was around then and he took a lot of time trying to teach Nathan how to play golf and fish, two hobbies that he never took an interest in.

His mind wandered back to his parents again. His dad was a good man, but when he thought back on his childhood, he realized how little he really knew his dad. Dad had worked a lot of hours and came home late often. When he was there, it was great, but he just wasn't there enough. He wasn't a bad father by any means. He was a good provider and he would manage to take some time off each year for them to do something as a family. They went to baseball games together, actually a lot of baseball games since Dad was a serious sports fan. Dad put the fan in fanatic. Nathan was only two years old when the Reds last won the World Series, but Dad told him so much about it that he almost felt like he had been there. Well, he had been there, since his parents had tickets for game 2 and couldn't find a babysitter.

He thought about Dad and Grandpa, how alike they were and how much he loved them both, and how he missed them both. He had never really told his dad what he meant to him. Being shy and an age where you didn't get overly mushy with your parents, a lot had remained unsaid. And his dad had been taken from him by a drunk driver. Now he was the age where he realized the importance of saying what needed to be said and the opportunity was gone. At least he had seen Grandpa's death coming and hadn't let the opportunity pass.

These thoughts and his grandmother's frantic writing took them almost to West Virginia, where they stopped at yet another truck stop and filled the gas tank, answered the call of nature, and then proceeded. The drive through West Virginia was breathtaking. It had been years since Nathan was on this highway, and that time he was 12 years old riding in the back seat while his father drove. He appreciated the scenery more now than he had then, and the road rolled on, mile after beautiful mile. Before he knew it they had passed Morgantown and he was taking I-79 north to I-70. He went past towns he vaguely remembered, regretting not paying more attention when he was younger. The miles and the hours rolled by in a blur, with his thoughts ranging from his parents and all he still wanted to tell them, to Phoebe and what he hoped he would be able to tell her, to his grandmother who was still sitting in the passenger seat writing her life story, or whatever it was she was so urgent to write down. He determined then not to make the same mistake that he had made with his parents.

"Grandma?"

"Hmm...you say something?"

"I love you...I appreciate everything you and Grandpa did for me. Just wanted you to know that."

"Well, that was certainly out of the blue," she thought to herself and out loud, "That's nice of you to say that. I love you too. Always have. You're a good grandson. But all grandmas think that of their grandsons."

"Maybe so. I couldn't have a better grandma though."

Myrtle contemplated what Nathan had just said, wondered what prompted him to come out with that all of a sudden, and figured that maybe it was a good sign. She looked over at him and once again he appeared to be in a different place, so deep in thought he was. "He really is a contemplative boy," she thought to herself. "Takes that after me, I guess."

Four hours later, four hours that seemed like about 20 minutes due to an unplanned nap that took her by surprise, Myrtle looked up to notice that the car was stopped in a parking space in front of Dick's Sporting Goods.

"Where are we?" She asked.

"We're in Fairfield, just a few minutes from Mark's house."

"That was fast. When I last looked up were barely in Ohio."

"Well, you were out like a light."

"I was just inspecting my eyelids for holes."

"Ha ha, I'll have to remember that one."

"Why are we stopped at this place?"

"We need to do some shopping."

"I can't think of anything I need from here."

"You need some new clothes."

"I have plenty of clothes packed. I can't think of anything I need."

"You need something to wear to this," Nathan said as he fished the folded up pieces of paper out of his pocket and handed them to her.

She unfolded the papers and saw two tickets for the Cincinnati Reds vs. the Chicago Cubs for the following afternoon. She just stared at them for a moment. She had grown up not far from here before she went away to college and had followed her beloved Reds all those years since, although from afar. She hadn't attended a game in Cincinnati in nearly 40 years. She had been trying to make sense of the route Nathan was driving, but hadn't wanted to say anything. She knew the most direct route would have been I-80 right out of New Jersey and straight across the country.

"We're going to the game?"

"Yes, we're going. Unless you're no longer a fan."

"Oh, you know better than that. Thank you Nathan. Really, thank you."

Myrtle picked out a couple shirts and a cap, and they proceeded to the home of Mark and Evelyn Rutherford.

"Let's just go on in for now and I'll come and get our bags later," said Nathan.

Nathan was reaching toward the doorbell when it was flung open and he was engulfed in a crushing bear hug. Mark was 6',4", weighed every big of 245, and all of it was solid. He had played football in high school and then again at the University of Cincinnati. He had hoped to play in the NFL, but a knee injury in his senior year put an end to that. Apparently he was still keeping in good shape, Nathan thought as he was trying to catch his breath.

"Good to see you buddy," said Mark as he mercifully pulled back. "Has it really been 14 years? And this must be the lovely lady you've told me so much about," as he greeted Myrtle with a courtly bow and a kiss on her hand.

"Why, aren't you the gallant one," exclaimed Myrtle. "Nathan has told me a lot about you as well, most of it good," she replied with a wink.

"Yeah, 14 years. Time flies, doesn't it?" Nathan replied.

"Will you people get in here and sit down before the food gets cold?" Came a voice from somewhere inside the house.

Mark said, "We might as well not keep her waiting. Evelyn's been slaving away over the stove all day."

They all made their way into the dining room and were seated. Evelyn had indeed laid out quite a spread. Nathan had not realized how hungry he was, since they had only snacked during the drive from New Jersey, and now the aroma wafting from the table had his mouth watering. On the table was a glazed ham, mashed potatoes, green beans, biscuits. corn on the cob, a bowl of mixed cut up fruit, and if Nathan's nose did not deceive him, something sweet was in the kitchen waiting to be brought out for dessert.

The guests being somewhat famished, conversation was at a minimum for the first few moments, other than "Could you please pass me more of those potatoes?" and "That ham is absolutely scrumptious," and "Could I interest you in another helping of these beans? They were just picked earlier this afternoon."

When they had eaten their fill and Evelyn had cleared the table, Mark said to Nathan, "Tempest Games, huh? That's quite a good gig. How'd you manage that one?"

"I went there straight out of college. They weren't quite as big then."

"Right place, right time, if you ask me. You came along and they release a couple blockbusters. What do you there anyway?"

"A bit of everything, but my specialty is the AI on single player games."

"So I have you to blame then? I haven't been able to get past the third level on Special Forces 2 for the last week. I'm getting my butt kicked."

"That's because it's a *tactical* shooter, Mark, not one of those twitchy run and gun things that other studios put out every year. The AI just has good tactical awareness and they're good shots. You have to outthink them."

"Yeah, whatever you say. You probably just made them hard to annoy people like me anyway."

Evelyn came back with dessert plates and a peach cobbler and while she was serving it out, Mark changed the topic.

"So, Nate, you seeing anyone?"

"Well...not really."

"What do you mean 'not really'? Either you are or you aren't."

"I've had a couple dates over the years, but nothing that worked out."

"Sometimes you can't just wait for it to work out. You have to go get it."

"That's easy for you to say. You never had trouble talking to girls."

"Well, you'll be 30 before you know it. It's about time you figured it out. It's not really that hard. You just have to have to say, 'What the heck' and go for it. Yeah, you'll get rejected a few times, but that's part of the game."

"I guess you know what you're talking about. Anyway, I'd better go bring in our bags. Dinner was excellent, by the way."

Nathan brought the bags in and Mark asked, "So you're taking your grandma to the game tomorrow?"

"Yep, 1:10 start time."

"Good. You guys can go to church with us, and I'll drop you at the ballpark, save you the parking. There's a movie out Evelyn's wanting to see and we can catch that at the Levee while you guys are at the game."

4

M ark dropped them off at the main entrance to Great American Ballpark, said he would pick them up at the same spot when the game was over, and left. Nathan wasn't much of a sports fan, but the look on his grandmother's face was almost magical. It was almost like 40 years had been erased. She was grinning from ear to ear, and if he wasn't mistaken she was almost skipping. At any regard, he was having a hard time keeping up with her heading to the gate. They bought a program, peanuts, hot dogs, and soft drinks, and went to their seats by the dugout.

When he bought the tickets, Nathan hadn't figured on the number of steps they had to walk down to the seats, and Myrtle began to lag behind as the steps took their toll on her knees.

"You know the last time I attended a Reds home game?" Myrtle asked as they finally sat down.

"Game 1 of the 1976 World Series against the Yankees?"

"That was it. How did you know?"

"Maybe because you told me twice last night. Grandpa was a Yankees fan and you never let him forget about that Series either."

"Those were good times. Hasn't been a team like that since, except maybe '90. That team was pretty good too."

A man seated to their right had overheard their conversation and interjected, "Did I hear you right? The last game you attended was the Series in '76?"

"That's right. What a team that was. Never see another team like that."

"You got that right, lady. Best there ever was, if you ask me. Those were good times to be a Reds fan. What kept you away all those years?"

"Got married and moved to New Jersey in the late 50s. My husband was from there, huge Yankees fan. We came here for game one and attended game four in New York. I think I enjoyed it more than he did. Just never really got the chance to attend another one here, always coming here at the holidays and all. Saw them play the Mets in New York a few times over the years, and a couple times in Philly."

"So what brings you back now?"

"My husband passed away recently. I'm moving in with my grandson here."

"He live here in Cincinnati?"

Nathan replied, "I used to, until I was 14. I moved in with Grandma here when my dad died back in '02 and now I have a job in San Jose."

"San Jose," the man responded, somewhat astonished, "You're moving in with him out there?"

"That's right. We're on the way there now and Nathan here surprised me with tickets for the game and we detoured through here on the way," Myrtle said with barely concealed delight.

"Man, that's the best story I've heard in a long while. I hope the Reds give you a good game to remember. Not been the best season and the Cubs are on fire lately. This guy they got going today has been dealing. Going to have to get to him early."

"I think they'll win. They won the last time I was in town."

"Maybe you bring the team luck. You should have come around more often these last couple years. Could have used a bit of luck."

"I don't know about that. I went every chance I had when they came to New York, and they still lost a few of those."

"Well, can't win 'em all."

"I didn't have these kind of seats in '76. We were way up. It's something else sitting down here."

"I try to sit this close when I come. You can watch the pitchers better from down here."

"You like to watch the pitchers?"

"Yes ma'am. Most important part of the game."

"That's right, but the way people talk about the 70s teams, all you ever hear about are the hitters."

"Well, I don't know about that. That team had a decent pitching staff."

"They sure did, but that's not what people remember. So, you followed that team?"

"I guess you could say I did."

"Were you lucky enough to attend of the World Series games that year?"

"I was at all four."

"Wow, call me jealous now. Did you have good seats."

"I didn't have a seat for game 1. I was on the mound for that one, but I had a good seat in the dugout for the other three."

"Wait, you're..."

"Yes, ma'am, that's me, but I don't think I had the pleasure of catching your name."

"Myrtle, Myrtle Callahan. It's a real pleasure meeting you Mr. Gullett."

"Just call me Don, and the pleasure was all mine."

As the game got underway, Nathan found his attention wavering, especially since Grandma was engrossed in a never ending analysis of every aspect of the game with her new found friend. He heard glimpses of the conversation, always dealing with some strategy or that: Should he swing away or bunt here? He should try to hit it to the right side. Maybe they should walk this guy and set up a double play. I wonder if they'll bring in the lefty here. On and on she went, hardly sitting back in her seat the entire game, hanging on every ebb and flow.

Nathan didn't get the fascination with sports, but it was a joy to observe Grandma. She really was in her element, enjoying a day at the ballpark watching her favorite team, and her joy was infectious. Those sitting around them were smiling from ear to ear and kept looking at her to see her reaction whenever a good play was made.

The game ended in a victory for the home team, which delighted most of those in attendance, none more than Myrtle, and she gave a thorough post game analysis all the way out the main gate, to the car, and throughout the entire thirty minute drive back to Mark's house.

The first part of their dinner conversation consisted of another account of the game, just in case anything had been missed during the car ride, until Evelyn, finding a pause in the flow, saw fit to interject a change of topic, much to the relief of everyone around the table, Myrtle excluded.

"So Nate, tell me more about your job? What exactly do you do there?" Evelyn asked.

"Right now I'm one of the programmers working on the single player games. Most games have a single player campaign and then an online multiplayer part. I program the AI for the single player campaigns. I did the AI for that game Mark likes to play."

"AI, you mean how the in game characters behave?"

"Mostly. I have two parts to that. I have to program how the player's squad mates behave so the player feels like he's playing with a team that will react accordingly to what he is doing. Then you have the enemy who have to behave in a believable manner as well. That's where Mark thinks I've made them too hard."

"You've done that the whole time you've worked there? You went there right out of college, right?"

"Yeah, but I didn't start doing AI. I started out doing some basic animation stuff at first, programming how characters move around, a lot of other really basic stuff like doors opening in rooms, or things you would see in an outdoor scene like ripples on water, trees swaying in the wind, that sort of thing. I did that for three years until

I got promoted to what I'm doing now. In fact, I'm up for another promotion, at least I think I have a good chance of getting it."

"That sounds great. What would that entail?"

"It's a supervisory position. I would head up a team with other programmers reporting to me, so I would have to supervise artists, AI people, and the animation people doing what I used to do. It would mean a lot more responsibility, but also a bit more pay."

"That would be great. When you you find out about that?"

"I'll probably know something by the time I get back to work. Which reminds me. I need to touch base, since they were expecting me to be flying back after the funeral, and now it's going to take a few days longer to get back. I'll shoot an email to my boss in the morning before we set out."

5

In the morning, Nathan fired off a quick email to his boss letting him know it would take a bit longer to make it back and they ate a quick breakfast, said their goodbyes to Mark and Evelyn, and set off. They were just pulling out when Myrtle said, "You know where Oxford is, Nate? Just head that way."

"I've been there a couple times, but not since Dad was alive. He took me up there to visit friends once and another time to go to a Miami football game."

"Just go west on 275 and head north up 27, Colerain exit."

"Ok, but why do you want to go that way?"

"Actually, we're going a little past Oxford. I have something I want to show you. Since you surprised me, it's my turn to surprise you."

While driving up 27, Nathan's cell phone rang, startling them both. He saw the number on the caller ID and said, "Looks like work. I'd better take it."

Putting his bluetooth on his ear, he pressed the button to take the call and answered.

"Nathan, Frank here. Just got your email. So what's the delay?"

"I'm bringing my grandmother back with me."

"Couldn't get her on the same flight or something?"

"We're not flying. She has a thing with flying, medical condition or something."

"You're driving back here, with your grandmother? How long do you figure it taking? We were kind of expecting you back. We have to get a patch out this week and we need you working on it."

"I have a laptop with me. I can work on things a bit at night when we stop."

"I'm not sure that's going to cut it. I wish you would have told us ahead of time."

"I didn't know ahead of time. This was kind of sudden."

"Well, Nathan...I don't know. Keep an eye on your email. I'll be in touch."

With that, Nathan's boss ended the call, and Myrtle, hearing the tone of the conversation, asked, "Is something wrong at work, Nate? That didn't sound good."

"Everything will probably be ok. Frank was a little miffed that I'm going to be getting back later than originally planned, but I have the PTO days, so it shouldn't be a big deal."

"Honey, I don't know if that sounded like everything is ok. You said you were in for a promotion?"

"Yes, supervisor position. I'm qualified for it and I have the seniority. There's no reason to give it to someone else."

"Unless that someone else is there when you're not, and doing everything he can to impress the boss."

"I don't know about that."

"Nate, I've been around the block a few more times than you have. I've seen that sort of thing happen before. Why do you think your grandfather went into business for himself?"

"I just assumed he always wanted to open up a garage."

"He had another job right after college, thought he would be there his whole life, but he got passed over for a couple promotions, guys who didn't know the job as well as he did but were always the boss's yes man, and he finally got fed up and left. He was always a good mechanic, so it wasn't that hard to get the proper certifications and open up the shop. He wasn't much of a businessman at first and we struggled for a couple years until he got the help he needed and got everything sorted out right. You know the rest of the story."

"Yeah, six locations in New York and New Jersey. Callahan's has a good reputation. Will probably be a still going strong when I'm your age."

"And I couldn't be more proud of what he built, but it all started because he didn't know how to play office politics. You just watch things there. The more things change..."

"You don't think they'll pass me up do you, for someone who doesn't know the job as well as I do?"

"That sort of thing has been going on in companies since way before your time, dear. Anyway, when you come to Oxford, just stay on 27 and go on out of town into Indiana. I think I can remember the roads."

Nathan drove into Oxford, spotted the United Dairy Farmers and pulled in.

"What flavor do you want, Grandma?"

"Flavor?"

"Milkshake? We can't leave this area without having a UDF shake can we? That's the one thing I missed after coming to live with you guys. Dad used to take me."

"Strawberry sounds good, but just a small one."

Nathan came out a few minutes later with the milkshakes and then proceeded out of town and into Indiana. Myrtle looked deep in thought, and finally popped up, "Hwy 101 South. You'll take 101 south from a small town called Liberty."

They came to Hwy 101 and Myrtle remarked that Liberty didn't seem too different since the last time she was there. Nathan headed south and had been driving for a few minutes when Myrtle said, "Take that next right, that's the road."

"West Dunlapsville Rd.?"

"That's it, I'm sure of it, " and shortly after Nathan made that turn, "Take this next left and take that road until it ends. There should be a driveway at the end when we get near the water." Nathan made the left turn on West Hoppes Rd. and eventually the road came to an end, with a small gravel drive turning off.

"Take the gravel road, Nate. I wonder if it's still there."

"You wonder if what is still there? Doesn't look like anything's back here. You sure you remember this place right?"

"I could never forget this place."

Just then, Nathan rounded a bend in the gravel drive and came upon a badly kept parking lot next to an even poorer kept building, little more than a shack, which sat no more than 50 yards from the shore of Brookville Lake. A small wooden pier jutted a few yards into the lake with an assortment of metal rowboats and canoes tied up. A sign advertised prices for renting the boats.

The building, a weather beaten affair with wooden siding that had been painted over more times than anyone could remember, a flat roof, and old metal gutters that leaked in spots and had also been painted to somewhat match the siding, was much as Myrtle remembered it, although somewhat more run down looking than it had been 58 years ago, and still had the same faded sign on the roof, *Jarhead Bait & Tackle.*

"This is definitely the place,"exclaimed Myrtle with barely contained youthful glee.

"This old place? Is this the big surprise you had for me? Looks like it's seen better days."

"Let's go inside and see how much has changed, shall we?"

"Ok, but before we go in, you have to tell me what's so special about an old run down bait shop."

"Why dear, this is where your grandfather proposed to me."

"Wait a minute, Grandpa proposed to you at a bait shop in Indiana? What were you doing here anyway?"

"We came here to see my parents. Dad insisted on meeting Patrick when things started getting serious, so we took a trip here that summer. After we went to church with my parents, Patrick and I came up here to go fishing."

"And he proposed to you here at the bait shop?"

"No, silly. We rented a boat and went out on the lake. It was quite romantic, I assure you. Let's go in the shop and see about getting a boat, just for old time's sake."

"Ok, Grandma, but do you think anyone's here?"

"Someone has to be driving that," she said, pointing to a black pickup truck that looked like it had also seen better days.

As they approached the door they could hear what sounded like gunfire and shouting from inside, followed by a man exclaiming, "Come on man, quit cheating. How do you get me in the back every time?" Myrtle was perplexed at what she heard, but Nathan was already grinning as he pushed open the door.

Upon entering he spotted the source of the noise, a rather large man with his back to the front door, completely filling up a protesting office chair and clutching an Xbox controller in both hands while still yelling at the tv. Right as Nathan walked in, the man yelled once again, "Man, this thing cheats. Always shooting me in the back and I can never see them before they shoot. Darn monkeys."

Next to the man's chair was an equally large dog that seemed immune to his master's tirades and only acknowledged their entrance with a slight lift of his head and an almost imperceptible whine. "Holy smokes, that is one large dog,"Myrtle thought to herself. Nathan walked around the counter, stood next to the man, and said, "The game's not cheating. The enemy just have good situational awareness, which you apparently don't."

"You ever play this game?" the man asked without turning around.

"Oh, maybe a couple times."

"Here then, see if you can do any better," the man replied, turning around and handing Nathan the controller. Nathan took the controller and appraised the man before he sat down at the xbox. He was indeed a large man, probably close to 300 pounds, but it wasn't all flab. There was some muscle underneath the padding, perhaps not that toned any longer and certainly not what it used to be, but still there and probably still formidable. He had close cropped hair, and a couple days' stubble on a round friendly face.

"I'm sure I can, just watch."

Nathan took the controller and said as he played, "Look here. You just ran into the room. If you take your time and watch your surroundings, you will see one bad guy over there before you enter the room. You can take him out with one shot, then move quickly to that cover here, take out the other guy over there, and then move quickly to that side of the room. If you have the rest of your squad take up a covering position right here, they can sweep the rest of the room and take out the rest of the bad guys as they try to take you out while you're moving. Just like that, see?"

Before the man took the controller back, he stuck out his hand to Nathan and said, "I'm Thad, and you are?"

"I'm Nathan."

"Well Nathan, you're pretty good. How'd you get that good at that game? I've had a hard time with it."

"I work for Tempest. I programmed the AI."

"So you helped make the game? Man, I'm impressed. I know how to turn my computer on and get on the internet, and I love to play games, but I wouldn't know the least thing about how to make one."

"Mister, is that dog friendly?" asked Myrtle at that moment, as the dog lifted its 250 pound bulk off the floor and started approaching her.

"Oh, Oliver don't bite nobody. He might lick you to death is all."

"What kind of dog is he? Is he part horse?"

"He's an Old English Mastiff. You heard of them?"

"I've heard of them, just didn't realize they were that big. What does he eat," asked Myrtle as she scratched the dog's ears.

"He eats whatever he wants. What brings you in today? Don't get many customers this time of day, just a few people come in for bait in the morning mostly."

"My grandson and me were thinking about taking a boat out for a bit, just to look around the lake. You know, I was here with my husband back in '58. Your place had the same sign, and you kind of look like the fellow who was here, but you can't be. He'd be in his 90s by now."

"That was my granddad. He started this place after the war."

"After the war?"

"Yep, World War II. Grandpa was a Marine, got wounded at Iwo Jima and was sent home, married Grandma in '45 and opened up this place. Been in the family ever since. I took over when I got out of the Marines and needed a job. Dad didn't want to mess with it. Suits me just fine though. I get to fish as often as I'd ever want and it brings in enough to pay the bills."

"That's nice. So, how much for one of the boats? You got anything with a motor?"

"I got a trolling motor I can put on one of the rowboats, and I'll let you take one out for nothing, seeing as you met my granddad."

"Oh, that's nice of you, but we can pay you for the boat."

"That won't be necessary. It's my treat, but if you want to fish some I can sell you some bait."

"I'm not sure my grandson here has ever handled a fishing pole in his life."

"Grandpa took me out a few times, but I never caught anything," Nathan said.

"Well, I'll tell you what," Thad replied, "if you want to fish, I have a couple extra poles around here. I can let you use one as long as you bring it back in one piece."

"Oh, you don't have to bother with..." Nathan was saying when Myrtle interrupted, "Nathan would love to borrow one of your poles."

Thad disappeared outside to prepare the boat while Myrtle and Nathan looked around the shop. Not much had changed since she had last been there, except for the tv in the corner and the slightly newer cash register. Some of the pictures on the wall were the same and there were newer ones added, mostly photos of various customers holding up a vast array of impressive catches. Myrtle wandered over to one wall where a Marine Corps flag hung proudly and underneath it were photos of men in uniform. One she recognized and pointed out to Nathan, "Look Nate, here's the man who ran the place back in '58, and look, here's the young man who's in charge now, looking pretty trim if you ask me."

"Wow, he's changed a bit since then. That must have been a few years ago, looking at what he looks like now."

"Watch what you say, young man. Things have a way of catching up with you when you hit your 40s."

"Meet the family," Thad said from behind them as he came back in, "The oldest one is my grandpa. You can see the purple heart right there on his chest. The other two are my great uncles who were in Korea, and you probably recognize the handsome fellow in the other photo."

"When was that photo taken," asked Nathan.

"Oh, nearly twenty years ago. I was 23 in that picture, and in a bit better shape then too."

"So military service runs in your family?"

"Yep, all but my brothers."

"Well, you'd think you would be better at shooters then," Nathan said playfully.

"Watch it, buddy. That fellow there will testify to how well I can shoot."

Nathan followed his pointing finger to a mounted head of a 12 point buck on the wall opposite the Marine flag.

"I got that one just last year. Friend of mine has some acreage down in Cincinnati. Lets me hunt there every year. Anyway, your boat is ready. Left you a couple poles and some live bait. There's also a stringer there if you want to keep your catch. I usually toss them back though. Cleaning them's too much trouble."

Nathan and Myrtle got settled into the boat, a sixteen foot aluminum row boat with two bench seats, with a trolling motor affixed to the stern. There were oars in the bottom of the boat, the fishing poles and containers of bait, a tackle box, and a cooler. Thad quickly showed Nathan how to operate the motor and said, "That won't go too fast, but it will get you around to all the best spots without you wearing yourself out with the oars...and you can help yourself to what's in the cooler."

"Thanks Mister," Nathan replied as he shoved off and operated the motor. It didn't take long for him to get acquainted with operating the motor and steering the boat in roughly the direction he wanted to go. It was really quite enjoyable. The last time he had been in a boat, his grandfather had done everything while he just sat there and enjoyed the ride.

"Nate, honey, just stay close to the shore here on the left and go around the bend."

"What's back there?"

"The lake bends around to the left just up there. You see where it branches off that way? It goes back into those trees."

"You can remember all that from all those years ago?"

"When you get to be my age, the stuff long ago is easy to remember, but what you had for lunch yesterday is a challenge."

Nathan steered the boat back the inlet into an area where the lake narrowed and the shore was lined with trees. There was a fair amount of shade near the shore, which made the temperature more pleasant. He looked at his grandmother and she was just sitting there with a smile on her face and her eyes shut. He had rarely seen her happier.

Without opening her eyes, Myrtle said, "You going to try your hand at fishing a bit?"

"I don't know. Let me see what's in this cooler first."

Nathan opened the cooler, found it full of ice, cans of Coke, and bottles of sweet tea. "What you want Grandma, Coke or tea?"

"Do you have to ask? I'll take the tea."

Nathan got his grandmother a bottle of tea and a Coke for himself and began to prepare one of the fishing poles. He got it fixed as well as he could remember according to what his grandfather had taught him; there was a hook, a sinker, bait, and a bobber. He dropped the line in the water and sat there expectantly, an expectation that quickly turned to boredom as nothing seemed to be happening.

"Grandpa always seemed to catch something," he commented.

"Your grandpa caught three bass that day, then he proposed."

"He proposed after catching fish?"

"Yes. We were right over there near the shore. I could tell something was on his mind, but he just sat there with the line in the water. They were biting good that day. He threw back about six that were too small, but he kept three good sized bass. After the third one, he just had this big grin on his face, a big bashful grin, and he kept staring at me. You see, Nate, he was a bit like you, kind of shy like. He said my name half a dozen times and kept pausing, like he was trying to figure out what to say, and he kept looking down at the fish that were still moving around in the bottom of the boat. Then he mumbled at first and I had to ask him to repeat himself because I couldn't hear him. Then he just blurted out, never taking his eyes off the fish, "What do you think about marrying me?" Then he looked up at me, and he looked scared as heck, and I took one look at those big puppy dog eyes and all I could do was just lean over and kiss him. He took that as a yes. All that happened right here on this lake, in a boat much like this one. It all seems like yesterday. Oh, God..." she broke off, choking back the tears that were starting to flow.

"You ok, Grandma?"

"I think so. I just miss him so much. You spend all those years with someone who drives you crazy sometimes. There were times when just looking at him would make my blood boil and I thought he was the dumbest man on the face of the earth, times I was so mad at him I couldn't see straight. Now I look back and I can't even remember all the things he did to anger me, but I remember clearly the moments like that day at this lake, or the day we lost our first baby. He just held me without saying anything, just let me cry until I didn't think I could cry any longer. There was the day your dad was born, and then the day your dad died I didn't think I could make it, and there he was, my personal Rock of Gibraltar. You think you love someone at the beginning, but those are just emotions. You look at that person and your knees feel weak, your heart skips a beat, and you can hardly control your voice. Those times are great, but that's not really love. Nate, you don't know what love is until it's all you have, when that person does something to wound you and you feel so angry you want to scream, cry, and shout all at once and then you realize you have a choice to make. You have to choose whether or not what you said at the altar is true, whether you really meant it. When you have to make the decision to love someone, not necessarily because you feel like it at the moment, but because you know it's the right thing to do to follow through on the promises you made when you felt like it, then you know what love is. Love is not a feeling, Nate. It's a decision, and you know what? I love him more now than I did that day, and I will continue loving him until, Lord willing, I will get to see him again."

Nathan was so wrapped up in listening to his grandmother that he hardly noticed the bobber dipping under the water, until she said, "Nate, you're getting a bite."

Nathan tried to remember what his grandpa had taught him about fishing, but that had been almost ten years ago. Nevertheless, he felt the line go taught, gave the pole a jerk, and realized the fish was hooked. He reeled in the line, only to find a small bluegill, hardly bigger than his hand. He gently removed the hook and put the fish back into the water saying, "There you go little buddy. Swim away now."

Over the next hour he caught and released four more of the same and then when he least expected it, he hooked another fish and this time he realized he had a big one on the line. Myrtle exclaimed, "Oh, Nate, I think you got a good one there."

Nathan reeled in the line a bit and then, trying to position himself to get more leverage, lost his footing and started to fall. Just then the fish, no doubt realizing his moment of opportunity, swam deep and fast to get away, snatching the pole clean out of Nathan's hands, never to be seen again. Nathan landed awkwardly in the bottom of the boat, hitting his head on the bench seat and momentarily seeing stars.

He got himself back onto the seat and holding his head, noticed to his utter dismay that his grandma was laughing. She composed herself quickly and said, "Sorry honey, I shouldn't laugh at your expense so, but that was a rather comical sight."

"Wasn't so comical from here," Nathan said, rubbing his head.

"You're not bleeding, but you'll have a bit of a bruise, and a bit of a story to tell as well."

"Yeah, a heck of a story, and I lost that nice man's good fishing pole."

6

Nathan steered the boat back to the pier and Thad was waiting there, sitting on the pier with his feet dangling down, a fishing pole in one hand, and a half eaten peanut butter & jelly sandwich in the other. He gave them a friendly wave, reeled in his line, and went to secure the boat and help Myrtle up.

"Here you go ma'am," he said, offering her his hand.

"Thank you kindly."

"So how was it? You catch anything?"

"I caught some small ones and threw them back," Nathan said as he climbed out of the boat, "but the big one I hooked took the pole."

"What did you go and do that for? Oh, don't bother yourself about it. I've lost a couple poles before. Happens to the best of us."

"I still feel bad about it. You've been so generous."

"Don't worry about it. You fall in the boat or something? Heck of a bump you got there."

Myrtle piped in with a grin on her face, "My intrepid grandson thought it would be a good idea to stand up in the boat for some reason. That fish brought him right back down." she said, still laughing.

"So where you guys from? You live around here somewhere?"

"San Jose," Nathan replied, "We're heading home."

"You're driving all the way to San Jose? What are you doing that for?"

"Grandma's moving in with me. Grandpa died last week. She doesn't do airplanes."

"I see. You have quite a trip ahead of you. You ever get back this way, you have to stop by again."

Thad retrieved his gear from the boat and trudged back to the shop, glad he hadn't loaned the boy his best pole. There was something about the old lady that he liked. She reminded him of his own grandmother, a kindly woman who still knew how to live in her old age. Maybe he would find a woman like that one of these days. He set the cooler down next to his chair, turned his game console back on, and opened the cooler to see if there were any Cokes left. As he took one out, he noticed something else that wasn't there before. There was a folded piece of paper placed inside a plastic bag to keep it dry. He unfolded the paper and inside it was a check, made out with his first name and last name blank. The attached note read:

Maybe this will help you fix the place up a bit. Thanks for everything. Myrtle Callahan.

"Well, isn't that nice," he said to himself. Then he looked at the check and was speechless. It was made out for $15000.

Nathan looked at his phone and saw two missed calls from his boss. Must not have been a good signal on the lake. He decided he would call Frank back later. Whatever it was could wait. They got in the car and started back up the gravel road when Myrtle said, "So, where are we headed next? You have the trip planned?"

"You said you wanted to see Mt. Rushmore on the way. I looked it up. We have to get up to 90 to head that way, so I guess we can head through Chicago."

"Chicago...haven't been there since...I think it was 1956."

"You were still in college then. What were you doing in Chicago."

"The football team was playing Northwestern. There was this cute guy on the team I had a crush on. I went to most of the games that year."

"So you were stalking this football player. How'd that turn out?"

"Turned out pretty good. It was your grandfather. So, how you plan on getting to Chicago."

"Well, while you were making friends with Dogzilla back there,"

"His name's Oliver."

"Whatever, while you were dishing out belly rubs, I was checking the atlas and the GPS. We head up to a town called Connersville. There's a state route runs west out of there and picks up US 52 all the way to Indy. Then we take 65 from Indy to Chicago, well to Gary actually, where we pick up 80. That's a toll road. Then we take the loop around the west part of Chicago and get 90 from there. We should get there late enough in the day to miss the bad traffic."

"Sounds like you have it all planned out."

"I think so. Dad took me up to Chicago once. I remember how bad the traffic can be. I hope we miss most of it. I also remember all the tolls. He had one of those passes you put up on your windshield. I hope I can get one up there somewhere."

"Is that your boss calling again?"

Nathan was hoping to ignore the phone again, but he decided to go ahead and take the call, hoping Frank was in a better mood this time.

"Nathan, where are you? Please tell me you're making good progress."

"In Brookville, Indiana, heading west."

"I certainly hope you're heading west. Only in Indiana? How many miles have you covered since I talked to you last?"

"Oh, about 50, give or take."

"About 50 miles? You do plan on getting back here sometime this year don't you? We have to get this patch out, and AI balancing is part of that patch. You guys should have gotten on a plane."

"I told you. Grandma can't fly."

"Yeah, I think you said that. Well, you have to put the hammer down and get here by the end of the week. I know how far it is. No time to stop and smell the roses. I'm sure Grandma will understand."
Click.

Nathan just drove on in silence for a few moments, until his grandma broke in on his thoughts.

"That didn't sound too good," she said.

"I've never heard Frank that upset before."

"You ever taken time off before?"

"Not much. I usually end up cashing in unused PTO at the end of the year. I never manage to take all the days."

"So now you're learning something about the business world. Nobody cares. You might do a good job. You might know your job inside and out and think you're some important person to the company, but there were people doing that job before you got there and there will be people doing it after you're gone. If you're not the lead dog, the view never changes."

"Grandpa used to say that all the time. You might have a point. I just thought I was important to the company. I'm doing well for someone my age and I really do know the job. In fact, I know most of the jobs on the development team. I'm qualified for that promotion."

"Promotions don't always go to the most qualified, honey."

With that, Myrtle got out her journal and began writing as they drove through the Indiana countryside. Nathan took in the flat landscape with cornfields in every direction and thought that for flat land it could be quite scenic in its own way. It was mid afternoon on a sunny day with enough of a breeze blowing to ripple the tassels on the corn stalks, making wave like patterns across the fields similar to the water at the lake earlier.

He wondered what his grandma was writing in that journal of hers. She had written quite a bit since they had left New Jersey. He wondered also how she could write that much in a moving car and if any of it would be legible. His thoughts ran to his job and how Frank was coming down on him. What was he to do? Taking Grandma in was the right thing to do. Frank should realize that and cut him some slack. What was he supposed to do, abandon his grandma, or force her to fly when it might not be good for her health?

He loved his job and he was darn good at it, better than most his age. He loved video games, maybe more than he should, and he loved making them. Frank was being unreasonable. Didn't he see the sense in what Nathan was saying? He had a laptop with him. He could put in some work every evening on the way out there, probably even finish most of the AI balancing for that patch.

He was more than qualified for that promotion. He had worked his way up since starting there six years ago. He understood all of the different steps in game development, having worked in every phase of the development of the most recent release. Heck, he probably knew enough to develop the thing himself, given a good enough team around him. At that point a thought took root and it intrigued him. If he had a good understanding of what it took to develop a game, why did he have to be stuck doing it for someone else?

He knew the answer to that question. Companies like Tempest have multi million dollar budgets to throw at a game, which is why they released AAA titles every year. Even knowing what he knew, he would need a team of superstars to even hope of producing anything remotely close to the quality a large company can pull off.

Still, the thought wouldn't go away. He loved his work and he liked most of his co workers, but if his boss was going to force him to have to choose between his job and his family, he knew where that would likely end up.

As these thoughts crossed his mind, he also thought of Phoebe, the co worker he had a crush on. If he lost his job or quit, how would he go about asking her out, if he ever screwed up the courage to do so? When he was turning things over in his mind at moments like this, it was easy to imagine doing or saying the right thing, but when it came down to it, he was extremely non confrontational. He thought it was just his shyness, but maybe there was more to it than that. He liked everything to be smooth and he abhorred confrontation in almost any form. He simply wanted Frank to see the sense without there being any trouble.

He was so deep in his thoughts he completely missed the turn for Hwy 44 in Connersville and had to turn around to back track. He made the turn and was headed west when Myrtle paused from her journaling to state that she had to use the restroom. They came to a town called Glenwood and found a small convenience store where Nathan pulled in for his grandma to use the restroom. He waited a few minutes and when she wasn't coming back, he went in to see what was wrong, only to find Myrtle arguing with the store clerk about use of the restroom.

"Can't you read the sign on the door, lady?" the clerk was saying, "It says no public restrooms."

"Sure I can read the sign, but I simply can't wait to get to the next town. You have to have a restroom here."

Nathan walked up and asked, "Is there something wrong here?"

"Yeah, this lady can't read the no restroom sign."

Nathan took one look at his squirming grandmother and another look at the young store clerk and said to him, "Look, my grandma here has to go. The next town is Rushville and I don't think she can wait that long. What harm can come from letting her use your bathroom? Where do you go?"

"I go to the bathroom in the back."

"You mean the one through that door?"

"Yeah, but it's not public."

"It is now, buddy," Nathan said as he began leading his grandma that way "unless you want to be the jerk that made an old lady pee herself."

"Ok, whatever dude."

When they got back to the car, Myrtle said, "Thanks. I don't think I could have held it another five minutes."

"It was nothing really. I don't know why that clerk was being such a jerk about it."

"Just following the rules. And by the way, Mister, if you see my grandson anywhere..."

"You're funny."

He pulled out and the drive resumed its previous pattern, Myrtle scribbling away in her journal and Nathan mesmerized by the wind across the corn fields, at least until he passed through Rushville and headed on into Indianapolis, corn stalks being replaced by skyscrapers.

Indianapolis came and went with hardly a notice and they found themselves on what seemed to Nathan to be one of the most boring stretches of road he had ever been on. The mesmerizing beauty of the cornfields was now becoming monotonous, but the traffic was relatively light and he was able to once again set the cruise control and get into a groove where his mind wandered. For someone who had little experience with long distance driving, he was fast becoming acclimated to it and found it oddly relaxing. He didn't quite understand how truckers did this day after day, but days like today it was enjoyable. The weather was mild, the music on the radio was still keeping his interest, and the miles blended one into the other at a rate that startled him. In what seemed like a few minutes but was in reality over an hour, he found himself passing Lafayette. Chicago was no great way ahead, especially as fast as the time seemed to be passing, and he almost regretted that he had planned on stopping there for the night. Maybe if Grandma didn't mind they could push on a bit farther.

By the time they got to Merrillville, the situation had changed and he was now no longer sure about his desire to push farther. He had not bothered to change the radio stations to get any local weather, so the storm that rolled through from the northeast took him entirely by surprise. One moment the skies were blue, the next there were some ugly clouds and then the wind kicked up strong blowing across the highway, catching the tow behind trailer broadside on and testing his ability to keep the vehicle in the lane. Then the rain hit, coming down in a torrential deluge that made visibility minimal and slowed him down to under 45 mph.

He merged onto 80/94 west heading toward Illinois and pulled into the first service plaza he came to, where they sat to wait out the worst of the storm. There Nathan produced an umbrella from the back seat and they ventured inside as fast as Myrtle could manage, which was not nearly as fast as Nathan would have preferred with the rain coming down as hard as it was. Nathan remarked on her speed of movement and she replied, "They don't call me Myrtle the turtle for nothing."

"Who calls you that?" Nathan asked.

"Your grandpa was the first. It wasn't that I couldn't get around fast back then, but I was never one to want to move that fast. Patrick, though, was always moving like he had a deadline to beat. I never understood why anyone would want to walk that fast, but that was him. I would always lag behind. We weren't even married yet the first time he called me that, but it was in good humor. The longer we were married, the more he learned to slow down some when he was with me, but I could tell it drove him crazy."

"Yeah, I remember how fast he walked when I would go somewhere with him, but I never minded. Myrtle the turtle. Now that's funny."

"Hey Nate, look over there. You can buy one of those toll passes there."

"Ok, I'll be right back."

Nathan purchased the EZPass and they waited a few more minutes for the storm to subside into something of a steady hard rain instead of the deluge they had arrived in, and they went back to the car to continue.

"Were you planning on calling it a day around here, Nate?"

"I'm not sure. I had figured it would be a good place to stop, but I think we should get west of the city before we turn in so we won't have to mess with it in the morning."

They did indeed push on west of the city, making it to Rockford before deciding that they were both in need of a hot shower and a hot meal, not necessarily in that order. They settled on the Baymont Inn for no better reason than it had a Cracker Barrel next door and Myrtle could think of no better hotel than one next to a Cracker Barrel.

The hot meal came first, then the hot showers at the Baymont, and then they both stretched out on separate beds to wind down, Myrtle with her journal and pen and Nathan with his iPad. He didn't tell his grandma, but he had downloaded a journal app and he was going to try his hand at writing down his thoughts. It seemed to do

Grandma some good and he certainly had a lot on his mind he wanted to sort through.

He hadn't driven a very large number of miles that day, but perhaps the combination of the activity at the lake then driving through the rain had tired him more than he was aware. He opened the app, wrote a few lines, and fell fast asleep, the iPad falling next to him on the bed. Myrtle saw this, smiled, and went over to tuck him in. "He's never too old to be tucked in." she thought to herself. She slipped the pillow under his head, reached down to take off his shoes, and picked up the iPad. The screen was still active when she picked it up and she saw what kind of app was on the screen. She smiled briefly, set the iPad on the dresser, and went to bed.

7

Nathan finally screwed up the courage to ask Phoebe out and surprisingly she immediately said yes. His heart didn't just skip a beat, it danced a jig there in his chest and he was filled with a happiness he thought he could never know. What they couldn't figure out was where to go on their first date, until she surprised him by suggesting Cracker Barrel. Of all the places to go on a date, why did she want to go there? Cracker Barrel was a fine place to grab a meal, sure, but it was not the place he imagined going on a first date. Maybe something a little more upscale with cloth napkins and candlelight, someplace a bit more romantic. No, that's where she wanted to go, and she was being surprisingly insistent on going there, right away so it seemed. "I'm hungry and ready for breakfast," she was saying.

Then Phoebe's face started to fade and it was no longer her voice he was hearing, but that of his grandmother, gently shaking him awake and wanting to get breakfast. His mind swam up from the depths of his dream, most unwillingly, and finally he sat up in bed, somewhat awake.

"There you are Nate, finally with us. We forgot to set an alarm and we appear to have overslept. We ought to be going."

"Grandma, it's central time here."

"Oh, ok, but we've still had enough sleep, and I'm getting hungry."

Thirty minutes later they were sitting in Cracker Barrel waiting on their breakfast to arrive and discussing the next leg of the trip. Myrtle inquired, "Where's that big mall? Is that on the way?"

"The Mall of America? That's in Minneapolis, "he said as he was checking mileage on his iPad, "about five hours from here, but it would add a few miles to our trip. We'd have to make our way back down to 90 from there. Might add three hours to the trip."

"Well, I was wanting to see it, but I don't know about adding that much time to the trip. You do need to get back to work."

"You know what, Grandma. I do need to get back to work, but I told Frank what was up and I'm not going to cut short our trip. If you want to go there, we'll stop there."

"But what about work, Nate? You're not irreplaceable."

"I know, but that's a two way street. No job is irreplaceable either, and you're family. Family comes first."

"I appreciate that, Nate, but you have to think about your future. I won't be around forever, you know."

"And that's why I want to make the most of whatever time we have. I can always get another job. I can't always get another grandma."

Then their food arrived and the conversation took a back seat to eating breakfast. When they had finished, paid the bill, and gotten back to the car, Nathan picked up right where they had left off. He had a knack for doing that, and it sometimes caught people off guard. Something started had to be finished, and if he was interrupted, he had been known to pick up an old train of thought a day later, almost as if he had never moved on while the other party had forgotten all about the unfinished conversation. Patrick had been the same way, thought Myrtle.

"I've been thinking about family and priorities and all that," he said as he was pulling out of the parking lot, "People prioritize things above their families and then when someone is taken from you the regrets come. What do you regret? Do you wish you could have spent more time away from that person or that you could have worked more? No, you regret the things you never said when you had the chance. You wish you had another hour, another day, another week, just to tell that person one more time how you felt, but you don't have another chance and you don't realize it until it's too late."

"You have some of those regrets, Nate?"

"You bet I do. You're not supposed to lose your parents when you're only 14. I never saw that coming. How often do you think I wish I could have said more to them, told them more how much I loved them and appreciated them? But no, I don't have that chance, and when I had the chance, I was a stupid teenager who didn't think that was important. I didn't know I wouldn't have the opportunities later. One minute I have parents that are getting on my nerves and the next day they're gone, and now that I'm a little older and appreciate them, they're not around for me to tell them. It was kind of the same with Grandpa, but at least I had some good talks with him and was able to say mostly what I felt, so there aren't as many regrets there, but with Mom and Dad...I'm not making that same mistake again."

"Oh, Nate, I miss your dad more than you know. After all, he was my son, and parents aren't supposed to bury their kids. I'm sure he knew how you felt."

"Maybe he did, but I never really got to tell him once I figured it out. That chance was taken from me and I...oh...I don't know. I just feel cheated."

"I don't know what to tell you, honey. That's part of life though. Sometimes people leave us too soon and there are always regrets. There was always something more we could have said or done. I would love to have one more day with your grandfather to tell him how much I love him. I never felt like it was said enough, especially the last few years when we both pretty much knew where things stood. You never feel like you said or did enough until it's too late."

"But you had a whole life with Grandpa and I only had fourteen years...and now I can't do anything about it, but I still have you left and I don't want to have the same regrets later, so we're going to take as much time as we need on this trip. So if you want to detour to see some giant mall, we'll stop at that mall, and then Mt. Rushmore, and whatever else looks interesting on the way, and if Frank doesn't like that..."

"Well, Nate, you maybe ought to set that cruise control before you have another regret. The police aren't as forgiving."

He looked down and realized he was doing nearly 80 mph, so he backed it off and set the cruise. The remains of yesterday's storm had finally left them and the drive north through Wisconsin was certainly more relaxing than last night's drive in the rain. Nathan had never been to Wisconsin before and found the drive rather enjoyable.

"You ever been through here, Grandma?"

"Your grandpa and I went up to Milwaukee once, but I've never been in this part of the state. Quite pretty."

"Yes, it is. Just let me know when you need to stop. Looks like there are a lot of towns between here and Minneapolis."

Myrtle started to take her journal out, but she put it down and just stared out the window, enjoying the rolling hills of central Wisconsin in the late summer. She was thinking about what Nathan had been saying earlier, about regretting the things he hadn't said to his parents. This had been her experience as well. She hadn't lost her parents young like he had, but she still found herself with many things left unsaid at their passing and now all of a sudden it was coming back. He had dug it up with his words and now she was feeling a bit of the same sadness that Nathan had spoken of. Why was it that people often took one another for granted until it was too late? Perhaps that was the way with most people. You just had these people in your life who made it better, and you assumed that was the way things were supposed to be; you never really tell people how much you appreciate them until it's too late. Maybe you do so more with friends than with family, but she was now wondering if that wasn't the case with most relationships people have.

She thought of all those people she had lost over the years: her friend Shirley who had died in an auto accident in her 20s, her parents and grandparents, several high school classmates, her son Martin and his wife, even several pets she had over the years. How many of them had she simply taken for granted, like they were just part of her life, meant to be there, and that they knew what they meant to her? Nathan had figured that out early, but she now realized that she had been doing what Nathan was regretting, and that she had done so her entire life.

That was often the way with people. Most people go through their lives chasing deadlines or chasing things they think they need, only to realize too late that they missed out on what is most important in life. You get to the end of your life and you start taking stock, and you realize that the things you often overlooked were the most important things and the things you strove for were the least important. The moments that seemed like interludes in your life were in reality the most important moments and those moments you thought were the all important goals turned out to be the unimportant interludes. Those conversations you had with your grandma on her front porch, when you really wanted to be playing, all of those quiet times between the big moments of your life, those were the important moments. Those were the times that really defined you. Those were the moments that stick out when you realize that more of your life is behind you than is in front of you and you want to figure out if any of it really meant anything.

Now it made sense. What did she remember the most about the years she had with her husband? Was it the big moments, the vacations they took together or the times she watched him play football back in college? No, as much as those moments were fun, it was the quiet conversations they had sitting on the couch, sometimes not talking about anything important, but just being in one another's presence. It was the dinners they had in the house, times they just sat there in companionable silence and didn't even speak, going to the shelter to pick out a puppy, and coming back with a puppy and a kitten because they couldn't choose between the two, watching the two romp around the house in reckless abandon and the laughter they had at their antics. Their marriage thrived not in the big moments, but in the small every day moments that seemed so unimportant at the time, but that now flooded her memories. They strove to make the big moments, but the small moments made them.

Nathan looked over and saw the far away look on his grandma's face and wondered what she was thinking about. As much as he thought he knew her, there was way more about her that he never really knew, and he realized at that moment that she was more important than the job he was going back to. She was a deeper woman than he ever imagined, and a wise woman as well. He had always figured that people her age simply acquired wisdom by virtue of having lived that long, but he saw in her that it wasn't entirely the sum of the years lived but what she did with those years.

Yes, he loved his grandmother, but like other people in his life, he hadn't always been too good at telling her. He was an introvert and he knew the limitations that put on him, but there was only so far he could let that hinder him. At least understanding that part of his personality had helped him to a degree. He understood why he was uncomfortable staying too long at parties and why he spent so much time in introspection. This trip was a fine example. As much as he had some wonderful conversations with his grandmother, they had also covered several hours of driving in total silence, her lost in her journal writing and he in his thoughts. Maybe he spent too much time in his own head.

He had passed Madison a few miles ago, had seen signs for towns like Waunakee and DeForest, was coming up on an exit leading to Lodi, and was seeing several billboards advertising attractions at Wisconsin Dells. Indoor water parks? Yeah, that would never fly where he lived in California. These people knew what to do with the long winters, he figured. No time to stop and check those out though, not if he wanted to get to the mall and give his grandma some time to walk around the place before it closed. Maybe they should have gotten out of bed earlier.

They rolled right on past Wisconsin Dells, passed Mauston, New Lisbon, and Tomah, when Myrtle announced her need for a restroom. They came before too long to Black River Falls and Nathan pulled into the Flying J and parked in one of the RV spots, right next to a Winnebago that looked like it had passed its prime 25 years ago. The Winnebago was idling but had thick curtains in all the windows, which lead Nathan to believe that the occupants were probably sleeping, which he found odd for the early afternoon. Maybe they had been driving all night to beat traffic. He realized he had to use the restroom as well, but he decided to wait for his grandmother to get back so he could leave the car running and keep the air conditioning going. It was becoming a rather warm day and he didn't want to shut it off.

Finally Myrtle came back and asked Nathan if he planned on topping off the gas while they were there, to which he replied, "Not a bad idea. Let me go in and take a pee real quick and then I'll grab a pump."

THE OCCUPANTS of the old Winnebago were indeed sleeping through the day, but not for the reasons Nathan had surmised. They had also been on something of a road trip, starting out in Los Angeles and passing through Las Vegas, Salt Lake City, up through Idaho to Montana, across Montana and North Dakota, down through Minnesota, and now into Wisconsin. Only the driver knew their final destination, and he wasn't sharing the information with anyone. It was one truck stop after another, no more than one or two nights at each location, normally driving from early morning to early afternoon and sleeping through the afternoon until evening.

It was the evenings that Cassie Ferguson dreaded. There had been another girl, a teenager named Melanie, but she had been given over to someone else in St. Paul. They were held against their will by a smelly unkempt man in his 50s known only as Mike. Mike used threats against family members as leverage to try to keep her in line.

How he knew so much about her family, she had no idea, but the threats seemed real enough.

Cassie was awake at the moment. She wanted to cry, but the tears had all but dried up at this point. She was becoming hardened to her situation, which had been a living hell these last few weeks since being abducted near her home in Long Beach. She was only 18, just out of high school, and working as a server at a small diner not far from home, hoping to start college if she could save up enough money. She was a very attractive girl and when a man she waited on at the diner, claiming to be a Hollywood agent, told her about an audition coming up, she jumped at the chance. He said all the right things and she dared to dream. By the time she and the other girls who showed up for the audition figured out what was really happening, it was too late.

Cassie had been forced to do unspeakable things since then, sometimes with private customers and sometimes at truck stops. Most of the truckers declined, but enough paid to make the venture profitable, at least for Mike and the man who Mike reported to, a man who had more Mikes reporting to him and giving him a share of the profits. She saw none of the money, and she really cared nothing for the money anyway. She wanted free of this hell. Lot lizards, they were called, the derogatory slur people in the trucking industry called young women like her.

She overheard enough conversations between Mike and his employer to get the gist of what their plan was. The idea was to service the west coast only, but the law had gotten close on a couple occasions, so now they were making their way across the country in an effort to distance themselves and then maybe set up operations in another state. Cassie twisted herself in her bunk to try to get more comfortable. Mike had taken to handcuffing the girls to their bunks during the day since Melanie had tried to run away in Montana. She didn't get far and two days later Mike followed through on his threat and Melanie's sister was involved in an accident. That ended any other escape attempts, but the handcuffs were used since then as an extra precaution.

Cassie heard another vehicle park next to them, right next to the window her bunk was near. With enough wiggling in the bunk, she managed to get her face next to the heavy curtain and eventually she was able to get her free hand to the edge of the curtain as well. The curtains could not be drawn since Mike had fastened the edges to the wall of the RV, but with enough working back and forth, trying to remain as quiet as possible so as not to wake Mike, she managed to tear the corner free, and eventually one whole side of the curtain. She pressed her face up to the glass and looked out. Parked next to the RV was a Chevy Tahoe with a U-Haul trailer hooked on and a young man sitting in the driver's seat.

Cassie dared not make too much noise for fear of being discovered by Mike, but she needed to get this man's attention somehow. She needed him to notice her, and notice that all was not well. She had no paper or anything to write a note with, so that was out of the question, and rapping on the window would certainly wake Mike, so that wouldn't work either. She just stared out the window and willed the stranger to turn his head and notice her. There, he saw her. Hopefully he would figure it out. He smiled back and waved, then went back to looking straight ahead. "Darn," she thought, "he just thinks I'm being friendly." She then went to moving the curtain around and he looked a bit longer this time.

Just then a petite elderly lady came out and got in the passenger seat, had a brief conversation with the young man, and he got out and went inside. Cassie kept moving the curtain and staring at the Tahoe, and eventually the woman looked over, taking a much longer look than the young man had.

As Nathan was walking inside to use the restroom, Myrtle looked over at the Winnebago parked next to them and saw a young girl staring out the window at her. She had one hand on the curtain and was attempting to wave the curtain around, but it appeared that only part of the curtain was loose. She thought there was something right odd about this girl. She looked quite young, probably in her late teens, and she was quite pretty, would look prettier if she didn't look so uptight about something. She looked scared, that was it. That girl looked downright terrified.

Myrtle's heart told her that this girl needed her help, but she was not quite sure what was going on or how to help. She got out of the vehicle and walked over toward the RV. The girl took her hand and held a finger up to her lips and Myrtle immediately understood that she couldn't make any sound. Myrtle had seem something on TV once about trafficking and although she couldn't be sure, she thought this was what was going on. Just then, Nathan was returning from the restroom and started to say something, but Myrtle put her finger to her lips to silence him, then came close to him and said, "Did you notice that girl looking out of that window over there?"

"Yeah, she seems friendly. She was waving."

"Take a closer look. Something's not right.

"Yeah, she looks kinda scared of something."

"Remember that piece on the news the other day about trafficking?"

"You think that's what's going on?"

"That girl is terrified. Just look at her. She motioned for me to keep quiet, so I'm thinking that the person holding her is probably asleep in there. We can call the police, but I don't know how long it will take them to get here, and we don't want him waking up and taking off."

"Look at how he's parked. There's not enough room to back that thing out of that spot. He'd have to pull forward to get out. Hop in."

Myrtle and Nathan got in the car and Nathan pulled forward and then parked broadside in front of the RV, blocking it from being able to pull out. Myrtle smiled approvingly, as did the girl in the window, and Myrtle already had her cell phone out and was dialing 911.

"911, what's your emergency?"

"I'm at the Flying J on...what's this road Nate...Hwy 54. There's an old RV here, a...Winnebago it looks like, and there's a young girl peeking out the window, looking scared as hell. I think she's been kidnapped."

"Can you talk to the girl."

"No, she's motioning to keep quiet. I think the kidnapper is in there asleep and she doesn't want to wake him, but she's sure been trying to keep my attention. She's young and very scared."

"Ok, ma'am, I'm getting an officer headed that way. Is this a good number to contact you at if we need to?"

"Yes...yes it is."

"Ok, we have an officer close by. He should be there shortly."

Five minutes later two squad cars came into the parking lot, lights flashing, and parked either side of the RV. One officer positioned himself near the door of the RV and the other approached Myrtle. "Officer Murphy ma'am. You the lady who called?" the officer asked her.

"Yes, officer. Something's up with that RV. You see the girl in the window?"

The officer took one look and said to his partner, "We need to get in there ASAP."

The other officer drew his weapon and they made quick work of the lock on the door and opened it quietly. What they saw inside made their blood boil. There were cots along the walls and on one of them was the girl who had been looking out the window. On a cot in the back was the man responsible, sprawled out and snoring loudly. Murphy approached and resisted the urge to beat the man to a pulp, instead simply slapping him to wake him up. When Mike woke up, he found himself looking straight at the stern face of Officer Murphy, holding a pair of handcuffs and saying, "You have the right to remain silent..."

Outside, the other officer found Nathan standing there and approached him. "You the one who parked in front of him?" the officer asked.

"Yep, didn't want him pulling away before you got here."

"That was quick thinking...I don't think I had the pleasure of getting your name."

"Nathan, sir."

"It's Jones, Nathan. Officer Kevin Jones. Is the other lady with you then, the one who called us?"

"Yes, that's my grandma."

"Your grandma's a hero, Nathan."

"Yeah, she's pretty special. I wouldn't trade her for the world."

8

It didn't take long for the local media to catch wind of what was going on at the truck stop and eventually reporters from network affiliates in LaCrosse and Eau Claire began showing up to do pieces for the evening news. Before they arrived, the police had time to conduct their own interviews of the rescued victim and to contact her closest relatives to arrange for transportation back home, the next available direct flight from Minneapolis. Officer Jones had found two cell phones, a laptop, and a tablet in the Winnebago and the information contained on these devices would in the coming weeks, when shared with Federal authorities, help bring down one of the largest trafficking operations in the country, resulting in the rescue of hundreds of young girls.

Myrtle was glad enough to accept Cassie's thanks, but when the reporters arrived later, it all became a bit too much. She wasn't sure if she should be called a hero, but each reporter was using that language. She did what anyone would have done in her situation. She saw someone in trouble and she called the police. How often did people do that every day? She happened to be in the right place at the right time, all because of her bladder. If not for that, they would not have stopped. Maybe it was destiny, or divine providence, or dumb luck, but she had been there. Maybe the Lord just saw fit to use her that day, and for that she felt grateful and humbled. Maybe someone else would have done the same thing. Either way, this girl was going back to her family and the low life who was exploiting her was going to jail. All in all, that made for a pretty good day.

A young reporter was currently speaking on camera, preparing opening remarks for her piece that would air on the late local news that evening. She had been told the reporter would be waning to get some remarks from her as well, and sure enough she was coming over with a microphone.

"I'm here with Myrtle Callahan, a woman many are calling a hero. Mrs. Callahan, can you tell us what happened here this afternoon?"

"Well, it started because I had to pee. I asked Nathan to take the next exit and this is where he stopped. I went in to use the restroom and Nathan went in when I came back to the car. We were parked next to the RV right over there. I saw that young girl peeking out the window and she looked right scared. I just did what anyone else would have done in my shoes. I saw someone in need and I called someone to help. You would have done the same, I'm sure."

"Well, I can speak for myself and most of our viewers in saying that we're glad you were on the spot to do what you did."

With that, she motioned for the cameraman to cut recording and he went to put the camera away for the trip back to the station. The reporter approached Myrtle and said, "We're off camera now. So you're traveling with your grandson. Where you guys headed?"

"We're going to California. Nathan lives out there and I'm moving in with him."

"And you're driving all the way out there?"

"Yeah, I don't handle flying too well."

"Where did you start out from?"

"We started in New Jersey. I just lost my husband and I'm selling my house and moving in with Nathan. We're going to take the scenic route."

"Wow. I'd actually like to do that one of these days. Well, Mrs. Callahan,"

"Just call me Myrtle."

"Ok, Myrtle, it's been a pleasure meeting you. So, are you guys going to continue on now?"

"I don't know. We were going to go to the mall in Minneapolis, but maybe we'll stay here and go there in the morning."

This scene was repeated three more times with reporters from the other network affiliates, and by the time the last reporter left, Myrtle was worn out and there was no question of continuing on. Nathan lead her inside where they went into the drivers' lounge in the truck stop and sat down wearily in two chairs. There were four truckers in there watching TV and Nate asked one of them, "You fellows don't mind if we sit down here for a bit and rest?"

"No problem," said the trucker, "room's hardly ever full here."

Another man came in just then and asked Myrtle, "Excuse me, but are you the lady who nabbed the kidnapper?"

"The police nabbed him. All I did was make a phone call."

"You're far too humble ma'am. I don't know if I would have noticed anything wrong."

"If you had seen that poor girl's face..."

"Well, maybe...anyway, name's Thomas. I'm the manager of the Comfort Inn over the other side of the highway. The girl's staying there tonight. No direct flights until tomorrow. We have a nice room waiting for you if you want, on the house. You can stay as long as you want until you continue on your way."

"That's too kind. You don't have to.."

"Yes we do have to. It's our way of saying thanks. We're never booked full anyway. Just come on over when you're ready."

Nathan would have loved to go over to the room right then, his limit of social interaction having been reached long ago, but that wasn't to be. When the truckers, who knew what had happened earlier, learned who they were, they were subjected to another round of congratulations and even a couple heartfelt hugs. The last trucker, a large man on the north side of 250 pounds with a full beard, shoulder length hair, a t shirt that was about a size too small to adequately cover his protruding paunch, and two massive tattoo covered arms, approached Myrtle and gave her a hug that nearly took the breath out of her. He handed his phone to one of the other men and said, "Jerry, you care to grab some shots for me?" He then positioned himself between Myrtle and Nathan, put one massive arm around each one of them, and pulled them closer to himself.

"Y'all don't mind getting a couple photos with me do you?"

"Not at all," replied Myrtle.

Jerry snapped a couple photos and a couple more of Nathan and Myrtle by themselves and the large man then approached and, handing Myrtle a business card said, "Richard Washington's the name. I'm with the organization on the card."

Myrtle looked at the card and read *Truckers Against Trafficking.*

Richard said, "A lot of truckers are part of our group. We always try to keep an eye out for situations like you came across today. A few trafficking rings have been stopped by observant truckers. I was wondering if you wouldn't mind me getting your story for our web site, and if we could use your photos. Lot of folks would love to read your story."

"I guess that would be ok," replied Myrtle

"Great, you tell me what happened," he said as he took a small digital recorder out of his pocket and started it.

Myrtle recounted the story again, starting from when they pulled off the exit to when the police arrived and took the suspect into custody. When she was done, Richard shut off the recorder, thanked her for letting him share her story, and went immediately back to his seat to email the photos and audio file to someone who would put it all together.

Myrtle sat back down, only to feel a tap on her elbow. When she turned, she saw the same face she had seen looking out the window of the RV. The face belonged to a petite black girl with a shy smile; she was really quite pretty now that she had been able to take a shower and wasn't as terrified. When Myrtle looked at her, she first looked down at the floor and then looked back at Myrtle, as if unsure of what to say.

"I'm Cassie," she said in a soft voice. "I'm mighty grateful." She then looked shyly down at the ground again and Myrtle said to her, "That was awfully brave of you, trying to get our attention like that."

"Yes ma'am...I...I'm glad you noticed. I talked to my mama a minute ago. She wants me to thank you too. We're both most thankful," Cassie managed to say before the tears came again. She fought back the tears and then reached out and embraced Myrtle. Myrtle just put her arms around Cassie's small frame and said, "There child, you're safe now. That man's never going to hurt you again. He'll never hurt anyone again."

By this time, they were both crying and finally when Cassie stepped back she noticed Nathan standing a couple feet away and offered him her hand. They shook hands, she thanked Nathan and all he could think to say was, "You're welcome...heard the officer say you're flying back to California. What part you from?"

"I live near Long Beach."

"You going back to school when you get back?"

"I just got out of high school, can't afford college yet. I've been waitressing to save up the money. I want to go to college. None of my family's ever been to college."

"Well, Cassie, I wish you luck. I'm glad we could be here to help."

"Yeah, I am too. Well...the officer is going to take me to the motel now. Thank you."

They sat back down for a few minutes and Nathan finally said, "You know what I could use right now? A good hamburger."

One of the truckers replied, "Culver's across the street there. Pretty good burgers. It's on me. You think I can ride over there with you? Can't park the truck over there."

Nathan looked at Myrtle and she nodded her head. He replied to the trucker, "Ready when you are."

On the way out to the car, Myrtle spotted a rack of greeting cards, purchased one, and five minutes later, the three of them were sitting in Culver's waiting for their food. The trucker said, "Man, I'm so rude, didn't give you my name. I'm Mack. Mack Turner."

"Nathan Callahan. Where you from, Mack?" asked Nathan

"When I'm home, which isn't often enough, I have a little house in Ohio, little town you've probably never heard of."

"Try me."

"Ever hear of Carlisle?"

"Sure, I grew up not too far south of there, in Woodlawn. I lived there until I was 14, then I moved in with Grandma when my parents died."

"You said Woodlawn?"

"Yeah, why?"

"What year was that?"

"2002. My parents were killed by a drunk driver. I was only 14 at the time."

"Man, we were practically neighbors. I was 18 then. We lived in Sharonville. I moved out the next year. Weird that we never met."

"Yeah, weird."

Their food was ready and they spent the next few minutes eating and speaking little except for Nathan saying, "Man, this is a pretty good burger. Wish we had this place where I live."

They finished eating, refilled their drinks, and resumed their conversation.

"So Nathan, where you live now?"

"I'm out in California, San Jose."

"What are you doing out there?"

"I'm a software developer. I work with a video game developer called Tempest."

"I've heard of them. They make that shooter I suck at. Good game, but I'm just not that good at shooters. So what are you guys doing passing through Wisconsin?"

"My grandpa died and Grandma decided to sell the house. Couldn't bear to put her in a nursing home, so she's moving in with me."

"Isn't that something. You taking the scenic route or something?"

"You could say that. You figured that out pretty quick."

"I've been driving that truck for 5 years now. I know the highways pretty well and the quickest way to San Jose isn't heading west on I-94 in the middle of Wisconsin."

"Grandma wants to see the Mall of America and Mt. Rushmore, and knowing her she'll probably find something else on the way. I don't really know what route we'll end up taking."

"Wow, I would love to do that. I always know what route I'm taking, and it's usually the same ones over and over, and mostly at night. That's what's frustrating about trucking. You see the country without seeing it. You pass so many interesting places and don't have the time to stop at half of them. I must have passed within 20 miles of the Grand Canyon a dozen times and I've never seen it. So, you guys were rolling down the highway and Grandma here has to take a pee, and you just happen to pull into the J when that uh...dirtball was taking a nap in his RV. Talk about timing."

"That's pretty much how it happened. The girl was looking out of the window and Grandma put two and two together pretty fast."

"Well, I'm pretty impressed. I've been keeping my eye out every-where I go and I've never spotted one yet. My niece Trudy was nabbed by one of those outfits and she was missing for two years. A trucker spotted her captor in Casper of all places. She came back and she hasn't been the same since, wakes up with nightmares half the time. Dude whored her out all over the country, sometimes to five or six guys in a night. I hate those ___ traffickers. Oh, pardon my French," the last part added in response to Myrtle's disapproving stare.

"Didn't sound like French to me," replied Myrtle.

"Sorry, ma'am."

"Oh, no problem. You live to be my age you've heard worse. Just watch it in front of the ladies, ok?"

"Yes ma'am. Say, you guys look pretty pooped. What you say we head back and you can get to your hotel and get some rest?"

"Yep, that sounds pretty good."

They got back to the hotel and Mack handed Nathan a card.

"Here's my cell number, and I'm on Facebook. Keep in touch, ok?"

"Sure thing, Mack. Nice meeting you."

They finally got in the car and drove over to the Comfort Inn. When they pulled in there were two young men waiting to take their bags in for them. One of them said, "You must be the Callahans. We've been waiting for you. Just follow me."

He put their bags on the cart and they followed him, stopping briefly at the front desk so Myrtle could hand the desk clerk a card with instructions to give it to Cassie when she got to her room. He opened the door to a suite, took their luggage in, and said, "You need anything, don't hesitate to call the front desk."

Nathan stretched out with his iPad and was mindlessly browsing the internet while his exhausted grandmother collapsed onto the bed.

"Oh, Nate, that was the most eventful potty stop I've ever had."

"Yeah, it's all over the news around here. All the local news channels have the story online and they're going to run it on the evening news. I won't be surprised if it goes national."

"Well, I'm past the age where I care about my fifteen minutes of fame. What matters is that poor girl has her life back, but how she'll get over what was done to her, I'll never know. Such a sweet creature still, for all that. I will pray for her."

Down the hall, that same young lady was sitting on the bed talking on the phone with her mother and still wiping tears from her eyes, when there was a knock on the door.

"Hold on a second, Mama, someone's knocking on the door."

She went to the door and looked through the peephole. It was the clerk from the front desk. She opened the door and the clerk handed her an envelope and said, "This was left for you at the front desk."

Cassie thanked him and locked the door before sitting down and resuming her conversation with her mother. She put the phone on speaker and set it down so she could open the envelope. She read the card while listening to her mother. The card read:

DEAR CASSIE,
   It broke my heart to hear what all you have been through recently. I

pray that the Lord will give you comfort and that you will find great joy in returning to your family. I also heard you say you were working to save money for college, so please allow me to lend you a hand with that. God bless you.

Myrtle Callahan

SHE WAS SETTING the card aside when she noticed that a piece of paper had fallen out of the card and when she picked it up she could hardly believe what she was seeing. It was a check made out to her in the amount of $20000.

"Oh my..." she cried.

"Is something wrong dear," asked her mother.

"No Mama, nothing's wrong," she said through her tears, "Nothing's wrong at all."

9

Nathan had certainly slept better. It wasn't that he stayed up too late, but his mind kept going back to Cassie and what she had been through, and it disturbed him greatly. Before going to bed, he had read quite a bit about trafficking online. Between what he read and what little he heard from Cassie, he was able to put together a fairly thorough picture of how these trafficking operations worked and what their victims went through.

It was not a pretty picture and he was highly disturbed by what he had learned. Human trafficking was pretty much the modern world's slavery and if the statistics were to be believed was the fastest growing criminal enterprise in the world. Most of the victims appeared to be from other countries, and most were forced into labor and not sex, but the sexual exploitation made for bigger headlines. He saw all manner of estimates about the number of girls and women brought into the U.S., figures ranging from 10000 to 50000. In truth, the numbers were probably rather hard to pin down because many of the victims appeared to be simply undocumented immigrants.

While rarer than the victims kidnapped overseas, there were victims here in America as well, as he knew all too well by what he had witnessed earlier. The traffickers used all manner of tricks to capture their victims, but outright kidnapping was not that common due to the extra risk involved. Often the victims were from poor families, but not always, and were lured by offers of good paying work in another city, or by a smooth talker promising an acting or modeling audition. Their captors knew a lot about their families and would make threats against a sibling or parent, or would take revealing photos of them and threaten to send those back to their families. Threats of violence against family or threats of ruining a girl's reputation with family members often proved highly effective at keeping the girls in line.

Sometimes girls were kept in one city and forced to work in underground brothels and sometimes, as was the case with Cassie, they were moved from city to city as customers in one city tired of them or the captor wanted to try another market for higher profits. They would also be used as prostitutes in truck stops along the way to other locations, which explained the cities that Cassie had passed through since being taken.

What he read troubled him greatly, but equally disturbing was the fact that he had known so little about it until now. He had lead a good life by comparison, even taking into account losing his parents at a young age. He had never been through such an ordeal, and his own concerns about his job situation or dating life seemed to pale in comparison.

Those thoughts had invaded his dreams and were still on his mind as he awoke and went through his morning routine. When he had showered, dressed, and packed all of his things, he then woke his grandma, who had apparently slept like a log and took a while to wake up.

"Oh, Nate, have we overslept again?"

"No, it's not that late. I just couldn't sleep any longer."

"Lot on your mind?"

"Yeah, thinking about Cassie. I did some reading. I wouldn't recommend that before trying to sleep. Seems like a lot of those jerks prey on minorities."

"I watched something on TV about it a couple weeks ago. They go after a lot of poor girls and minorities."

"Yeah, same thing I was reading last night. Bunch of sick bastards. Well, I'm going to take my stuff to the car while you get ready."

Myrtle was ready a few minutes later and after they had breakfast in the hotel, they set out on I-94 toward Minneapolis.

"How far to Minneapolis?" asked Myrtle

"Looks to be about 2 1/2 hours, give or take. It's about 140 miles, so it depends on what kind of traffic we see getting into the city. Not much to pass through between here and there. There's that town the TV reporter was from."

"Eau Claire?"

"Yeah, that's it. That's the only large town between here and there."

"You know Nate, there's one thing you can take from yesterday. Don't take anything in your life for granted. Be thankful for everything you have."

"Yeah, I know what you mean. I'm never going to gripe about anything again."

"I'll remember you said that," Myrtle said as she was opening up her journal and fishing a pen out of her purse. Nathan caught this and didn't say anything further, but got lost in his own thoughts as he drove on. Close to Eau Claire he made a quick stop at a cheese shop off one of the exits. Myrtle asked him as he was getting out of the car, "Do you need to use the restroom or something?"

"No, just figured we couldn't pass all the way through Wisconsin without buying some cheese. I'll be right back."

Ten minutes later he came back with several one pound blocks of smoked cheddar, smoked swiss, colby, colby jack, pepper jack, and a small bag of cheese curds. He cut a few slices of smoked cheddar, retrieved two drinks from the cooler, and pulled back onto the highway.

"You know, Nate, I've never been one to eat a lot of cheese, but this is rather tasty."

"I guess they know a thing or two about making cheese in this state."

"How much did you buy?"

"Enough. About 15 pounds, all different kinds."

"I'd say that will last a while."

"You know, the scenery is really quite nice around here. I had always imagined I was a big feature guy, but this is nice."

"Big feature guy?"

"Yeah, you know, the big spectacular stuff you see on calendars and postcards. Ocean views, mountains, you know, big stuff."

"I've never heard anyone use that term before."

"Well, it just popped into my heard. Made sense at the time."

"I guess it does. Life is kind of like that, in a way. The big moments are fun, but most of life is made up of small moments. You don't want to miss those. Your grandpa and I had some big moments, but I find myself remembering the small ones. Sitting in the kitchen eating breakfast, sitting on the back porch watching the sun set, sitting in front of a fire on a cold night. Those are the things I remember fondly."

"Since you put it so eloquently..."

"Oh, come on, I'm not that eloquent. I just miss him and everything reminds me of him. When you're with someone that many years..."

"Yeah, I can't imagine. You know where this reminds me of? Remember when you and Grandpa came to visit and we took that day trip to eastern Ohio? I think I was around ten."

"When we went out to Hocking Hills?"

"Was that the place? Where we went hiking and saw that cave?"

"That was it. You're right. This countryside is similar in a way. Very enjoyable on a day like this."

"You know, when you said you couldn't fly, I wasn't too excited about driving. I wanted to get back fast and get back to work. Now I'm kind of enjoying this. I wouldn't trade it for a fast plane ride back now."

"I hope you're still saying that in a couple days, being cooped up with an old lady all this time."

"That's not so bad. You're a good passenger. You don't complain much, but you do have to stop and pee too often."

"When you get to my age, if that's the only thing wrong, you rejoice. You know what they say though. The old grey mare ain't what she used to be."

"You're still kicking a lot better than a lot of mares your age."

"That's nice of you to say so. I'll tell you what. There are some days I feel half my age and other days I feel every one of my eighty years."

"You know what amazes me about you though? You take everything in stride. You lose your husband and you keep moving. Then you just agree to pick up and move all the way across the country like you're moving across the street. It's like nothing affects you."

"Don't get me wrong, Nate. Things do affect me, but you get to a certain point in your life that you can't let life beat you. Things happen and you have a choice. You can curl up and die or keep on living your life. I can't change anything that happens. All I can control is the attitude I have toward what happens. I take what life throws at me and make the most of what I have. Sure, I cried when Patrick died, and I still miss him terribly, but I don't think he'd want me just moping around."

"I just don't know if I could take it as well as you do."

"Honey, you learn to. Death is part of life, and you can't let it beat you. It's a little easier to handle if you know what's on the other side, or more precisely who. All that "he's in a better place" talk you hear at funerals? You might think it's trite, but sometimes it's actually true."

"I think it's true in Grandpa's case, but a lot of times it's just fluff to comfort people."

"That might be true a lot of the time, but your grandpa was ready to go. He told me that death would be like walking through a door from one room to another, and since he knew who was waiting in the other room, he wasn't too worried about it."

"You think he was trying to comfort you?"

"Perhaps. He was like that. Even in his pain, he was looking out for me, but either way, he really believed it. There was a man who followed the Lord. He wasn't worried about death because he was confident where he would end up."

"That's what I admired about him. It was matter of fact, nothing preachy with him."

"He was a real as it gets, that's what he was. That's what I loved about him, and why I still love him. Death isn't goodbye, only see you later."

"I have a feeling when we see him later, he's going to show us his favorite fishing spot."

"Yeah, Nate, you're probably right. By the way, you heard any more from your boss?"

"Not since that last conversation."

"What do you think will happen?"

"I really don't know. And to be honest, I really don't care."

"Of course you care. It's your career."

"I didn't mean it like that. I've just been thinking about what you told me. I know a lot about my job. I was involved in a lot of the development of the last game the company put out. If things go south there, I could land a position at any number of companies in the same area. I could even start out on my own if I had some good people with me."

"That would be kind of risky wouldn't it?"

"Maybe a little, but I have a lot of money saved up. I could live a couple years without a paycheck probably."

"I thought things were expensive out there."

"The cost of living is higher, but I get paid well and I really don't spend much. I have my apartment and my internet and cable bills, but that's about it. I don't go out much. Eating out is no fun alone and it's a lot cheaper to cook."

"You know, you could do something about that eating out alone thing."

"I hear you. I've been thinking a lot about what you said."

"Your friend Mark told you the same thing. You have nothing to lose by going for it. You want me to go and tell her you like her?"

"You're joking, right?"

"Maybe, maybe not. If you don't want me to do that, you'll just have to beat me to it."

"Good luck with that. You don't even drive. You think I'm going to run you over there so you can go play matchmaker?"

"Why not? It could be fun."

"I could just see it now. I walk by her desk and she says, 'Hi Nate, guess what you grandma just told me?'"

Myrtle had no response, but only because she was laughing. Sometimes she had an odd way of laughing where her whole upper body would just shake up and down and her eyes would be squinting, but no sound would be coming out. The smallest bit of wit could set her off, and this time she went on like this for a good five minutes. Nathan was wondering if she would need to come up for air. It was clear that the whole notion was amusing to her and soon Nathan was smiling as well. He hadn't seen her laugh like this since before Grandpa died. It did him good to see it.

"You do know it's not polite to laugh at the expense of others," he said.

"Oh dear, I'm sorry, but I couldn't help it. Myrtle's Matchmaking Service. Kind of has a ring to it, doesn't it? Maybe a new business venture for me. All you single friends will be lining up. I'll be rich."

"You're already rich."

"You didn't have to remind me. You're not doing so bad yourself. I looked up what people like you make."

"You looked it up?"

"I DO know how to use the internet. I'm not completely clueless."

"Well, I'm not as loaded as you are."

"That was all your grandfather's doing. That business is doing well and I don't have to lift a finger."

"How much do you have in the bank anyway?"

"None of your business, young man. It's plenty."

"How much have you given away since we left?"

"Oh, those couple checks? That was nothing."

"Say that to the recipients. You changed that girl's life."

"Maybe. Her life has already been changed. I just did something nice for her. After what she's been through, she deserves it."

"I've been thinking about her ever since. I feel bad about what she went through, but I'm really happy that we were there when we were. Maybe someone else would have stopped, but I'm happy it was us. I'm going to remember that day for the rest of my life."

"And just a few minutes ago you were getting on me about my bladder."

"That was the best timed pee break ever."

"Right place, right time. Or the Lord's timing. I just feel humbled that I could be used that way."

"Yeah, me too. How much did you give her anyway?"

"Oh, twenty grand. It won't even be enough to pay all of her college."

"Twenty grand? That depends on where she decides to go to school. It will be a good start. That might not seem like a lot of money to you, but to a poor girl like her? That's like winning the lottery. How about the guy in Indiana? How much did you give him?"

"Not as much. I think around fifteen."

"Fifteen thousand? You're certainly being generous."

"Like I said, I have plenty and I'll never live long enough to spend it all. Not with more coming in every month from the business. Don't worry, Nate. There will still be plenty left for you when I kick the bucket."

"Don't talk like that. You still have plenty of years left in you."

"None of us are guaranteed anything. Anyway, why be blessed with all this money and not use it to bless others? What am I going to do with it anyway?"

"Well, when you *do* kick the bucket, at least the preacher won't have to lie at your funeral."

Myrtle lapsed into another fit of laughing and then pulled out her journal and began to write more. Nathan turned up the radio and before he knew it, they were pulling into the parking lot of the Mall of America.

"We're there already," said Myrtle, "that was pretty quick."

"Yep, we're there. I'm not sure what you do in a mall this big, but I looked up some things online. They have an aquarium here and a maze made of mirrors, a lot of stores, and quite a few eating places. We could probably get lunch while we're here."

"The aquarium sounds interesting, Nate. Don't know about that maze."

They ended up going through both, the aquarium being more enjoyable than the maze.

"Nathan, that maze gave me a headache. I think I could use some lunch now."

"That place looks interesting," Nathan said as he pointed across the way.

"Bubba Gump Shrimp Co.?"

"Yeah, you like seafood."

"Sure, let's try it."

They went to lunch at Bubba Gump and though the food was good enough, actually really good, Nathan found himself wanting to change the topic when he realized that his grandma had an inexhaustible memory of quotes from Forrest Gump and was more than happy to share them with every restaurant employee she could come across. When they were finally done and had paid the bill, Nathan said, "I knew you liked that movie, but I didn't know you could quote the entire thing. How many times have you watched it?"

"Oh, I don't know, not more than a dozen times...well maybe more than a dozen. I don't remember. Your grandpa and I saw it at the cinema the night it opened and we saw it again the next night. We lived through everything in that film, so it kind of hit home."

"I guess so. I didn't know you knew so many of the lines though. I'm impressed."

They walked around aimlessly until they came to a bookstore, where they were both at home. Nathan picked up a couple novels and Myrtle got a novel and another journal book. He could't believe she had already filled one, but as much as she wrote while he was driving, maybe he shouldn't be that surprised.

When they were approaching the counter, an employee stopped them, took another look at Myrtle, and then stuck out her hand.

"I knew I recognized you. I saw you on the news last night. I'm Vanessa. I'm so glad to meet you."

"Hello Vanessa," Myrtle said, "You saw me on the news?"

"Oh yes, from the truck stop. You're the lady that called the cops on that kidnapper."

"I thought all the news people were from Wisconsin."

"I was visiting my parents in Hammond last night. They get the Eau Claire station. Anyway, I'm just so glad to meet you. Seeing that story made my day. Nice to see some good news for a change. So, you passing through or something?"

"Yep. On the way to California"

"Wow, I've always wanted to go there."

"Me too."

"So you've never been there either?"

"Not yet anyway. I'm moving in with my grandson here. I just lost my husband."

"Oh, I'm so sorry to hear that."

"Thanks. I'll be ok, though. We saw it coming for a while. Cancer. Not the best way to go."

"Yeah, my grandpa has cancer."

"Do yourself a favor," Nathan said, "Tell him how much you love him. Even if you think he knows it already. You'll regret it later if you don't."

10

Nathan pulled out of the mall and headed south on US 169. As they were leaving the city, Myrtle asked, "So, which way are we headed?"

"You still want to go by Mt. Rushmore, right?"

"Yes, I do. Your grandpa was going to take me out west, before he got sick."

"So we can take this road for a bit to a town called Mankato, then there are some state routes that will take us down to 90. Thought it would be a nice change to get off the interstate for a little while."

"How long has it been since we had lunch?"

"Oh, I'd say about three hours."

"How far is that town you mentioned?"

"Looks like between an hour and an hour and a half."

"Let's stop there for supper then, if that's not too soon. I'm in the mood for a good steak. How about you Nate? When's the last time you had a good steak?"

"Oh, it's been a little while, couple weeks at least."

"So get online and see if there's anyplace up ahead to get a good steak. Nathan read a few reviews on his phone and an hour and 20 minutes later they pulled into Charley's Restaurant in Mankato.

"The online reviews for this place were good," Nathan said as they were getting out of the car.

"Let's hope they're right. I haven't had a good ribeye in ages."

They were seated and made their order, ribeye and baked potato for Myrtle, sirloin and fries for Nathan.

"Lord knows that was the best ribeye I have had in a long time. Ask the waiter for a box and I can have the rest of it tomorrow."

"Mine was pretty good too."

"I can see that, as fast as you went after it. You have to take your time with something that tasty."

"You sound just like Grandpa."

They pulled out of the parking lot and Nathan opted to take State Hwy 60 down to Worthington and then I-90 west through South Dakota. His plan was to spend the night in Sioux Falls, spend the next day driving across the state, spend another night and then have the entire following day to see Mt. Rushmore. He had no idea how much walking around his grandmother would want to do, but it would be best to start in the morning and just let her go until she got too tired. If they left early enough, he could drive a little farther while she napped in the car.

The drive down Hwy 60 was a welcome change of pace from the interstate driving he had done so far since leaving New Jersey. Grandma was in her journal again and Nathan was in one of his introspective moods where he went between thinking about his job and beating himself up over his romantic shortcomings. When he got in these moods, the miles rolled by and the time went by fast. He had dreaded this trip when Grandma first said she couldn't fly, but now he was enjoying it. He could almost see the allure of the road that truckers spoke of...almost. How in the world people could do this day in and day out he would never understand. Well, they probably couldn't understand how he could sit at a desk all day.

He was in one of these moods when he rounded a bend in the road and was brought abruptly to the present, by what exactly he wasn't sure. Maybe it was simply the right angle of the shaft of sunlight coming out of the high thin clouds, the way the wind was rippling the crops in the fields, or the glint of the sunlight off the water of a small lake not far north of the highway, or maybe it was the combination of all of these factors, but it broke through his thoughts and all he could do was just utter an audible, "wow."

"You say something, Nate?"

"This countryside is really pretty, is all. I just noticed it."

"It doesn't look much different from where you grew up."

"Maybe not. I think I just get so lost in my own head that I don't notice what's around me."

"If I had to spend too much time in your head, I'd probably get lost too."

"Well, I guess it could be a scary place for an old person."

"Listen young man, my head's not such an empty space either. When you get to be my age, there's so much stuff up there it can be hard to sort through it all. You slow down because you're sorting through all the useless stuff in your head, and that's why we old folk notice things young people don't. Nathan, honey, there's beauty all over the place if you just slow down enough to notice it. Getting slow in your old age is the Lord's way of forcing us to take the time to notice what he created."

"Yeah, and his way of teaching young people patience," Nathan said with a slight chuckle.

"You watch it kid. You're not too big for me to turn you over my knee."

"You'd have to catch me first. They don't call you Myrtle the turtle for nothing, remember?"

"Careful, you get me laughing too much we'll have to make another stop."

"Speaking of stopping, we have two options. We're about an hour from Sioux Falls, but it's still early. We could push on to Mitchell and stop there for the night, then get up early tomorrow and make it the rest of the way across the state. Then we can either see Mt. Rushmore tomorrow evening or get up early the next morning and take half the day."

"How about we stop to pee in Sioux Falls and spend the night in Mitchell then?"

"Fine with me, I'm just along for the ride."

"You know what I'm noticing? I can't remember ever seeing this many motorcycles in one day."

"Now that you mention it, we've been passed by I don't know how many bikes since we got on 90, and that wasn't that long ago."

"Maybe this is a popular highway for bikers."

"Must be, but they're all heading west like we are. You seen any going the other way?"

"Can't say that I have."

Arriving in Sioux Falls, they stopped at the Flying J, on the lookout for anything suspicious as they pulled in. Nothing suspicious this time, however, just Harleys everywhere and burly bearded men milling about. He couldn't recall ever seeing a rougher looking assembly. He used the restroom, bought a few more drinks, and had just finished putting the drinks in the cooler when one of the bikers standing nearby addressed him.

"Hey, how you like the Tahoe? Been thinking of getting one."

"Uh...it's ok. I like the way it drives. It's just a rental though."

"How is it on gas?"

"Not too good, but it's the only thing the rental place had with a hitch for the trailer."

"Where you headed?"

"Left New Jersey a few days ago, heading for San Jose."

"Moving out there?"

"I live out there. My grandma's moving in with me. Grandpa died last week."

"You taking your grandma across the country? Wow, that's epic. You must have a lot of time to talk," the biker said, sounding to Nathan like he was getting choked up.

"Yeah, we talk a lot. She always has a lot to say."

"Son, that's great. I would love to do that, but I lost my granny last year. Hell, I wish I had just another day to talk to her, or even five minutes. Lot of things went unsaid. Don't let that happen to you. You don't want the regret."

"I hear you. Lost my parents when I was young."

"What do you mean *when you were young*? You're still young."

"Happened when I was fourteen. They went out to dinner, got hit by a drunk on the way home."

"Whoah man, that must have been rough."

"It was. I got over it as well as anyone could, but it's the regrets that still bug me. I was just a teenager, and you know how teenagers are with their parents. Talk about things left unsaid."

"Yeah, that sucks. I think I need to call my mom before we pull out."

"So, you with all these other guys?"

"Got a couple buddies I'm riding with. These other guys are all headed the same place, I reckon."

"Where's that?"

"You don't know much about bikers, do you son?"

"No, not really, never met any."

"Heading to Sturgis, ever heard of it?"

"I saw it on the map. Taking Grandma to Mt. Rushmore before we head south for I-80."

"Hope you have your reservations out there. Might be hard finding a room. You take care."

"Yeah, you too."

Myrtle came out of the restroom and said, "Sure are some rough looking fellows in there."

"Oh, they're just rough on the outside. I seem to remember you telling me something about books and covers."

"I might have said something like that once."

"Yeah, they're probably all softies anyway."

"So the guy you were talking to was a softy?"

"He misses his grandma."

"So did he say why there are so many of them here."

"He said they're all headed to Sturgis."

"Well, there must be something going on out there."

11

Remembering what the biker said about the availability of rooms, Nathan called ahead and reserved a room for them at the Hampton Inn in Mitchell, one of the few rooms left there, and they headed west on 90.

"How far until this town we're stopping at, Nate?"

"A little over and hour, looks like. The town is Mitchell. They had a brochure in the truck stop about it, says they have some sort of building made of corn there. I have got to see that."

"I have the brochure right here. Says here that the outside is decorated with corn and is changed yearly. The whole building isn't made of corn. It was built back in 1892 and has had all sorts of uses over the years. They play high school basketball games there and have different kinds of shows."

"So you want to go by and take some photos?"

"I'd rather just get some rest for now. We can swing by there in the morning."

They drove on in silence for a while, listening to the radio and Myrtle once again writing in her journal. "She's going to have enough in there to publish a book by the time we get home," Nathan thought to himself.

Nathan passed a small town called Alexandria, saw that Mitchell was less than a half hour ahead, and then the engine sputtered momentarily and died. He coasted to the shoulder and stopped. This was a rental and was apparently in good working order when he had picked it up in New Jersey.

"I wonder what's wrong with the car," he remarked.

"Did the engine just quit, no warning?"

"Yeah, just died there, no warning at all."

"Nate, honey?"

"Yeah?"

"When's the last time you put gas?"

"Uh...somewhere back in Wisconsin I think. I meant to back in Sioux Falls, but I got to talking to that biker and it slipped my mind."

"Well, I think you've found out what's wrong. What are you going to do?"

"We just passed a town a mile or so back. I guess I could go back there and get some gas. Might be a bit of a walk."

No sooner had he spoken than he saw three motorcycles slow down and stop just behind them. One of the bikers got off his bike and he recognized him as the man he had spoken to back at the Flying J.

"What seems to be the problem?" asked the biker.

"Would you believe I ran out of gas?"

"Now...wait a sec...aren't you the guy I talked to back at the J, the guy taking his grandma to Cali? How in the world did you run out of gas 40 miles after leaving a gas station?"

"Absent minded, I guess."

"Son, that's beyond absent minded. How the hell do you park next to a gas pump for ten minutes and then run out of gas 40 miles down the road? Thanks, kid. I needed the laugh."

"We stopped to use the bathroom. Wasn't thinking about gas."

"Well...whatever. There's a gas station back there in Alexandria. I could give you a ride back there and we could get some gas. Hop on," and to his two friends, "You guys care to keep granny here company while we run and fetch some gas?"

Nathan hopped on the back of the bike and before they set off he said,"My name's Nathan, by the way."

"Jim Masterson at your service. And my friends over there: the carrot top's Andy and my darker friend there is Jose." Andy and Jose both offered a wave.

They rode back to Alexandria and pulled into the gas station, only to see out of order signs on the pumps. Nathan went inside and inquired of the clerk,"So, the pumps are out?"

"Yep, been down for a couple hours, dang computers. Can't say when they'll be back up."

"Are there any other gas stations around?"

"On ahead in Mitchell is your best bet. About 15 or 20 minutes."

"Ok, thanks."

They rode back to where the car was parked and Jim spoke with the Andy and Jose before saying to Nathan, "Looks like the closest place to get gas is Mitchell. That's nearly a 40 minute round trip to get gas. We can't leave Grandma here that long in this heat. How do you think she'd feel about riding along?"

"I'd love to," Myrtle exclaimed before Nathan had a chance to reply.

"Ok, we're going to need some gear for these folks," Jim said, "I've got an extra helmet and jacket.

"I've got an extra helmet and a couple extra pairs of chaps," Jose said.

Andy replied, "I think I'm good for another jacket."

"That ought to do it," Jim replied.

"Ok, Grandma," Jim said, "We need to get you dressed."

"You can call me Myrtle."

"Ok, Myrtle, you need to put these things on. It might get hot, but safety first. Just slip your legs into these as best you can. I know they're not your size, but we don't have time to go shopping. Now, slip on this jacket. Ok, now here's a helmet. You can put that one when we're ready to pull out."

Nathan and Myrtle were both wearing chaps and biker jackets

that were a few sizes too large and the sight of his grandmother dressed like this was enough to drive Nathan to laughter.

"Laugh all you want, honey. If Patrick could see me now he'd be rolling too. I imagine I must look quite fetching in this getup."

"Oh, you have no idea," Nathan said as he took several photos with his phone.

"So, let me get this right, these things on my legs are called chaps?"

"Yes," Jim said, "and the rest is pretty self explanatory."

"I've seen other bikes going by with women on the back. Do you have a word for that too?"

"Well...there is...but I don't reckon it fits in this case."

So they were off, Nathan on the back of Jim's bike and Myrtle on the back of Jose's, for the short ride to Mitchell. Neither Nathan nor Myrtle had ever been on a motorcycle before and the ride was nothing short of terrifying for Nathan. Myrtle, on the other hand, was having the time of her life. She found the whole experience exhilarating, reveling in the sense of speed. It might have seemed somewhat scary for someone her age, and maybe it should have been if she had given it any thought, but she wasn't thinking much about it. It was just plain fun. Maybe the fun came from it being a new experience, and at her age there were few experiences that could qualify as new.

They pulled into a gas station where Nathan purchased a small gas can and filled it. They strapped the can on the back of Andy's bike and Nathan said to Jim, "Our hotel is just a few blocks from here. Maybe we can drop Grandma off before we go back to the car."

When they arrived at the Hampton Inn, Nathan noticed the look of sheer happiness on his grandma's face and commented, "Why, you look like you were having a ball."

"Yes, indeed I was. Did you not find it quite exciting?"

"No, I did not. I found it quite terrifying."

"Come on Nate. Where is your sense of adventure? One would think you were the old man and I the young woman. I feel like a spring chicken. Why, I feel like I'm in my 40s again."

"I'm glad you enjoyed yourself. I don't think motorcycles are for me, no offense to our present company."

"Oh, Nathan, you're just afraid of risk. You need more excitement in your life. You just might learn to enjoy it. I had a ball. Jose here sure knows how to show a lady a good time."

"Why, it appears that Jose is blushing. I don't think I've ever seen that before," remarked Jim.

Myrtle was in the process of removing the jacket when Jose waved his hand for her to stop and said, "No, ma'am. You keep it. A souvenir from your ride."

"Why, thank you very much, young man."

"No, thank you ma'am. It's been a long time since anyone called me a young man."

After the reservation was confirmed and Myrtle was resting comfortably in the room, they made the trip back to the car. After he got the car started, he shook each of their hands and said, " Thank you so much for everything. I really appreciate it."

"The pleasure was all mine," replied Jose, "Your grandma is a great lady."

"Yeah, she is. Maybe you'll keep a better eye on your gas gauge from now on," Jim said.

"Yeah, I'll do that. Thanks again."

As the bikers sped off into the distance and he eased onto the highway, he felt all of a sudden a bit lonely. Alone time was something he usually cherished, but this time it was different. The last time he had been alone had been before the funeral and he had grown used to having his grandmother around, even if she was keeping quiet and writing in her journal. The drive to Mitchell wasn't long, under 20 minutes, but it felt longer for some reason. This was a strange feeling for Nathan and he wasn't quite sure what to make of it. This trip, for its relatively short duration, was changing him.

He hadn't realized it during all those years he lived with his grandparents, but Grandma was really pretty smart. Why hadn't he noticed it until now? She was always a sweet old lady, everything a young man could want in a grandma; she had qualities Nathan could not readily identify, just that they seemed to be the quintessential qualities most good grandmothers had. Not that he had much other experience with grandmothers, his maternal grandmother having passed when he was a small child, but he couldn't imagine having a better grandma.

Now he was seeing something else, something he admired but never noticed before, and he couldn't put a finger on it. Grandpa was a larger than life persona and he had more than adequately filled the void left when Nathan's father died, not only teaching him honesty and integrity, but modeling those virtues. He didn't just teach Nathan how to be a man; he showed him.

Now that Grandpa was gone and he was viewing his grandma out from under his shadow, he saw her in ways he had never noticed. She wasn't like many old people. Many people her age were afraid of change and a set in their ways, but not Grandma. Sure, she complained about things changing at times, but she also knew how to change with the times when necessary, and seemed more comfortable with it than he was. When he saw her with the bikers earlier, it was like he had a glimpse of who she had been as a young woman.

Before Grandpa's death, he loved her much like any other boy loves his grandma, but now he was getting to know her better and he was coming to the realization that she was the kind of woman he hoped he could marry some day. She was fun, not some stick in the mud old person who had lived life and was just now waiting to die. She was still trying to live, to cram as much as she could in however many days she had left. He wanted to be like her when he got old, and he wanted to get old with someone like her.

That thought brought Phoebe back to mind and thinking of her brought to mind something his grandfather had said on one of those attempts at fishing.

"Grandpa, I'm not catching anything. Aren't the fish supposed to bite sometimes?"

"Well, Nate, they don't call it catching, they call it fishing. Pardon the cheesy analogies, but fishing is a lot like most things in life. You have to prepare the bait and drop the line in, and even then the fish isn't always going to just come up and jump on your line. You have to do some work. You have to know where to cast your line and sometimes you have to reel it in a bit, make the bait move some to attract the fish. Sometimes you really have to go after the fish because he's not just going to come and jump in your boat without you doing everything you can to attract him and then hook him when he finally goes for it.

It's like that with most things in life. You don't just sit there and expect fish to jump in your boat. You have to go out there and go after what you want. Heck, if I didn't get off my butt and finally ask your grandmother out, where would I be? A girl like that wasn't going to sit around forever and wait for me, and if one of my buddies hadn't told me she was interested, I might have never done anything. The world isn't going to hand you anything, boy. You have to get off your butt and go and get it."

The funny thing is, he couldn't remember if they caught any fish that day or not, but now he remembered what his grandpa had said like it was yesterday and not twelve years ago. Had he heeded his advice? Mostly, at least where his education and career were concerned. He knew what he wanted to do and he had pursued his education with a dogged determination. His determination had paid off, landing him the job he wanted with the company he wanted, and now he was sitting in a pretty good spot in his career. There was only one missing piece in his life and now he figured his grandfather's advice applied there as well, if only he could muster up the courage to do what needed to be done.

He pulled into the gas station, filled the tank, and then went to the hotel, stopping at the front desk for another key before going to the room. He found his grandma sitting in the bed, her journal open beside her with the pen sitting across the open pages, still wearing her biker jacket, with a slight smile on her face and a tear running down her cheek.

"Everything ok, Grandma?"

"Yeah, Nate, everything's ok. I was just thinking about your grandfather."

"Yeah...I was too. You know what else I was thinking about? That you and Grandpa were baseball fans, your team is playing tonight, and there's a sports bar right down the street. I saw it when I was going to get gas."

"Oh, Nate, you know I'm not one to hang out in bars."

"This is a sports place, with lots of TVs and games on. We can watch the game, you can have a tall glass of tea or three...it'll be good for both of us."

"Ok, just give me a minute to fix my hair after having that helmet on."

A few minutes later Nathan and Myrtle walked into Blarney's Sports Bar and Grill and found a table facing one of the TVs and a young woman came over to wait on them.

"We've already had dinner," Nathan replied, "but we might want an appetizer and something to drink, and do you think we could get the Reds/Pirates game on the TV right there?"

"Sure thing. What kind of drinks can I start you out with?"

"I'll take a Coke and my grandma will probably take iced tea if you have it."

"We have tea. Would you like sweet or unsweetened, ma'am?"

"Sweet would be good," Myrtle replied

"Ok, I'll be right back with your drinks and I'll see about getting your game on."

Nathan looked over the menu and said, "Beer battered onion rings. You think you can help me with those?"

"You know those things give me heartburn."

"Well, I'm going to order some. You're welcome to help me with them."

The server arrived with their drinks and Nathan ordered the onion rings. She said, "Ok, I'll be back with those in a few minutes. If you need anything, my name's Elaine."

Nathan answered with a shy smile, "If we don't need anything, is your name something different?"

"Huh...ah...ha ha, that's a good one. Thanks for me making me laugh. I needed that."

The TV changed just in time for the first pitch, their onion rings arrived, and against her better judgment, Myrtle did indeed eat nearly half of the basket while watching the game. After two drink refills, a trip to the restroom, and about three innings of the game, Myrtle took a sip of her tea, sighed, and said, "I miss your grandpa, Nate. He would have liked this place."

"Yeah, he took me to a place like this once, near Edison I think. I miss him too."

"You know, dear, I think he would be awfully proud of you."

"After today, I'd say he would be more proud of you."

12

They ate the free hotel breakfast and got in the car. While Nathan drove there, Myrtle pulled out the Corn Palace brochure. He didn't need GPS to find the place as he went north up Route 37 from the hotel, 37 becoming Burr Street, from which a left turn on 6th Avenue took them straight to the Corn Palace, which they could hardly miss as they drew near. Myrtle read from the brochure as Nathan drove, so by the time they reached the corner of 6th and Main where the building stood, they felt that they knew everything they needed to know about the large arena/multi purpose facility thad had been there over 100 years. She read about the mosaic murals decorating the outside of the building, murals made entirely of corn and changed on a yearly basis.

The brochure did not do the site justice, and Nathan and Myrtle spent more time than they had imagined they would walking around the perimeter and marveling at the images made entirely of corn, taking photos of every part of the exterior, and even posing in front of the larger than life image of Elvis with a microphone. When they got back in the car, Nathan remarked, "That was actually more impressive than I imagined."

"I know, Nate. I can think of better uses for that much corn, though."

"Well, it certainly is unique."

As they got on I-90 heading west out of Mitchell, Myrtle commented that Mt. Rushmore could not be too far away and Nathan replied, "If we drive straight there we could get there by late afternoon, so maybe we can take our time, spend the night in Rapid City, and see it tomorrow. That way you can have all day if you want. I'm not sure what there is to do there other than look at the mountain."

"Are we going to find a room in Rapid City? You remember what our biker friends told us."

"I made a reservation online while you were in the bathroom this morning."

"Good thinking, kid. Is there anything to see before we get there?"

"Well, I did some browsing online last night before I went to sleep. We're going to pass right by the Badlands and there is a loop road you can take through there. The pictures online looked amazing. We can take lots of photos there. There's also this place called Wall Drug. Looks like a major tourist trap, but it's supposed to be famous. We might have to stop there."

"Yes, I've heard of Wall Drug, Nate. You see the bumper stickers everywhere you go. You remember our neighbor back in Jersey? He had a sticker on his pickup."

"We're about three hours from the Badlands, and if it looks anything like I saw online, you're going to be taking photos until the cows come home, so you might want to make sure you have good batteries in your camera. I'll just use my phone."

"You kids and doing everything on your phones. I'll never get used to that."

Myrtle took out her journal and began to write, so Nathan once again lapsed into his usual introspection as he drove. By now, the sixth day of their trip, he was becoming accustomed to it and his mind tended to rehash the same topics. He had remembered so many forgotten conversations he had had with his father and grandfather, had rehearsed countless reasons why Phoebe was the perfect girl and countless other reasons she was beyond his grasp, had let himself feel that there was a glimmer of hope, had beaten himself up over his inability to make a move, had tossed his job situation back and forth, and had gone back through the whole cycle again.

All of this had really accomplished very little except make him frustrated by his shortcomings, but it was also making him realize the wisdom in what his grandfather had told him years ago, about seeing what you want in life and just going after it. That was Grandma. She had an adventurous streak that he never knew she had. That's not a trait he normally associated with people her age, but she was showing it throughout the whole trip. He had been terrified on the motorcycles; she had taken to it with a joyous abandon. Now he was beginning to wonder about her medical inability to fly. Maybe she wanted to have one last adventure after all and saw this as the chance to do just that.

If that was the case, he should feel manipulated, but he didn't. He didn't really doubt what she said. It was like everything else she faced. Make the most of it and enjoy yourself. She was acting like a younger woman, with a level of energy and vigor he could scarcely believe. Maybe it was therapeutic, something she needed after recently losing her husband. Maybe it was good for both of them, since they were both mourning the same man for essentially different reasons. This was probably what Grandpa would want them to do, have some fun and live a bit. That was how he approached life after all.

After 200 miles and three more bathroom stops, they reached the turnoff for Hwy 240, the loop road through the Badlands. It did not take long for him to see why this road was listed as one of the great scenic routes in the entire U.S. There wasn't much vegetation to look at, but the rock formations took his breath away. There were numerous places to stop and take photos, and they took advantage of every one of them. They hardly spoke to one another except to marvel at the rocky spires jutting up and the vast pallet painting the rocks as the sun hit from different angles, the bands of colors marking the different strata in the rocks, the shadows cast from some of the taller peaks. It was a scene of utter desolation, but of an eerily beautiful desolation. Every time they thought they had seen everything there was to offer, there was another type of rock formation or the sun hitting another formation in a manner they hadn't seen before.

They were so caught up in the scenery that they lost all track of time and when Nathan finally glanced at his watch, three hours had gone by and he was feeling hungry. He grabbed two apples from the cooler, passed one to his grandmother, and said, "Here, we haven't had anything since breakfast."

"Thanks, Nate. I hardly noticed that I was hungry."

They soon came to the end of the loop road and crossed I-90 into Wall, and Nathan made a point of looking for Wall Drug, which in a town that size could not take long to find. He saw a sign for the Wounded Knee Museum, remembered something about that from a forgotten history class years ago, and turned to head to the museum. Finding the museum closed, he went across the street to a small gift shop, which was empty save for an elderly American Indian sitting behind the counter.

"Help you with anything, young man?" asked the man.

"I was wondering about the museum across the street, if it was going to be open any time soon," replied Nathan.

"Won't be open 'til next spring, had a fire a couple years back."

"That's a shame. I wanted to check it out."

"You know what it's about," asked the man emotionally.

"I heard about it in history class when I was a kid, but I don't remember much. I didn't pay attention enough in class, I guess."

"Would you like to know about it?"

"What can you tell me?"

"I can tell you a first hand account, the story my grandfather told me when I was young. He was there."

Myrtle had wandered into the store and hearing the conversation between her grandson and the man, she kept her mouth shut to see where things were going. As there were no customers in the store, the man arranged a couple chairs for them all to sit down on and began his story.

"My grandfather was a young man at the time, only fourteen years old. He saw the soldiers come into the camp that morning, demanding that our people give up their weapons. Many did, but many did not. He heard a commotion in the middle of the camp and kept his distance. He stood back and observed a struggle between two men over a gun, heard the gun go off, and then all hell broke loose.

The single shot rang out and was followed by a volley. He saw people falling to his left and right and wanted to fight the soldiers, but he only had a knife. He saw the soldiers through the smoke firing volley after volley, firing and stepping back, and with each volley more fell. Our people were writhing on the ground and still more fell. He heard some singing the death song then, but he was not going to sing that song yet. He wanted revenge.

He managed to get a weapon from one of the white soldiers and as he was lifting it up to fire, he drew their attention and several began to fire at him, but all missed. He ran toward a ravine that several other people were fleeing to, but the ravine was full of the dead and dying, and many others trying in vain to escape the fire that was being poured into them. He saw babies there, young women, old women, young boys much younger than he was, and he was filled with anger. He saw an infant trying to suckle from his dead mother's breast. Soldiers were firing into the ravine and many were struck down there.

One time when the smoke cleared he saw that the soldiers also had another kind of gun he had never seen before that had revolving barrels. These guns were firing into the camp and mowing down many of our people. Then he saw through the smoke a riderless horse and ran toward it meaning to use it to escape. When he mounted the horse, his brother saw him and also mounted. Soldiers fired at them and this time my grandfather was hit in the arm. Another bullet took his brother in the chest. They galloped that horse as fast as they could and made it away, receiving no other fire.

His brother died later that evening from his wound, but my grandfather was able to get his wound treated.

The soldiers killed 300 of our people that day. They killed unarmed women, children, old men, babies, and young men in their prime. Many of our people were dumped into mass graves, and the government awarded the Medal of Honor to many of the soldiers who had done the killing. The Medal of Honor for an act so dishonorable."

By this time tears were streaming down the old man's face and Nathan and Myrtle sat there dumbstruck. Myrtle knew the story, and by now Nathan could remember it from history class, but hearing it from this man seemed to drive it home, seemed to make the story more alive. Nathan moved silently to the man's side, opened his arms, and enveloped him in an embrace, saying to him, "I'm so sorry."

"No need for you to apologize, son. You weren't there, and I wasn't either."

"No, but I can't think of anything else to say. It breaks my heart."

"You know what you can do for me, for us? You can read this," handing Nathan a hardbound copy of *Bury My Heart at Wounded Knee*, "and then maybe you can visit the place where it happened and pay your respects there. This book will give you all the details, names and dates and all that. You can't undo what happened, but if there were more people like you willing to try to understand, and willing to extend a little respect and kindness to an old Lakota, then that would go a long way toward healing. It would be a good start."

"Where did it happen?" asked Nathan.

"Oh, not more than a two hour drive from here, south down by the Nebraska border."

"Well, we have to go south anyway, so we'll stop by. By the way, I don't think I got your name."

"You can call me Sam."

"I'm Nathan, and this is my grandmother, Myrtle."

"There is no way this young lady can be your grandmother."

"God bless you, but you have a silver tongue," Myrtle said, "Nate and I will stop there to pay our respects and to give our regards to your grandfather."

Myrtle also gave Sam a hug and they took the short walk to Wall Drug. After speaking to Sam, neither was in a light hearted mood, and walking around Wall Drug is nothing if not light hearted. They visited many of the shops, purchased a few souvenirs and some western themed art that Myrtle thought would look good in Nathan's apartment, which she had yet to lay eyes on, grabbed a quick bite to eat, had a glass of free ice water, and even managed to get some photos of each of them sitting on the saddle of the giant jackelope outside.

Of all the silliness in the place, the jackelope had to take the cake. The darn things were everywhere, and some of them were quite convincing, a real testimony to the skill of a taxidermist with a sense of humor. After seeing a few of these rabbits with antlers attached, Nathan had to ask a local what the deal was and the only answer he got was, "Why that's a jackelope." He wasn't gullible enough to think the creature was real, but likewise he couldn't readily figure out why it was such a popular item. Just weird South Dakota humor, he figured, but it was at least mildly amusing.

They loaded up their souvenirs, went by the gift shop to say goodbye to Sam, and made the drive to Rapid City, where they checked into the Holiday Inn Express. As they were pulling in, Nathan remarked on the close proximity of Boston's Restaurant and Sports Bar, where they found themselves 20 minutes later after checking in and leaving their luggage in their room. Once again Myrtle was able to watch a baseball game and sip a glass of iced tea, while Nathan went through numerous Coke refills while reading the book Sam had given him. Nathan was a fast reader and by the time the baseball game was over, he had read through nearly half the book and was wiping away tears with his napkin.

Myrtle, who had read the book years ago, had a good idea what Nathan was going through and didn't speak to him about it. She watched the game and occasionally looked at her grandson, who never looked up from the book except to sip his drink. A book like that must have a powerful impact on a boy as soft hearted as Nate, she thought to herself.

Back in the hotel room, Nathan said little and sat down to continue reading. Myrtle, realizing that any attempt at conversation would not be welcomed, opened her journal and began to write.

My grandson seems greatly moved by his experiences today. He was never one to show any interest in history, thought it one of the most boring subjects in school. I remember his complaints about dry history and all the stupid names and dates. Now he made a direct connection with an amazing man, who if I had to venture a guess is probably near my age if not older, a man who is directly connected to a real historical event he studied in school. Nathan is soft hearted to a fault, and hearing that story seems to have broken that soft heart of his. He's over there reading through Bury My Heart and trying to hide his tears, but he's better just letting them out. My reaction was much the same when I read it, what, 40 years ago? Has it really been that long?

Every time I write here I wonder about the rapid passage of time. I feel like I married Patrick a week ago and now he's gone. I met him 60 years ago and was married to him for 58 of those years, and it seems like it all went by in a blur. Here I am old and I'm not sure how I got here. Wasn't I a young vibrant woman just the other day? Well, I feel like a younger vibrant woman lately. I thought this trip would be tiring for my old bones, but if anything it's made me feel younger, almost like it's a grand adventure, the kind I longed for when I was young. Now I'm having my adventure, a few years later than I wanted to and without the man I wanted to have it with, but maybe there's a reason for that.

I thought I would have this grand chance to impart some elderly wisdom on my grandson during our trip, but I find myself learning as much from him as he could learn from me, or maybe I'm learning more about him. That's it. I'm learning more about him than I am from him and I'm learning that he's a little more complex than I thought, but also a lot like his grandfather. He has that same introspective habit that Patrick had, and gets that same faraway look about him when he's lost in his thoughts. There's so much going on in there and there's so little ability to let it out. That's how my husband was, God rest his soul, and Nathan is more that way than he was. He's a loving creature and such a caring soul. I remember the times as a young boy that he would cry at the news. He never thought I noticed and he thought he was so good at hiding it, but every time there was a sad story, his heart break for people he never knew.

Now he's come face to face with one of the saddest stories of our nation's history and he's been told the story by someone who is closer to it than a history text and it's like the tragic news story a thousand fold. He's come face to face with the heartbreak of a people and his own heart is breaking for them. Maybe if there were more people like him, there would be more reconciliation. Maybe it would be a step in the right direction.

This trip has been more than I imagined it would be. While it's true that the doctor said flying might not be the best thing for my health, I must admit that I wanted to go by road for selfish reasons. I've always wanted to see the west, to have this one last adventure. I know Nathan didn't want to at first, but now it seems to me that he's enjoying it as well. Maybe enjoying isn't the word for his experience this afternoon, but I know he's getting as much out of it as I am. Maybe he just needed a break from work, more than he thought he did.

Myrtle had more on her mind, but her eyelids were getting heavy, so she shut the book and drifted off. The last thing she saw was her grandson still reading, and still wiping tears away.

13

Nathan was pulled from the depths of sleep by a pressing need to use the bathroom. Normally he would fight the urge and try to get more sleep, but this time he was glad to be awake. His dreams had been disturbing, disjointed images of children in danger while he was powerless to help them. He wiped the sleep from his eyes and ambled into the bathroom. Returning back to the bed, he noticed his grandmother sitting at the desk, dressed and ready to go.

"How long have you been up," he asked her.

"Couple hours, I think. I'm ready to go when you are."

"You're telling me you've showered and I slept right through it."

"Well, you were out like a light, but you were tossing a lot."

"I was having weird dreams."

"Care to talk about it?"

"Not really. I'm going to get a shower."

Nathan returned from the shower and as he was packing his suitcase, Myrtle asked him, "So, bad dreams?"

"Yeah, and weird. You know the dreams you have when you're not feeling well and everything's kind of disconnected, one image after another and nothing making any sense?"

"I only have those when I'm sick or feverish."

"Same here, but it was weird. Kids were always in trouble and I couldn't do anything about it. I wanted to help them, but I couldn't. It was frustrating."

"How late did you sit up reading that book?"

"Not sure about the time. I finished it and went to sleep."

"You finished the whole thing?"

"Yeah, just couldn't put it down."

"What did you think of it?"

"Man, I'm not sure what to think. It bothered me, made me think. I'm still trying to sort out how I feel. I mean, I'm still proud to be an American, but our country has dome some shameful things."

"The shame isn't yours, Nate. Your ancestors weren't there."

"I know that, but...oh, I don't know. My family never owned slaves or killed Indians, but those events are still shameful. I still think we live in a great country, but we have some pretty big skeletons in the closet and most people are just trying to keep the closet door locked. Maybe we need to deal with it before we ask people to get over it and move on."

"You can't change the past, Nate."

"No, but we can change the future. Let me just grab a donut from the breakfast bar and we can head out. Anyway, I've been doing too much thinking. Slavery was one thing. We freed them and then spent the next 100 years trying to make them equal, and we've mostly done that. There's still racism, but black people are equal by law. But with the Indians, it's different. We've just swept that all under the rug and ignored it. How many of those people still live in poverty on reservations? They live on the fringes of society and everyone else just wants to ignore them."

"This has really gotten to you, it seems."

"Yeah, you know I've never been that interested in history, but talking to Sam hit me. It's not just history with him, but family history. He drove it home. Well, you know I've always had a soft spot for people who are hurting, and all Sam did was bring his people's pain to my attention. Now I'm trying to deal with it. It's not comfortable."

"No, honey, it's not comfortable. It must be a lot worse for someone like you. You have your grandfather's empathy. Did you know he cried for ten minutes on the way home one day because he hit a squirrel?"

"A squirrel?"

"That's just how he was. He was a big softy, and you're just like him, but not as good at hiding it. You've lived a sheltered life until now, but since we left New Jersey, you've come face to face with suffering. Cassie's situation bothered you a lot too, didn't it? I think you just have a lot more empathy than most people. You know what it is? You care. You actually give a darn about other people and about their suffering. That's a rare trait these days."

"I guess you're right. I've always been that way. You know I never watched the news with you and Grandpa much. I was obsessed with programming and pursuing the career I have now and I think I blocked a lot of things out, or just didn't notice much of anything else. By the way, why did you want to see Mt. Rushmore anyway? There are a lot of things to see across the country."

"I'm not exactly sure. I've always found it interesting looking at pictures of it, and there is a lot of history carved up there. Your grandpa mentioned it a couple of times too."

"I've never given it much thought myself. I'm always so busy with work."

"Don't you get vacation days?"

"I get PTO days, about three weeks a year, but I never use all of them."

"PTO?"

"Paid time off. A lot of companies do that now instead of having vacation and sick days. With sick days, you can't use them if you're not sick, and people who never get sick would never use them. Tempest went to PTO about the time I started there. You just get so many days and you use them however you want. If you don't use them, you get paid for them, so I just get an extra check every year."

"That makes sense. Why don't you use those days?"

"I don't know. Just never needed them I guess."

"Everybody needs time off. Even the Lord took a day off when he was done."

"I just never thought about taking a vacation. Never thought I needed to."

"You don't have to go anywhere. Just taking the time off will do you some good. Do you think you're doing the company a favor by not taking time off? You think you'll impress them or something and it will pay off?"

"It's not that..."

"Come on Nate, I wasn't born yesterday. Your grandfather thought the same thing before he started his business. He would work extra hours and not take time off, and then he found out that all that didn't help him one bit. Not taking those days isn't going to impress somebody there who will all of a sudden put you on the fast track for better promotions and raises. You'll be worth more to them if you take the time off you're allowed to take. You have to recharge."

"I guess I've never really thought about it like that."

"Oh, you've thought about it, but you think you can show them what a hard worker you are and it will help you out. Believe me, it won't."

"I'm using a few of them right now."

"But would you be using them if your grandpa hadn't died?"

"Probably not."

"See, I was right. When you go back to work, you'll find that the time off did you some good, even if it took someone dying to get you to take it. Speaking of work, it's been a while since you've heard from your boss."

"The last time I heard from him, he wasn't exactly happy. No news is good news."

"You think you should follow up with him, see how things are?"

"I figure if anything changes he'll let me know."

"You just don't want to deal with it right now. You're putting it off. That's your one flaw. You don't like conflict and you're really good at avoiding it. The problem is that sometimes when you have to deal with it, it's bigger than if you had dealt with it sooner."

"You're really on my case today."

"Sometimes you need it. You know, you are your father's son, and your grandpa's grandson. They were both the same way at times, but you take it farther. You think that things will just happen, so you go through life figuring that you can stay out of conflict, do a good job and live a good clean life and the good things will just happen. Well, honey, the world doesn't operate that way. You do a good job and some other guy gets the promotion or the raise because he did the thing you abhor, he just went and asked for it. You're interested in some girl and you conduct yourself like the perfect gentleman around her but she ends up with the same guy who took your promotion, because he just went after what he wanted instead of thinking it would come his way by right."

"You see the signs? We're almost there. You have your walking shoes?"

"I have everything I need. Walking shoes and fresh batteries in my camera. Don't think you can just go and change the subject so quickly. We'll pick it up later."

When they arrived, they saw signs for the Lincoln Borglum Visitor Center and the Presidential Trail, and Myrtle, feeling energetic suggested they walk the trail first.

"You sure you feel up to it," Nathan asked.

"It's only a half mile. We can take it slow."

And take it slow they did. Myrtle hadn't accounted for the number of steps and her knees were on fire before long. They made numerous stops along the way and finished the walk an hour later, a walk that was worth it in the end because of the better views of the sculptures. Myrtle took photo after photo of the mountain as well as the surrounding area, including the two half tame deer that were watching them from a few yards off the path.

When they arrived back at the visitor center, they were more than ready to sit down and view the 15 minute film that explained how the faces were carved. They walked around to view the other exhibits and

Gutzon Borglum's studio, they purchased the usual assortment of overpriced souvenirs and t shirts, and then made their way back to the car, having spent nearly three hours there, most of that time spent resting Myrtle's worn out knees on the walking path.

While there, Nathan heard about the Crazy Horse Memorial that was currently under construction and when they got back to the car he mentioned it to his grandmother and suggested that they stop there on the way south. It appeared to be about a half hour away. A half hour away it was and they soon stopped there as well, and although the mountain sculpture was still a work in progress, it was already quite impressive. Nathan followed the signs to the Welcome Center, where Myrtle was happy to find out that bus rides were available to the base of the mountain. They boarded one of the buses for the short ride and once again took several photos of the sculpture in progress, which when completed will depict Crazy Horse, mounted on a horse, and pointing into the distance. Some of those details could already be made out and Myrtle and Nathan were both immensely impressed by the details already present.

Back at the Welcome Center there was also a historical film that they viewed and then Nathan saw signs for a museum entrance. They made their way into the Indian Museum of North America, where Nathan became engrossed in the displays of artifacts and art work, photographing everything in sight. Myrtle tagged along and although she was fascinated by the exhibits, she was even more fascinated by observing her grandson. He looked like the proverbial kid in a candy store, she thought.

The gift shop turned out to be the candy store. As Nathan loaded his numerous purchases in the car, more books and artwork, Myrtle said, "You know, Nate, for a kid who never cared for history, you're showing a lot of interest now.

"It was never real before. Either I didn't have good history teachers, or I just never paid attention."

"Maybe it was a bit of both, but you seem to have forgotten one small detail."

"What detail would that be?"

"Where are we going to spend the night? You didn't sleep much last night, so who knows how far you'll be able to drive."

"I looked online when you were in the bathroom. There's a small town in Nebraska, not much of a drive from Wounded Knee. The Super 8 has rooms. Not what we're used to, but it's a room."

"Sounds good," Myrtle said as she retrieved her journal from her purse and began to write. Nathan once again let his mind wander as he drove. He thought about Wounded Knee, remembering what Sam had told him and what he had read before sleeping. The whole thing saddened him, but not just what happened but how indifferent most people were to it. He had been the same way most of his life, thinking history to be something in the past that wasn't worth his attention.

"I think you're right," he said.

"Huh, you say something?"

"I think you're right."

"I heard you the first time. I just wanted to hear you say it again."

"I've been thinking while you're over there writing War and Peace."

"I haven't written that much."

"It just seems like it. How many of those books have you filled up."

"I filled the one I brought with me and a few pages in the one we got in Minneapolis."

"You must have a lot on your mind."

"What happens to one of your computers when you've had it a while?"

"The hard drive gets filled up with a lot of useless junk."

"Exactly. Writing it down helps clean out the hard drive."

"I didn't think you knew so much about computers."

"I pay attention when you try to tell me about them. Occasionally something sticks."

"Well, I run through things in my head a lot. I guess for the same reasons. You said I try to avoid conflict. I think you're right. I'm always looking for the smoothest path and where has that gotten me? Sure, I have a good job and I had to study hard to get there, but it didn't seem hard at the time. It was something I was interested in. I've been thinking about work, and about Phoebe, and I think I've had the same approach all along. I think that if I do what's right, work hard at my job and be a good friend to Phoebe that things will fall into place."

"How's that been working out for you so far?"

"Well, work's been ok. That's about it. I think I always thought that's how things worked because when you observe other people that's what it looks like. You see a couple and they're just friends. Next thing you know they're engaged, and from the outside it looks like something that just happened. I've been rather naive, haven't I?"

"You could say that. You know what else, Nate?"

"What's that?"

"I have to pee."

"So what's new? I'll see if there's anything coming up."

After the pit stop, Myrtle got in the car and opened her journal. Nathan turned the radio to a jazz station and continued heading south. Before long, he was approaching Wounded Knee. When he arrived at the memorial, he was surprised at what he found. He half expected to see a well cared for facility with a visitor's center and a gift shop, but he was wrong. There was a gate set up over a roadway, some signs that had a brief history of the massacre, a fenced in area with some tombstones, and a vast grassy plain with a gradual slope to a hill on one side and the Wounded Knee creek in the distance. Having recently read the account, he recognized the hill as the place where the Army had placed the Hotchkiss guns that were used to mow down so many of the victims, and most likely some of their own people as well.

He just stood there for a moment, partly sad that there wasn't more of a memorial there, and then he noticed a few native people hanging around, a rather bedraggled lot, and some approached him to ask for money or any help he could offer. This saddened him and touched him at the same time. Back home he had grown hardened to panhandlers because he figured many of them didn't seem to need help but only wanted booze. Maybe that was the case here as well, but he doubted it, and the sight of some of the children tore at his heart. He parted with all of the cash he had on him and most of the snacks and soft drinks he had in the cooler. He noticed an old woman away from the rest and he approached her.

"Is this all there is here," he asked her.

"What more did you expect?"

"I don't know. Something like what you see at other historical sites, something taken care of and respectful of what happened."

"Young man, this tells our story best. We're the forgotten people. Most would rather forget what happened here."

"People shouldn't forget. How could people forget?"

"Remembering is uncomfortable. Most would rather forget. What brings you here, young man?"

"You can call me Nathan. I'm taking my grandma to California. We stopped in Wall yesterday and I met a man there who told me about this. Said his grandfather was one of the survivors. I had to come and pay my respects."

"Well, Nathan, you can call me Diane. Glad to meet you," she said as she brushed a tear from her cheek.

"You ok, Diane?"

"Yeah, I'm ok. Just touched. A lot of white folk come to visit. Most of them are curious or act like they have some guilt they're trying to get rid of. You're not like them."

"Thanks. I don't know about the guilt thing. None of my family were involved. I don't know. I learned about this in school when I was younger, but it went in one ear and out the other. History wasn't my thing. Then hearing the story from Sam made it more real. We had to stop."

"Did you say you met Sam up in Wall?"

"Yeah, old guy in a gift shop. You know him?"

"You could say that. Sam's my brother. Our grandfather was one of the survivors. So he told you the story, did he?"

"Yeah, he told me, and gave me a book to read. I told him we'd come here and pay our respects, try to honor the victims."

"Oh, you have honored them, and you honor us too. Who is this young lady with you?"

"I'm Myrtle, Nathan's grandmother," Myrtle said, "Pleased to meet you, Diane."

Myrtle approached Diane, gave her a hug, and handed her an envelope before heading back to the car. Nathan said goodbye and joined his grandmother. As they pulled away, Diane opened the envelope and read the hastily written note.

I am humbled to visit the site of such a sad day in our nation's history and I am equally humbled to have met a living relative of one of the survivors. I am not only saddened at what has happened, but at how your people continue to live. I see many here who look to be in great need, so accept this as a small attempt on my part to help with that need. I trust you to put it to good use. Myrtle Callahan.

Diane was about to put the note back in the envelope when she noticed something else, a check for an amount that made her gasp, and brought another tear to her eye.

14

They left Wounded Knee and drove down to Chadron, NE, but ended up at the Best Western when the only rooms at the Super 8 turned out to be smoking rooms. They were both hungry, so they dumped their bags in the room and went across the street to the Country Kitchen to have supper. They placed an order and while they were sitting waiting for their food, Myrtle said, "You know, Nate, seeing those people today broke my heart. I've never seen such poverty up close. I know you feel the same way."

"Well, we are Irish. The Irish have had a rough way to go. Maybe they're a kindred spirit."

"I don't know if you can compare the Irish situation with theirs, honey."

"Not the way things are now, but there are similarities. You know all of these books I've picked up today and the one I read yesterday? It's got me thinking. Now you're more of a history person than I am, so correct me if I get anything wrong, but what happened to the native people here isn't an isolated thing."

"I think I know where you're going with this."

"It seems to me that as long as people have been running around on the earth, the person you don't want to be is the person who's native to a certain area. Those people are always getting run over by more powerful people who want their land. All over the world, it's always been the stronger people taking whatever they want from the weaker ones, and it's only rather recently that humans have come to the idea that maybe we shouldn't be doing that."

"For a kid who didn't like history, you sure remember more of it."

"No, I don't remember the names and dates, but the more I think about it the more things keep coming back. Little bits and pieces from high school and college. What I keep remembering is how this has played out all over the world and how people now are finally figuring out that it's wrong to prey on your weaker neighbors. Only now it's too late because most of the damage has been done. So what do we do? How can we treat those groups of people who had everything stolen from them? It's not like we can just give it all back. Think how complicated that would be. But tell me, Grandma, you've seen the Indians we've met the last couple days. Do any of them look like they're living the American dream?"

"Not sure I'm following you completely."

"It's not that hard to see. They're still living on reservations, basically second class citizens. Our government, or the government a hundred years ago, basically pushed them off their own land, settled it, and then put them on all these reservations, and few of them have ever assimilated into our culture. Sure, some do, but many of the ones we have met are still living where they were placed and the rest of us seem rather happy to keep them there. Out of sight, out of mind. I feel like there has to be something I can do, but I don't know what."

"Well, Nathan, you're young still, and young people are always thinking they can change the world, then you get older and get beaten down enough by the world and often you give up. That's why so much never actually gets changed. People don't hold onto that idealism you have and they give up. My advice. Don't give up. The few people who don't give up when they get beaten down are the ones who actually do change the world."

"Thanks, but I really don't know what to do, or what I can do. The whole situation seems pretty complicated, but it seems to me that the

people on those reservations have been there for so many generations that they don't really know a way out. It's like folks in the inner
cities. There are these cycles that go back generations and people
don't know what's available to them. Then coming in as an outsider
you're not always welcome if you try to tell people what they need to
do, even if you're right."

"Nathan, you just hit the nail on the head, but you have a sharp
mind. Keep at it and I'm sure you'll think of something, even if it's just
a small impact you can have in a small area. You make a positive
impact on even one person and you never know how far that can go.
That woman at Wounded Knee last night...what was her name...
Diane, that's it. Anyway, she seemed awfully touched by us just stopping by and by the humble attitude you showed. You lifted her spirits.
Maybe she will have a positive impact on her family because of that.
You might have done more than you will ever know."

"I hope so. I know you'll have an impact. I saw you give her that
envelope. Oh look. Our food's here."

The server put their dishes down on their table and then looked
at Nathan and said, "Sorry for eavesdropping, but I caught what you
were saying. I grew up at Pine Ridge. I wish more white people were
like you. Thank you."

"You're welcome. So you live here now?"

"Yeah, married a white guy and moved down here. He's like you.
If you need anything, just let me know."

They finished their meal and headed back to the hotel, where
Nathan sat down and opened the journal app on his iPad, since his
grandma was already in her journal book writing away. He pulled out
a small bluetooth keyboard, connected it to the tablet, and began
to write.

*Where do I begin? Tomorrow will be a week since we left New Jersey
and it seems like almost an age ago. Then again, it's been a fast week as
well. I thought at first that we would be in San Jose before now, but so
much has happened in these last few days and now I almost don't want the
trip to end. Grandma has surprised me in a few ways. I always knew she
was a smart woman. I mean, she has a college degree and all that. How*

many women her age got a degree? Not as many as nowadays. I'm really enjoying myself right now, even when Grandma nails me on something, and she's done that a couple times lately. She's right. I don't like confrontation, and I will try to avoid it at all costs, and maybe that's part of why I'm no longer in any hurry to get back.

I know I have a good job and I make good money, and that promotion should be mine if there's any justice, but what Grandma is saying about what happened to Grandpa and how that's just the way of the business world? Could she be right? That was years ago and companies are different now. This industry didn't even exist back then. Then again, she's been right about darn near everything else.

And what about this business about going after what I want and not waiting around for it? Have I not done that? I knew before I got out of high school what I wanted to do and I worked my butt off and got there, but do I really have everything I want? I know the answer to that. I want the whole American dream, the whole thing. I want to have a couple brats running around the house, those brats growing up and making me a Grandpa, and all this time growing old next to a woman. I want all the happily ever after white picket fence stuff. What have I done to get that though? I have always assumed that relationships just happened to people. That's the way it seems at least, but maybe Grandma's right. No, there's no maybe about it. She is right. Have I ever known her to be wrong?

If she's right, then I have a major comfort zone to get out of. Is Phoebe the one? Well, if she isn't, then the one must be one fine woman, because Phoebe is so...so what? I'm not even sure. Sure, she's good looking, but with her there's more than just her looks. She's humble, sweet, confident, and something else I can't put a finger on. Exotic maybe? Well, she's a foreigner, so that accounts for the exotic part, and maybe for the other qualities as well, qualities American girls don't seem to have as much of. Maybe that's it. Maybe I'm a bit old fashioned and she comes across as old fashioned, like maybe people in other countries raise their kids the way people used to be raised here before things changed.

What changed? I don't know. I'm in over my head here, out of my depth. I just know that I'm interested in her. She's the kind of girl a guy could make long term plans about, and if what Grandma says is true, about *the ticking clock and all that, she's going to be making those kind of plans soon, with or without me. I need to do something about that apparently, and that's what I'm not sure about. Well, when I get back home, I need to figure something out or screw up the courage to just ask her out.*

Maybe Grandma's right about me being young and idealistic, but I wasn't that way a week ago. I was just concerned about my career. I was happy with my career and the company I work for. Everything was going well. Everything except Grandpa dying, but we all knew that was coming, with the cancer eating away at him for the last couple years. Now we meet Cassie the other day and just happen to be in the right place at the right time. Now she's back with her family and I've been thinking about how I can help other people in her situation. I never thought about causes before. Then I meet Sam and the other Indians and my heart is broken again. I want to help them too.

Yeah, I want to help them, but I don't even know what to do. Just be nice to all the ones I meet? Just tell them I sympathize with their plight? No, I need to do something, just like I want to do something to help trafficking victims. I have a soft heart according to Grandma, but my head can't figure out what to do with what my heart is telling me.

Now I see why Grandma writes in her little book all the time. This is somewhat therapeutic, and it does help to sort out thoughts. She's still going strong over there and I'm thinking I want to call it quits and start on one of those books I bought.

With that, Nathan closed his journal app and opened one of the other books he had bought on the history of the Oglala people. The book was fascinating, and eye opening. He had always thought of the Sioux as one homogeneous group, had never realized that there were subsets of Sioux that all had their own identity. He was still reading long past the time his grandmother had closed her journal and gone to sleep and he realized that if he didn't close the book and get some sleep, tomorrow was going to be a difficult day driving.

He eventually did sleep and the morning started pretty much the same way the previous morning had started, with his grandmother coming back into the room to wake him after having already showered and eaten breakfast. He ate a bite, consulted the atlas, and then packed the car. As was their routine at this point, Myrtle asked him how far they were going to go and what route they would be taking.

"It looks like we can take Hwy 385 south for a bit, then take a couple other side roads down to Cheyenne, then it's pretty much 80 almost all the way home, well almost all the way. We have to take another highway south from just past Sacramento. Looks like we have about 20 hours of driving time from here to San Jose. Who knows how many days that will take us at the rate we're going, but we can probably be there by mid week even if we dilly dally."

"How much more can we dilly dally at this point?"

"I don't know. There are still a few towns to pass through. There's Cheyenne, Salt Lake, Reno, and the small ones in between. You might find some photo stops across Wyoming."

"You not in much of a hurry to get back, Nate?"

"Not in a hurry, but not stalling either, just enjoying the trip."

"When I said I didn't want to fly, you seemed disappointed. Now you're wanting to take your time."

"There is a joy in the journey. You know, wasn't that a line in a song Grandpa liked, one of those Christian singers he listened to?"

"Yes, I believe it was, but which singer escapes me at the moment. I have all his music packed in one of the boxes. You can probably find it when we unpack."

"You know, I liked some of that music, but I never told Grandpa."

"I think he knew. You always were an odd kid when it came to music. You never really liked what your peers liked. Are you still like that?"

"You hear what we've been listening to this whole trip, don't you? Modern pop just doesn't cut it and rap is too vulgar. That's what most people my age listen to these days. Hip hop is quite popular, but I can get cussed at anywhere without having to hear it in my music."

"That's something we agree on then. I don't understand that at all, but I think your grandfather had a more open mind than you or me. He didn't like it either, but he said that music was always people speaking from their own cultural experiences. Maybe that's what rap is, inner city people talking about their lives."

"You know, for an old lady you sure do keep up with things."

"That's how your grandpa was. You remember how he was always reading and watching news. He liked keeping up, said he never felt old that way."

"Well, when I was in college I met a lot of people from a lot of backgrounds, and there were people there who came from the inner city, some of the lucky ones who got out and were making something of themselves. They could talk about their struggles without dropping F bombs every five seconds or saying degrading things about women or calling each other the N word. There's a difference between speaking about your culture and your struggles and glorifying the negative aspects of your culture."

"You would know better than I would, Nate. I've heard some of it, gotten turned off by it, and never wanted to listen to it again. Then your grandfather was always trying to understand people. He would hear one of those songs and wonder what it was that made a young man so angry to say those kinds of things and he would try to understand."

"But he had a couple of his shops in some inner city neighborhoods, right? He would interact with them more than you did?"

"Yeah, Nate, his first shop was in a pretty rough area, but he always did good work and the locals would come to him. He got to know his customers, would always listen to them when they talked to him about their troubles."

"Man, I miss him. He was one heck of a man."

"Yes, he was. You're a lot like him in more ways than you know. He had that same habit you have of retreating into yourself and not coming back for a while. You just zone out. When we first met he had that habit of never looking directly at the person he was talking to. He would look down or at the wall behind someone, never in the eye. He was so painfully shy, just like you. You do the same thing, you know. You're always looking everywhere except right at the person you're talking to. You need to work on that, especially if you ever want to actually start dating. He got better at that over the years. Lord knows I was always getting on him about it.

You got his good qualities too. He was empathetic to a fault. His heart would break every time he heard a sad story from someone. There were days he would come home from work almost in tears because some customer had lost a family member. One time he had a woman bring a car in that was going to require an extremely expensive repair. It was the woman's only car and she was a single mother with three kids. She didn't have enough money to fix the car and couldn't afford to buy another one, and she couldn't go without a car with her job and having to take her kids places. Of course you know what Patrick did? He fixed the woman's car and didn't charge her one dime, even though it meant we struggled for a couple weeks."

"I heard that story at the funeral. That was the old black woman with the purple dress on, right?"

"Yes, I believe I saw her there."

"She talked to me for a while and told me that story. She said she didn't know what she would have done if it weren't for his generosity."

"That's right. All three of those kids of hers ended up going to college. That's just how he was. He couldn't bear to see others suffering. He must have given away thousands over the years. One time I went looking for a dress and when I asked him where it was, he had given it to some woman from church because I hadn't worn it in over a year."

"After talking to that woman at the funeral, it made me want to be like him. I mean, you can tell the life you've lived by the people who come to your funeral, and if they have to lie or not. I don't think anyone had to lie there."

"You can't ask much more than that really, that nobody has to lie at your funeral. Speaking of that, I haven't finished all my arrangements. Your uncle knows mostly what I want, but it hasn't all been written down yet. Maybe I should do that."

"Come on Grandma, don't talk like that. You're not that old yet, and you're as healthy as a horse."

"I'm already past my three score and ten, and none of us are guaranteed tomorrow."

"I know that, but it's depressing. Wait until we get home and then we can talk about that."

"Ok, but I want the same preacher. I like how he handled your grandpa's service."

"Alright, but seriously, can we talk about something else?"

"Sure, I just want to be ready."

"I'm not sure there's anyone more ready. It's just depressing to talk about it on our trip."

"You said we're going to pass through Cheyenne?"

"In about 3 1/2 hours, give or take."

"What's the next city after that?"

"Probably Laramie, if I can remember right. Why?"

"Just wondering where we're going to have lunch."

"I think Cheyenne would be too soon. We'll probably find something in Laramie. That's about four hours away."

"Sounds good."

Myrtle then pulled out one of the books Nathan had purchased and began to peruse it, ending their conversation, and prompting Nathan to turn the radio up. His grandma had figured out how to browse the categories on the satellite radio and when he turned the volume up he found it on a 50s channel. He had never listened much to 50s music, but he left it there and found some of it pretty good and some of it mildly amusing. He recognized some of the songs, and before long found his toe tapping and the miles rolled by in a blur.

By the time they were passing through Cheyenne, Myrtle had been writing in her journal for nearly an hour and Nathan changed the channel to one of those mellow blend channels that played a mix of mostly 70s music with some 60s thrown in for good measure. He found that he actually liked that music better than most of the newer pop music, and better than the 50s channel that, if left up his grandmother, would probably play non stop all the way to San Jose. They stopped to use the restroom in Cheyenne, at another Flying J truck stop, and Nathan overheard some other travelers talking about a big Abraham Lincoln statue at a rest area west of there. He asked and they told him it was at exit 323.

Leaving Cheyenne and heading west, Nathan found the rest area at the top of a long uphill grade and thinking his grandma would find it interesting, he stopped.

"There is no way you have to pee again, Nate."

"No, not that. A guy at the Flying J told me about this rest area. Check that out."

Myrtle looked out the window and there in front of them was what had to be a 30 foot high stone pedestal, granite from the looks of it, with an enormous head of Abraham Lincoln perched on top. She gazed at it in awe for a moment before retrieving her camera and telling Nathan she would be back shortly. Five minutes later, after taking several photos from a few angles, she came back and asked Nathan if he would take a couple shots of her with the statue in the background, and they even solicited the help of another tourist to take a couple photos of the two of them.

When they got back in the car, Nathan decided he would look up restaurants in Laramie and find someplace good for lunch, when he noticed a new email on his phone. The email was from Frank, his boss, and he didn't particularly want to read it at the moment, but decided to go ahead and open it.

NATHAN,

Frank here. I know I said I needed you back here ASAP and all, but we can wait. The patch is going to be bigger than we expected and the other teams will be a while getting their parts done, and knowing you, you'll have the AI fixes done with your usual speed, so just get here when you can get here. Of course if you want to fire up your laptop and work on things remotely, feel free to do that. Also, we're going to do another round of interviews for that supervisory position. There are a couple other guys who were promised interviews. You're still the best fit, but we have to talk to them too. Probably just a formality. Also, my sister in Minnesota saw you and your grandma on the local news the other day, something about you saving some girl from a trafficker. That's pretty awesome. Everybody's been talking about it around the office. Anyway, what I said earlier. Don't worry about it. You haven't taken much time off and you could use the break, and we all think it's something else you bringing your grandmother all the way out here to live with you. So we'll see you soon. Shoot me a message back and let me know when you know what day you'll be back. If you do any work remotely, just send me the files.

"Is that from work," Myrtle asked.

"Yes, take a look," Nathan said as he handed his phone over and pulled back onto the highway.

"That looks like good news," she said after she finished reading the email, "a different tone than the last one."

"Yeah, it's almost like Frank had a major change of heart. That's not like him to change his tone like that, but I'll take it."

"You find anything to eat in the next town?"

"You in the mood for steak?"

"Who isn't?"

15

They stopped in Laramie and after checking online reviews, they chose J's Steakhouse since reservations were not required there. They looked over the menu and placed their orders, and when the waiter left Myrtle commented, "So your boss seems more agreeable than he was the other day."

"Yes he does, but why the sudden change of heart?"

"It could be anything, honey. He thought you could use the break, or it's just what he said about the deadline not being as urgent. Anyway, what is a patch?"

"After a game comes out things come up after people have played it for a bit. No matter how well you test it, the players find problems and they have to be fixed. Sometimes it's a graphical glitch, or an exploit someone figured and and you have to fix it, or sometimes it's something with the multiplayer that needs to be balanced."

"You know most of that went over my head."

"I'm not sure how to explain it then. Ok, most people download games these days. Even with the game consoles where people buy a CD, the CD only has so much of the game on it. The rest is downloaded. If there is any kind of a problem with the game after release, the developer can make a file that is downloaded to the game file the person already had and that new file fixes whatever the problem is. We call it a patch because that's exactly what it does. When you have a pair of pants that has a hole, sometimes you just sew a patch over the hole and your pants are fixed."

"Ok, that makes sense. So you have work to do on this patch?"

"Yes, but apparently it's a big patch and everyone has something to do on it. My part isn't that big, just fixing some bugged behavior on the AI. AI is the computer controlled characters that are in the game. I have to do some balancing on them. Someone thinks they're too hard, so I have to tone them down a bit. It won't take me that long to do it, maybe a couple days, but some of the other fixes are apparently taking longer."

"I guess you know your job pretty well?"

"Not to toot my own horn too much, but probably better than most."

"So you think you have a good shot at this promotion?"

"Pretty much. There really isn't anyone more qualified, not with all the turnover we've had lately."

"Is there a lot of turnover in your industry?"

"You could say that. Tempest is still a fairly new company and there are some giants in the same area. There are a lot of software companies in that part of California, and not just games. Guys are always shopping for a better deal and there's a bit of jumping around."

"Have you thought of shopping around, as you put it."

"Not really. The company hadn't been around that long when they hired me and I've grown with them. I like being part of that. It feels like we're the underdog, a real us against the world kind of feeling."

"But you're not as much of an underdog as you used to be."

"What do you mean?"

"I started using that iPad you gave me. Did some reading waiting for you to wake up the other day. Your employer is becoming a big deal."

"I guess so. The latest game was a huge success. They've put out two titles so far and it could be a successful franchise for a few years. There are other projects in the pipeline as well, not to mention the new VR titles."

"VR?"

"Virtual reality. You seen those goofy looking headsets people wear on their faces? People wear those and when a game runs through that, you feel like you're in the game, not looking at it on a screen. Right now there aren't that many games in VR, but it's looking like the next big thing. The companies that are able to release some good titles will make a killing."

The waiter brought their food and was followed by the manager, a tall middle aged black man who said, "You guys the Callahans?"

"Yes we are," Nathan replied, "Why do you ask?"

"I thought so. I'm Tony. My cousin emailed me the news story from Wisconsin. Cassie is my niece. I thought I recognized you when you came in, so I had to see for myself. Your meal's on the house. Least I could do to say thanks."

"Thank you very much, young man," replied Myrtle, "Your niece is an incredible young lady. I was glad we were able to help."

"We're all very glad you were there ma'am, and we're glad that the...uh...unsavory person responsible is behind bars where he belongs. You folks going to be here in Laramie long?"

"Just stopping to eat and moving on. We're probably going to spend the night around Evanston," Nathan said.

"Well, the next time you're in Laramie, you'd better stop in again."

As they pulled out onto the highway after eating, Myrtle asked, "So this VR is kind of like 3D was a few years ago?"

"Not quite. 3D never really took off as much for games, but it's still used in movies. VR will be huge for games, but not so much for movies. With 3D, you're still viewing it on a screen, but with VR, you're actually in it. It's hard to explain if you haven't seen it first hand. You're not looking at the images on the screen. The scenery is all around you, like you're actually walking around in it. It's going to be huge in flight and racing games."

"Maybe you can show me sometime."

"When we get home. I have a headset on my computer and I have a couple VR demos you could view."

"So your company is going to go forward in this area?"

"Yeah, and if I get that promotion, I could work on some of that. I would love the challenge."

"There isn't much challenge in what you do currently?"

"There is and there isn't. I know my job inside and out, but I like learning new skills, but Frank has been hesitant to let me work in other areas because I'm good at what I do. He likes to keep people where they're good. It's his comfort zone. Makes his job easier I guess."

"But it sounds like now he might give you the promotion. What would that mean for you?"

"It will mean more money, but the part I'm interested in would be the extra responsibility. I would be supervising others, running a team kind of. I would still do a fair bit of programming, but I would have other people on my team and the team would have to handle different aspects of a project. I might have programmers, artists, graphics people, motion capture people, and AI people all reporting to me and I would have to coordinate their efforts. It would be a whole new experience, and a whole new challenge."

"Well, Nate, if I know you, you will be up to it. It sounds like you're kind of excited about it."

"You could say that. I didn't expect it at my age. It's exciting and scary all at the same time, but I think I'm up to it."

"Would that mean more hours at work?"

"It could. That generally happens when a project is approaching some sort of a deadline. There's a release date coming up for a new game, or a patch is going to go out by a certain date. Then people end up doing crazy overtime to meet the deadlines."

"It looks like we'll be home soon. You allowed pets in that place?"

"Uh, yeah...but I don't have any. Always been too busy."

"Sounds like you're going to be at work a lot. A little critter around would give me someone to talk to while you're out."

"You been giving that some thought recently?"

"Just a little. A house can get a bit lonely by yourself, and I've never lived by myself."

"Well, there's a shelter not far from home. They have lots of little critters."

"And another thing. I want to get involved in a church. Does yours have many people my age?"

"Well, I haven't been going regularly, just once in a while. There are a couple close to me that I've been to."

"Ok, Nate, but you know how I feel about that. We're going to pick one and you're going to take me every week. And you're going to stick around."

"Yes, ma'am."

"Speaking of that, tomorrow's Sunday. When we get to...whatever that town was you said we were stopping at, we need to find one for the morning. You can just pick one close to the hotel."

"The town's Evanston. We're still around four hours away from there, unless you want to push on to Salt Lake City."

"No, Evanston will probably be fine. You think they'll have one of those places where we can catch the game? They're playing the Cardinals this weekend."

"Darn near every town has a sports bar..."

"Oh look, the Reds are playing the Giants soon. It's not too far away, is it?"

"It's not too far. Traffic's a bear going up there, and it gets nippy at that ball park. I've been a couple times."

"How about a beach? I haven't been to the beach in ages."

"It's a bit of a drive, but that's nothing we're not used to by now. The water's darn cold though. Nothing you can swim in most of the time."

"Oh, I'm not much for swimming, even if the water's warm. I just like to sit there and take it all in, the smell, the sounds...it's absolutely grand."

"Ok, it's a date then. First weekend, we'll head to the beach for a day."

"Oh, you're bringing a date? That I have to see. Who is she?"

"That's not what I said."

"Maybe I'm hearing things then. Happens when you get older. Shame. I thought I was going to be meeting that fine young lady you mentioned from work."

"We're not dating, Grandma."

"Well, whose fault is that?"

"Yeah, I hear you. You know how shy I am."

"So was your grandpa. It didn't hold him back."

"So, what kind of church you want to look for in the morning?"

"Nice, way to change the subject. I'm sure it won't take long to find one near the hotel. You have that GPS there, or you can search on your phone like you do for restaurants. Oh, I have to pee."

"Again? Didn't you go at the restaurant before we left?"

"Yeah, let's see how your bladder holds up when you get to be my age."

"Nobody's bladder can hold out with that much iced tea. How many glasses did you drink back there."

"I don't remember, just find me a bathroom."

"There's an exit up ahead. We'll see what they have there."

The next exit had a gas station and Nathan pulled in and they both got out. Myrtle went to the restroom and Nathan bought some more drinks to put in the cooler and topped off the gas tank. After their experience in South Dakota, he rarely let it get below half. When Myrtle returned to the car, she went back into her journal as they rejoined the highway. Nathan thought he would never tire of the mountain scenery they were driving through, and Myrtle must have thought the same, trading the journal for a camera and snapping photos out the window.

It wasn't long before Nathan saw a rest area and it was now his turn to have to stop. When he was pulling into the rest area, Myrtle asked, "You have to pee now?"

"Yeah."

All that came from Myrtle was a vain attempt to suppress a laugh. When Nathan looked over, her eyes were squinting and her whole upper body was shaking in uncontrollable laughter, with small squeaky giggles coming out of her mouth.

"What's so funny," he asked, in a tone of feigned irritation.

"You are," she managed to say before another bout of laughter. How she could derive so much mirth from this situation he didn't know, but he found the laughter infectious and he was soon smiling as well as he went into the restroom. Coming out, he noticed one of those large wall mounted maps of the state with the location of the rest area marked and he took a moment to study it. The next town was Rawlins, and running northwest out of Rawlins was US 287. He followed the direction of that road and saw that it ran right into the northwest corner of the state, right past Grand Teton National Park and straight to Yellowstone National Park.

He stood there wavering back and forth for a moment. He needed to get back to work, but his boss had said he could take his time. Yellowstone seemed like a grand place to stop, and no doubt Grandma would love to visit there. Doing some quick mental math on the mileage, he figured it would add perhaps a day to the trip. One extra day to see Yellowstone, to see Old Faithful go off...yeah, it was worth it.

He got in the vehicle and pulled back onto I-80 and when he took the exit onto 287, Myrtle looked up and said, "You've gotten off 80. I thought we were going to take 80 all the way home."

"We'll get back to 80, but it might be a couple days."

"You really aren't in a hurry to get back to work."

"You saw the email from Frank. He said I could take as much time as I need, and we need to take another day."

"Joy in the journey?"

"Something like that."

"Is this a last minute decision, Nate?"

"Rest areas don't put those big maps on the wall for nothing."

"So what was on that map that got your interest so much?"

"Northwest corner of the state. There's no way we can see everything, but we owe it a day or two."

The rest of the drive north went by in silence save for the radio,

Nathan switching back and forth between 70s music and smooth jazz, both good stations for driving. As they went north, the terrain became increasingly mountainous and Myrtle found herself writing less and taking more photos out of the window. There were more restroom breaks, more than usual given the amount of tea and Coke they were going through. As they were leaving Riverton, Myrtle chastised Nathan for the amount of Coke he was drinking.

"Come on Grandma, you're drinking tea all the time. What's the difference?"

"Tea is better for you."

"I can't see what good it's doing you. It's never in you long enough."

"Same with those Cokes. You're going in to pee every time I want to stop."

"Well, you might have a point. I don't drink nearly as much of it at home. I guess the caffeine can't hurt with all this driving."

"Most of that's in your head. Get enough rest and you don't need caffeine. If you didn't sit up half the night reading."

"Those books are interesting. I'm catching up on all the stuff I ignored in school."

"So, where are we shutting down for the night."

"Figured we go up to Cody. They have a museum up there, a few motels, and churches to pick from in the morning."

Three hours later, they arrived in Cody and checked into the Best Western and then found a sports bar where they filled up on mediocre pub food while Myrtle watched the game. Nathan was online reading what he could of the history of Cody and at one point he stopped reading and turned his iPad so Myrtle could see it.

"Hey Grandma, take a look at this. This town wasn't always called Cody. Before it was named after Buffalo Bill, it was founded by this cowboy who stopped at some springs nearby to water his cattle. The settlement grew and became this town. That's not the best part. Look at the guy's name."

"Hmm, that name looks familiar, but I can't place it."

"Think back just a few days. My friend Mark knows a guy by that name, one of the musicians at his church. Mark introduced us to him when the service let out."

"Oh yeah, I remember him. Said he was a big Reds fan and hoped we would have fun at the game. Come to think of it, he reminded me of you in a way."

"That might be a stretch. I wonder if he's related to the guy who founded this town."

"You never know. Either way, it's a funny coincidence."

"Yeah, funny. I wish we could have talked to him more. Seemed like a nice guy."

When the game ended, they went back to the hotel and Nathan pointed out that there was a large complex of museums across the street and there were some churches nearby, one that had an early service. They could hit the early service, then the museums, and then depending on how much time they spent at the museums, go to Yellowstone. Myrtle figured a whole day would be needed at a place like Yellowstone, so Nathan reserved the room for two nights.

When Nathan came out of the bathroom in their room, he found that his grandmother had removed the book from his nightstand and put it back in his suitcase.

"What happened to the book I had out here?"

"You drove a lot of miles today, young man. You are going to get enough rest tonight."

He started to protest, found out that he didn't have the energy to mount much of a defense, and just settled down in his bed, removing his iPad to check his email. He had just connected the tablet to the hotel wifi and was waiting for his emails to download, when he shut his eyes for a second, opening them ten hours later.

16

Nathan awoke Sunday later than he had planned on, but feeling completely refreshed and glad that he slept that long. Myrtle was already showered and dressed in her Sunday best by the time he rolled out of bed and the first thing she asked him was where they were going to attend and what time the service started.

"I had one picked out with an early service, but it looks like that one already started," he replied as he glanced at the clock, "Let me check for another one that hasn't started."

A quick search on his iPad revealed two churches they had time to make and he let his grandma pick one before he headed to the shower. Less than an hour later, they were seated in a medium sized non denominational church, not big enough that they escaped attention as obvious first time visitors. Nathan was relieved when the service started, as he had already had his fill of social interaction.

He considered himself a Christian, had been raised attending church, but he was not as ardent as he had been in his teen years and his attendance was sporadic at best. He kept telling himself he would start attending regularly and would try to live out his faith more, but people who did that were something of a minority in the part of California he lived in and he knew few people his age who fit that description.

His grandmother was drawn right in, but Nathan's mind kept wandering until the familiarity of the music caught his attention. He knew the songs from his youth, but the style was upbeat and modern enough that he could remarked the similarities with Mark's church back in Cincinnati.

It all seemed to go by in the blink of an eye and before he realized it, the singing, preaching, praying, and more singing had all ended and people were getting up to leave. He felt stirred by the music and challenged by what the preacher had said, no new information really, but information he had needed to hear. As they left, he shook the pastor's hand with something akin to genuine grateful affection.

"Well, Nathan, that was really quite good. The music style wasn't quite my thing, but good. What did you think?"

Nathan had no words for what he was feeling and simply responded with, "It was good. I haven't attended much lately. Guess I needed that."

"Well, honey, this old lady needed to hear what he said as well. So, what are we up to today?"

"That museum looks interesting. Looks like it's several museums in one. I read about it yesterday."

Wandering around more museums might not have been the first thing on Myrtle's list, but the Buffalo Bill Center of the West was quite impressive. She was most fascinated by the vast art collection and the exhibits explaining how artists in the 19th century had helped shape the public image of Yellowstone. Many of the art pieces really brought the beauty of the park to life, in ways that the primitive photography of the time probably could not.

Nathan found the firearm exhibit far more interesting than he had figured it would be, no doubt due to his limited experience with firearms. Myrtle had even less of an interest in them than he did and took the time to rest her legs, catching up with him when he exited that part of the museum. The natural history museum was more interesting to Myrtle, but not as much to Nathan, although he was a dutiful enough grandson to feign interest.

The Plains Indians exhibit was another story. He pored over every exhibit with a keen interest, reading everything and taking numerous photos. He soon realized that his grandmother had fallen out and was once again parked on a bench waiting for him to join her. They soon went to the gift shop, Nathan straight to the books and Myrtle to the replica artwork.

By the time they exited the gift shop with another collection of books, art, and other odds and ends, they realized they had spent most of the afternoon there.

"Nate, my old knees can't walk another bit. We need to find someplace to grab some dinner and rest our bones."

"There's a restaurant near the hotel. We passed it on the way to the church."

They were soon seated at a table at the Sunset House Restaurant and were looking over the vast menu trying to pick something out. Nathan settled on the prime rib and Myrtle, feeling that she had eaten far too much beef on the trip, opted for the fish and chips, which the menu proclaimed to be the best in the state. She silently wondered how much competition there was for best fish and chips in a state like Wyoming.

After they placed their orders and the server left the table, Myrtle said, "That was a good service this morning."

"Yeah, it was."

"Is that all you have to say about it?"

"Pretty much. The music was good and the sermon was good. Made me think a bit."

"Made you think about what?"

"Oh, I don't know. Dad always took me to church growing up, and then I always went with you and Grandpa, and I do believe, but I haven't gone much lately and I kind of saw what I've been missing. And it made me think of Grandpa. You know when the preacher said that integrity was doing the right thing even when nobody was looking, when you do right even when you know nobody will notice or you won't get recognized for it? When he said that, I saw Grandpa's face as real as if he was sitting there with us. That was him. He always tried to do the right thing even if he was the only one who knew he had done it."

"Why do you think I fell in love with him? He was that way even back in college. Sometimes he would do things for people and try not to be noticed. Oh, Nate, I miss him so much, but I shouldn't complain. Having him all those years was a blessing. The Lord's been so good to me."

"Is that what you got out of this morning?"

"Yes, honey, it made me realize how blessed I've been all these years. I feel like the Lord has done so much for me and I don't deserve any of it. I mean, look at all the suffering in the world. Look at all those poor folk who don't have anything or those people in parts of the world who are persecuted and suffer so much. Or look at dear Cassie. You think these people love the Lord less than I do? Some of them are better Christians than I could ever hope to be, so why have they suffered and I haven't? Sometimes God doesn't make a lick of sense."

"You came out of church thinking God doesn't make sense?"

"Oh, I don't know. I just got to looking at my own life and how good I've had it, and Lord knows I'm grateful, but I see all of this suffering and sometimes I feel guilty. I lay my head on the pillow at night and I thank God for the life I've had and the blessings I've had and now I wonder why other people who are as faithful as I am don't have those blessings. But you're the one who opened my eyes, Nate."

"Huh? How did I do that?"

"You've got such a soft heart and it tears you apart every time you see someone else suffer. The way you were with those Indians in Wall and at Wounded Knee, the way you looked at that handicapped child at the church this morning. You might not know it, but you're more like your grandfather than you realize. I sit here and thank God for my blessed life, and then I see your heart breaking over others who aren't as blessed. I've been on this earth 52 years longer than you have and I've followed the Lord for most of that time, and I see in you what should have been in me all this time."

"I think you sell yourself short. You've always loved people."

"I suppose so, but seeing you these last few days and then hearing what I heard this morning...it made me think. It made me realize that no matter how long I live I will always have room to grow, and new things to learn. The minute you think there's nothing new to learn is the minute you need to be humbled."

"I guess you have a point. I know I have a good life, but I've always had a soft spot. Heck, it bothers me to see a dead animal on the road."

"I ABSOLUTELY CAN'T EAT another bite," Myrtle exclaimed as she stuffed one last fry into her mouth, "but that was really excellent. You want the rest of these fries."

"No way. I'm stuffed. I haven't had prime rib in ages. You know, this place is pretty good, and I only picked it because it wasn't far from the hotel and we drove past it this morning."

Back at the hotel, Nathan picked up the remote and turned on the tv.

"Would you believe all the political stuff on every channel," he remarked.

"'Tis the season," Myrtle replied.

"Well, I can't say that I like the season much, especially this time around."

"Yeah, Nate, not much to like on either side. Almost makes you wish for a good third party candidate."

"You want to watch this," Nathan asked as he stopped on ESPN, "Maybe you can catch the Reds highlights. They played a day game today, didn't they?"

"It was a 1:00 game, so it came on before we left church this morning. Sure, you can leave it there. And speaking of church, why haven't you been attending lately."

"Oh, I don't know. Busy, I guess."

"You work Sundays?"

"No. Oh, I don't know. I just get so busy during the week and by the time the weekend rolls around, I don't feel like getting out."

"Now Nate, that's a pretty weak excuse and you know it. You have no excuse now. I don't drive anymore, but I don't miss Sundays. You're going to take me, and as long as you're already there, you're going to stick around until I'm ready to leave. Do I make myself clear?"

"Yes ma'am," Nathan said as he stood at attention and offered her a mock salute, with a shy grin on his face, injecting humor in an effort to cover up the guilt he felt. He knew how important her faith was to his grandma, and he knew how important it was to her that he share it. It wasn't that he didn't believe, but it had never meant to him what it had meant to his grandparents. He didn't think he was on bad terms with the Almighty, but he simply didn't take it as seriously as his grandma did. He found the services a bit boring, the one that morning being an exception, but when it really came down to it, he simply didn't feel like getting out of the house on Sunday mornings. The couple times he had attended he didn't meet many people his age and had given up looking.

"Well, that figures," Myrtle said in disgust a couple minutes later.

Nathan wondered what he had said to elicit that response, but a glance at the television told him all he needed to know. The Reds had blown another lead in the late innings. It wasn't the best season and Myrtle was showing her obvious displeasure at the highlights.

"You know, every year can't be their year," he replied.

"I know, but some of these losses this year, blowing leads late. It's frustrating. But I'm old enough to remember better years. I should count my blessings. They've won four championships in my lifetime; I was too young to remember the first one, but I can remember three. Aren't any Cubs fans around that can say that."

"Is there even anyone alive who can remember their last one?"

"Well, Nate, joke all you want, but the way they're playing this year that might change."

"I guess we'll just have to wait for October to see. Man, I am becoming more like you and Grandpa."

"Why do you say that?"

"This is the most I've ever talked about sports in my whole life, and I'm making fun of the Cubs."

"The Cubs *are* an easy target." Myrtle then let out a chuckle.

"What's so funny?"

"You ever really think about sports and realize how silly it really is?"

"Never really thought about it. I sometimes poke fun at how silly a lot of fans are, especially where I life. Everyone is a Giants and 49ers fan and some people take it way too far."

"The fans are pretty silly, but the sports themselves are silly as well, and I'm saying that as a fan. I love to watch the games, Nate, but they're just plain dumb when you really break it down. I love baseball, but think about it. Many people will pay good money to watch two groups of grown men try to whack a little ball with a stick while the other group tries to keep them from whacking it, or tries to catch it after they whack it. The group that is better at whacking the ball and catching the balls the other group whacks is the winner. Then people like me are cheering them on and hoping the group of grown men from my hometown are better at whacking the ball than the group from someone else's hometown."

"When you put it like that."

"But you know what else, Nate? It seems so silly, and those fans you make fun of who take it so seriously don't really get it, but there is a beauty in it. Life can throw a lot of stuff at you, a lot of really negative stuff. It can really beat you up. You've taken some of those blows, Nate, and you're still standing. I can say that you're probably taken them better than many would have, but that's the beauty of sports. Life hits you pretty hard and through it all you have these silly games that grown men play for ridiculous amounts of money and for three hours or so, you can get so wrapped up in something that in the long run doesn't really mean anything, but for that bit of time it does mean something, and everything else in your life is set aside for the moment.

Sports can transcend the pain...and those boring mundane

moments of your life... and inject a bit more meaning. It can put a smile on your face when there's really no reason in your life to smile. Then there are times when it can do more than that, when it can bring hope to people and unite them. 1980 was one of those times, when a bunch of young people played a hockey game and beat a team they weren't supposed to beat and gave hope to all of us. So yeah, it can be really silly and meaningless, and then all of a sudden it's not silly and it has meaning."

"Wow. I've never heard anyone talk about it like that. It's just never been my thing. I like to watch football sometimes, but that's about it. Just a typical nerd, I guess."

"To each his own, but everyone needs a diversion when life gets weird."

"I play video games or listen to music. That's funny, since I make video games for a living, but sometimes playing ones that are made by a different company is relaxing. I think I might spend more time reading, though."

"You'll need to spend more time reading if you ever hope to finish half of those books you've bought this week."

"I've already finished one and I'm almost finished with another. Speaking of silliness, you want to leave it on this channel? The Sunday night game is coming on."

"Who's playing?"

"Red Sox and Indians. You care to watch that?"

"I don't give a flip who wins, but you can leave it on. Beats the political talk."

"Ok, you can watch that. I'm going to read a bit."

"You do that, but don't stay up until some ungodly hour this time. We're going to Yellowstone in the morning, right?"

"Yep, Yellowstone and then we have to make our way south again, so we'll pass through the Tetons if I'm reading the map right. Get your camera ready."

17

This time, Nathan actually beat his grandma out of bed, and by the time she stirred he had already packed the car and eaten breakfast. While she was showering and eating breakfast, he was navigating a Wyoming travel site reading about Yellowstone and what attractions would be of interest to his grandma, and he settled on what were probably the most visited areas of the park-the upper and lower falls, the lake, and Old Faithful. He consulted the map and had the car pulled in front of the hotel by the time she came out.

US 14 west out of Cody winds through numerous elevation changes, still navigable at a reasonable speed, but tempting to drive slightly slower to take in some of the most breathtaking scenery in the state. What would normally take roughly an hour took an extra fifteen minutes as Nathan found himself admiring the view and easing off on the gas as he did so, while Myrtle snapped away with her camera out of the passenger window. On two occasions she petitioned Nathan to stop the car so she could photograph a particularly beautiful vista.

If either of them had ever made a prior visit to Yellowstone, they may not have taken as much time to get there. Coming into the park the scenery improves with every mile and all the two of them could do was stare in wordless admiration, with the occasional utterance of "wow", or "Would you look at that."

They drove around the lake and went north to the area of the upper and lower falls, where they simply stood and stared at the falls, letting the sight and sound of the cascading water move them. Nathan looked at his grandma and saw the same look of amazement on her face that he had on his and said nothing, for fear of breaking the spell. There were numerous other people taking in the sight and it seemed to Nathan that each person reacted in a different way. Some people were exclaiming loudly and others were dumbstruck and staring, while others, far too many for Myrtle's liking, were taking selfies. "How narcissistic can people be these days," she thought to herself, "that they have to have themselves in every photo?" She waited for what seemed like an eternity with her camera held up, waiting for the selfie takers to move on so she could get what she wanted, a photo without any people in it. She pondered just how self centered the current culture had become that not only was there such a thing as a selfie, but that there was even a name for it. She remembered when she was younger, having to hand the camera to someone if you wanted a photo of yourself in front of something, and how people always wanted an unspoiled photo as well.

After she got the photos she wanted, they got in the car and drove down to the lake, finding a picnic spot near the water. They sat there looking over the water at the mountains in the distance, not speaking at all until eventually Myrtle broke the silence by mentioning that she had to use the restroom. When she had done that they got in the car and Nathan followed the signs for Old Faithful.

They drove there in silence as well, Myrtle taking more photos from the moving car, having to slow down for two bears that decided they needed to cross the road, and eventually arriving at the geyser with ten minutes remaining until the next eruption. Their mood here was much the same as it had been at the falls, but this time Nathan managed to position his grandmother in a good place for photos where she would have an unobstructed view. He found that when he mentioned to a few of the other tourists that his grandma desired to get some photos without people, most were accommodating. Myrtle managed to get the photos she desired and Nathan simply stood back and took video with his iPad.

After a visit to the Old Faithful Visitor Education Center, where they saw geological exhibits on how the geyser formed, and where Myrtle once again took advantage of the restroom facilities, they headed to the car. When Nathan looked at his watch, he was shocked that it had been nearly six hours since they had entered the park, and he had hoped to reach Evanston or Salt Lake by the end of the day. Running the mileage on the GPS, he decided that he would push on to Evanston. The four and a half hour drive would most likely turn into five hours plus when figuring in restroom stops.

After preparing sandwiches to eat on the way, Nathan pulled out and began the drive south along the Idaho and Utah borders. US 89 and US 30 run a rather twisty up and down route to Evanston, offering postcard views through Grand Teton National Park and along the Salt River Range farther south. Anyone traveling this route will soon run out of superlatives and this was much the case with Nathan and Myrtle. The journal book remained unopened and Nathan even turned down the radio. He had been dreading the mileage to Evanston after the time they had spent at the park, but this drive was one of the most delightful stretches of road he had yet traversed.

Somewhere south of Jackson, Myrtle said, "You know, Nate, I have never seen anything so majestic in my life," instantly thinking that any words she could say would fall short of describing half of what she had seen. In all her years, she had never been west and she found the photos and video she had seen to be entirely inadequate to describe it.

"Yeah, it's something. I didn't come this way when I came out after college. I came through some mountains, but today takes the cake. Still, you'll see more when we pass through Salt Lake. That's a pretty town."

"You were going to stop in Evanston. How much farther to Salt

Lake City? We could just push a little more and make it there, couldn't we?"

"I suppose we could. Depends on how I'm feeling. It's been a rather long day."

"It has, but we could have spent two days at Yellowstone."

"Probably. We only saw a small part of the park. That lake is huge."

"You know what amazes me?"

"What's that?"

"That there are people who could see what we saw today and still believe there is no God."

"You'd be surprised. I work with quite a few atheists."

"You didn't see so many of them in my day."

"There are a lot of them in my line of work, or it's that I live in California. That's not exactly the Bible belt."

"I'm sure they were in New Jersey as well. Maybe I've just lived a sheltered life. When I was young, everyone went to church regularly. That's just how it was. Even when I got older, Patrick and I just went and most of our friends did as well. When you hang out with a particular crowd, you can forget that there are people out there who are different than you are."

"I know what you mean, but my eyes have opened quite a bit since I moved to California, heck, since I went to college. You see everything on a campus these days, things that I'll bet you didn't see when you were in college."

"Nate, I was in college in the 50s. We didn't see much out of the ordinary then. There weren't even a lot of black folk on campus, except for the athletes. There weren't as many girls either."

"Things sure have changed in your lifetime. I thought I had seen a lot of change, but I'll bet the world is really different since you were young."

"You're right, but let me tell you something. I've been observant as I've grown old. You hear a lot of people my age talk about the good old days and how we should get back to how things were, but I'm not so sure that's a good idea. Not completely. Sure, more people

attended church then and families were together more, all that
Norman Rockwell stuff, but what kind of people do you see in all of
those paintings, Nate?"

"I don't know. Middle class people in small towns?"

"Well, that's the idea people like to perpetrate, but Mr. Rockwell
portrayed black folk in many of his paintings. He drew attention to
the inequality back then. But nowadays when people want to talk
about this ideal life, they don't use those paintings. I lived through it,
Nate. Growing up in a white suburb and attending white churches, I
didn't see much of it until things started getting stirred up down
south. We didn't have as much overt racism where I lived, especially
when I got to New Jersey, but it was more subtle. We didn't have the
separate water fountains and restrooms, but that didn't mean that
people weren't racists. They just hid it better. So yeah, a lot has
changed since then, and maybe a lot of it has been for the better."

"I guess you're right. But you're kind of old fashioned yourself,
just calling them black and not African-Americans."

"You know I don't go in for all that PC stuff. We need to quit with
the hyphenated American nonsense and realize that we're all just
Americans. Anyway, if that's the term to use, what do you call black
people in England or France? Where do you draw the line? What I'm
saying is that when you look back to the times when I was young,
your idea of what it was like is drastically different depending on
what color you are. I look back at my childhood and think of it fondly
and think America was a much better place, but a black woman my
age might remember having to drink from a separate fountain, use a
separate bathroom, or sit in the back of the bus. She might not want
to go back to that America."

"Well, don't you think our country is worse morally?"

"It depends on how you look at it. There are a lot of things that
have gotten worse, but I just think we keep trading sins every few
years. We get rid of one and think we've gotten better, but all we do is
replace it with something else. At the heart of it, people haven't really
gotten any better. Every generation has its immorality that they try to
overlook or justify. People tried to justify racism back then and now

we think we've gotten better because we passed all those civil rights laws and we treat black people better, but now how many unborn do we kill every year? Have we really gotten better?"

"Now I'm confused. So you're saying that we're really not getting better or worse? It seems that we don't discriminate as much as we used to, but then again there are the Indians. They've gotten the short end of the stick and everyone seems to have forgotten about them."

"I think you're beginning to see it, Nate. The founders wrote wonderful things in the Constitution and the Declaration of Independence about all men being equal, but we still haven't gotten to that point, have we? I think they laid out the ideal and we've spent over 200 years trying to live up to it, but we're still not there. America was founded on good principles, but America has never really measured up to those principles. We do a better job than most countries, but there's still a lot of room to grow."

"You don't sound like most people your age."

"I was married to your grandfather for 58 years. He was the history nut and there were times he would go on and on about this and that. I guess some of it stuck, more than I realized. Nate, honey, there were good things from the past that maybe we should bring back-people going to church more, being more respectful, families staying together more, kids respecting their parents more-that sort of thing. But if you ask a minority, I don't know too many of them who would want to go back to that time."

"Well, it's a shame we couldn't have kept the good things and gotten rid of the rest. Seems like we threw out the baby with the bath water."

"Maybe that's the case. All this talking, I'm getting thirsty. You know what would go down well?"

"Let me guess. Iced tea?"

"That would certainly hit the spot. Is there any left in the cooler?"

"I think you drank the last one back at Yellowstone. There's a town up ahead. I'll stop and see what there is."

Nathan took the next exit, found a gas station, and topped off the tank and the cooler. When Myrtle came back from using the restroom he said, "I think we'll push on to Salt Lake. There are plenty of motels and there is an interesting place we can have dinner."

"Let me guess, steak?"

"Let me congratulate you on your mind reading ability. There's a place online here, Ruby River. Supposed to be the best steakhouse in Utah and they make their own root beer. I haven't had a real root beer in ages."

"The rate we're going on this trip, we're going to turn into a couple of steaks."

"I like to say I'm a secondary vegetarian."

"What do you mean by that?"

"The cows eat the grass; I eat the cows."

"Well, I'm not entirely sure that's how it works."

"Funny thing, I don't eat that much of it at home. Maybe because it's no fun going to a nice place by yourself."

"Well, Nate, you could do something about that."

"I know, I know. I'm working on that."

All manner of retorts came to Myrtle's mind, each one more sarcastic than the last, so she remained silent. She pulled out her journal once again with the intention of writing, but the recent conversation had brought to her mind how much her grandson resembled her husband, and she shut the book and her eyes, reminiscing about her late husband and drifting off with the image of his face in her mind.

18

The drive through Evanston and into Salt Lake City was as uneventful as Nathan could wish, with his grandma napping the entire way, only waking up for restroom breaks. They hadn't done that much walking at Yellowstone, but maybe it was enough to wear her out. She hadn't napped much in the car up to now, spending the time she wasn't talking to him writing in her journal or taking photos out of the car window. He wondered about both, how legible her writing would be and how the photos would turn out. Grandma was as healthy as a horse, but at her age maybe it didn't take much to tire her. She was 80 after all.

Grandpa had been tireless, at least before the cancer had taken its toll. He was also an athlete in his youth and he kept himself in top shape even in his old age. Nathan was the opposite. He couldn't remember the last time he saw the inside of a gym. He wasn't in bad shape by any means, courtesy of a high metabolism, but he was still in his 20s. He knew it would catch up to him some day, especially with his appetite for good food and too many soft drinks.

Nathan pulled into the hotel, woke up his Grandma, and they checked in. They were only in the room long enough to dump their bags when Myrtle asked, "So where's that restaurant? I'm kind of hungry."

Nathan looked up the Ruby River Steakhouse and nine minutes later they were finishing their meals and washing everything down with frosted mugs of Ruby River's own hand crafted root beer.

"You know, I was never a big root beer guy, but this stuff is excellent."

"Your dad never took you to the Root Beer stand? It's not far from where you lived."

"That little place in Sharonville with the hot dogs and root beer?"

"That's the place. It's been there since the 50s, but I was already off to college when it opened. I went there a couple times when we came back to visit my parents, and your dad always bragged about it. I figured he took you."

"We went there a couple times, but I was small. I remember the loaded down hot dogs."

"They make their own root beer as well. It's hard to tell which one is better. I haven't had theirs in years. This one is good enough for a second glass. You want another one?"

"You don't have to twist my arm. I'll flag down the waiter."

The waiter brought two more glasses and removed their empty plates, and they sat for a moment contentedly sipping their root beer before Nathan finally broke the silence.

"You had a heck of a nap in the car. You sure you won't be awake half the night?"

"I didn't realize I was sleepy, but the sun coming in the window must have done me in."

"You were out like a light. Maybe Yellowstone wore you out as well."

"Maybe. I feel pretty good right now, but after that meal I think I will sleep like a baby tonight."

"Like a baby? You mean you'll wake up every two hours and cry?"

"Ha ha ha. Where'd you hear that one?"

"Some girl at work. They had a new baby at home. She would come in rather worn out some mornings."

"Your father did that to me. It took forever before he would sleep through the night. Your grandpa and I had to take turns getting up. We alternated nights."

"Dad said I did the same thing. He reckoned he was getting paid back."

"Yeah, it's a bit of a pain, but it's worth it, and when your kids grow up you sometimes miss those moments."

"You miss changing diapers?"

"Well...sometimes that was a bit messy, but you miss the intimate moments with a small one. It's really quite a bonding moment, very sweet. Maybe one day you'll find out first hand."

"Yeah, maybe. Let's not get too far ahead of ourselves yet."

"You'll be 30 before you know it."

"I know that. You don't have to keep reminding me."

"I'm a woman. It's my job to remind you."

"Well, I don't need to be reminded about that."

"It doesn't seem you've done anything about it."

"I'm working on that."

"Well, you'd better work a little faster. I want to see you happy before I die, and I'm no spring chicken you know."

"I am happy."

"That's not what I mean. I know you. You're too much like your grandfather. Something's missing. You and I both know what it is."

"Ok, can we talk about this somewhere else. We're in a restaurant."

They finished their root beer, paid the bill, and drove back to the hotel, where his grandma picked up right where she left off.

"Ok, Nate, I won't mention it again until we get there, but listen to me. I've been around the block a few times and I know a thing or two. I know you're interested in that girl at work, and from what you've said she might have similar feelings, but she's not going to just fall into your lap. Women aren't wired that way. You have to make the move, and you need to make it sooner than later."

"Yeah, I hear you. You've only said that about a million times since we left New Jersey."

"I'm just concerned about you, and I wouldn't mind having a great grandkid to spoil," she said with a sly smile.

"I knew you had an agenda."

"Oh Nate, I bug you because I love you."

"I know you do. I love you too. That's just a sensitive area, that's all."

"I know you're shy, but if you want what you've never had, you have to do what you've never done."

"That's catchy. Was that one of Grandpa's sayings?"

"I don't remember where I got it from. I heard it on the radio or TV."

"Well, I guess there's some truth to it. Anyway, I'm going to want to grab some sleep fairly soon, but before I do," he said as he fished a deck of cards out of his pocket, "what do you say to a few hands of rummy?"

"I haven't played since..."

"Since the last time we played with Grandpa in the hospital room."

"Yeah, we used to play all the time, play hand after hand and just talk."

Her voice trailed off and she wondered where he had gotten a deck of cards. Probably at the last gas station they stopped at. She sat silent for a moment, wiped a tear from her eye before composing herself and said, "Ok, a few hands before we go to sleep. You can deal."

Nathan dealt the cards and they played hand after hand, the conversation drifting away from Nathan's love life, which was what he had hoped would happen when he took out the cards.

"You'll never learn, Nate. You like going out in one move, and I've stuck you three straight hands."

"Grandpa always seemed to be able to pull that off."

"But if you remember, he would play those points if he saw you or me getting low on cards. You're holding them too long. If you ask me, I think your mind is elsewhere."

"I just haven't played in a while is all."

"Don't give me that. You played the last time I did. Your grandma's just better at cards than you are."

"You think you're better? How about this," he exclaimed as he played all of his cards at one go, a four card straight and three kings.

"Ok, you got me there, but look at the score."

Nathan's triumph was short lived as he added up the hand and realized that his grandma was still leading him by over 100 points.

"Yeah, yeah, but that still felt good."

"Winning feels better."

"Now I know you got that from Grandpa."

"Your grandfather did hate to lose. That's why he never wanted to play your computer games. He could never beat you at those."

"He always said staring at the screen bothered his eyes."

"Come on, Nate, you know better. He used computers at the shop before he retired and they never bothered his eyes there."

"But that was just text. Some people have physical problems with video games. Can't handle the fast moving images on the screen. It can make some people sick and give other people seizures."

"Well, Nate, I'm sure there's something to that, but I know my husband. He hated to lose."

"He always liked playing Madden, even when I beat him."

"That's just because he liked football, and he was hoping it would rub off on you."

"I guess I didn't catch the sports bug like you did. Even Dad was into it."

"You ought to try it. Everyone needs a diversion."

"I told you, my games are that. Well, that and reading now. I find I really enjoy reading."

"You aren't kidding. I remember how fast you went through those Harry Potter books."

"You would like them. They're not just for children."

"I don't know, Nate. Give me my Jane Austen any day."

"I couldn't get into that old stuff."

"You should try it. Those books aren't just for old ladies, you know."

"Maybe one of these days. You know those other ones Grandpa kept reading over and over? The nautical books?"

"The Aubrey books by O'Brian?"

"Yeah, those. Did you pack them?"

"I'm pretty sure they're in one of the boxes. You asked me to pack his books, remember?"

"I'm glad. I read the first one and I kind of liked it. I'd like to read the rest of them."

"You do know that O'Brian was a fan of Jane Austen don't you?"

"I wasn't aware of that."

"That's true. Her writing was a big influence on him. When you get to the second book in that series, you can see the similarities."

"You read O'Brian?"

"Sure, as much as your grandpa was always talking about those books, I had to read them so I could talk with him about them. I quite enjoyed them."

"I can't wait to read the rest of them. And, with that hand, you're at 500 points. You kicked my butt."

"What else did you expect. Say, I'm getting rather sleepy. See you in the morning, ok?"

"Sure, sleep tight."

"Don't say the next line. This place better not have bed bugs."

And with that, she climbed into her bed and was out like a light before he could think of a reply. He wasn't that tired yet, so he slipped out to the car, unlocked the trailer, and rummaged through the boxes until he found the books and found the one he was looking for, *Post Captain,* by Patrick O'Brian. He took the book with him back into the room and settled into bed and began to read, falling asleep somewhere in the middle of the third chapter.

19

Nathan woke up and looked across the room to see his grandmother fully dressed, sitting at the writing desk scribbling away at a furious pace, her bags already packed and waiting by the door.

"You in a hurry to get somewhere," he asked.

"Just woke up early and couldn't get back to sleep. Couldn't just sit there."

"You have breakfast yet?"

"No. I'm tired of these hotel breakfasts. Can we find someplace on the way?"

"Sure, there's a restaurant close to here. It's on one of those local guide things over there by the telephone."

Myrtle kept writing while Nathan showered and 30 minutes later they were pulling into Roberts Restaurant and soon after, their server was bringing their plates. Roberts specializes in traditional American fare, and the breakfast did not disappoint. Nathan looked at his plate and was ready to dive in when his grandma said, "Nate, maybe we should pray before we prey."

"Pray before we pray? Uh...oh, I get it. That was rather clever. Sure, go ahead," he said as he bowed his head. Myrtle, mindful of her grandson's voracious appetite and not wanting the food to get cold, kept grace to an extremely brief prayer of thanks, and upon looking up, saw that their server was standing there respectfully.

"I didn't mean to interrupt," she said, "I just wanted to make sure everything is ok."

"Everything looks great," Myrtle replied, "but knowing Nate, he's probably going to want another glass of milk before we're finished."

"Ok, I'll bring another one right out. By the way, I don't see too many people doing that before meals anymore. Next time you pray, you can mention me if you don't mind."

"Any particular reason?"

"All sorts of reasons, ma'am. I'd hate to bore you with all the details."

"Go ahead and bore me. By my age, I've heard it all."

"Oh, it's complicated. I have a two year old daughter at home and my husband just left me. Well, I caught him cheating and I kicked him out."

"Oh my..."

"Well, I'll get over him. Bastard's not worth the sorrow. Oh, excuse me... I have a daughter to raise now and I don't have much experience. All I've ever done is work in restaurants. I think I need to go back to school, but I don't know where to start. Day care will be crazy expensive if I try to take classes and I still have to work. Well, I've bored you enough. Got other tables to get to. I'll be back with that milk."

Nathan just stared at his food for a couple seconds before he started eating. The food was excellent, but he couldn't get his mind off the sad situation their server was in. His grandmother had not touched her food yet, but was instead rummaging through her purse.

"Did you catch that girl's name," she asked.

"Her name tag said Natalie."

"Probably not a last name on there. Most places put the server's name on the receipt these days. Let me see the bill when she brings it."

"What are you up to?"

"Sometimes all you can do is pray for someone, and sometimes you can help answer the prayer."

Myrtle pulled her checkbook out of her purse, filled out a check with the name line blank, and set it aside and ate her breakfast. Natalie came back with another glass of milk and a coffee pot.

"Would you like a refill on your coffee, ma'am," she asked.

"Yes, please."

"Ok, I'll just leave this with you," she said as she left the bill face down on the table, "No rush. If you need anything else, let me know."

As Myrtle continued eating, she turned the bill over and looked toward the top. Sure enough, the full server name was right there near the top, Natalie Peterson. She wrote the name on the check and tore a blank page from her journal book and wrote the following note:

DEAR NATALIE,

Please accept this and use it toward school. I hope it's enough to allow you to take the classes you need without having to work yourself to death. God bless you.

MYRTLE CALLAHAN

SHE FOLDED the check inside the note and finished her breakfast. When they had finished eating, Nathan paid the bill with his card and Myrtle handed the note to Natalie on the way out the door. They went out to the car and Natalie opened the note and read it, then read it again, looked at the check in disbelief, and looked at it again just to make sure she was seeing things right. She had to sit down in the nearest chair to control the tears that were running down her cheeks. Another server came by to ask if she was ok and she replied, "Yes Chloe, I'm ok, but can you take care of table 16 for me?"

"Sure thing, Natalie. What's up?"

"Got this from my last customer," she said, showing Chloe the note and the check.

"Holy...thirty thousand dollars? Is that real?"

"I think so. I don't know what to say."

"You should say thank you, if they haven't left yet."

"Yeah, I should. Can you cover for me for a sec?"

"Sure, go, before they leave."

Natalie ran out of the restaurant, tears still flowing, and saw the Tahoe with the trailer sitting still, Nathan checking mileage on the GPS before pulling out. She ran up to the passenger door and just stood there. Myrtle rolled down the window and then recognized Natalie.

"Lady, you didn't have to..." Natalie was saying.

"Yes, I did," Myrtle interrupted. "I'm old. I don't need it"

"I don't...how...thank you," she said through a new bout of tears.

Myrtle opened the door, got out, and gave Natalie a hug. When she pulled away, she said, "You make something of yourself and raise that little girl right. That's all the thanks I need."

A man came out of the restaurant and asked, "What are you doing out here? It's not time for your break yet."

Natalie showed him the note and the check and the man immediately softened his tone and asked, "These the people who gave you that?"

"Yes, this is Myrtle and...I don't think I got your name, "the last part directed at Nathan.

"I'm Nathan, Myrtle's grandson and chauffeur."

"Well," the man replied, "thank you for what you have done for Natalie," and to Natalie, "Take all the time you need here."

Natalie handed her phone to her boss, with the camera app opened, and went and joined Myrtle and Nathan. "Can you get a couple shots," she asked him.

More photos taken, more hugs, and Natalie went back inside to work and Nathan and Myrtle pulled out and joined the highway. By the time they got to the gas station and were filling up the tank, Natalie had taken a photo of the check and the note, along with the photo of her with Myrtle and Nathan, and had posted it all on Face-book, along with a detailed write up of what had happened. By the time Nathan was pulling off in Elko to use the restroom, Natalie's post was well on the way to going viral. They were becoming internet celebrities and they didn't even know it, mostly because Nathan was driving and Myrtle was writing in her journal. When they reached Winnemucca and took another restroom break, Nathan's curiosity got the better of him and he asked, "How much did you write that check for?"

"Thirty," Myrtle replied.

"She seemed awfully touched over a thirty dollar tip."

"Thirty *thousand,* Nate."

"Oh my...you gave her thirty grand?"

"Yes. I figured that would go a ways toward whatever she wants to study. College isn't cheap these days."

"Yeah, that should go a long ways. You think she'll use it for that and not waste it?"

"I'm pretty sure. You get to be my age you learn a bit about reading people. She's got no reason to lie to a stranger."

"Seems like a good chunk of change to give someone."

"Listen, Nate, I've got way more than I could ever hope to spend before I die. Your grandpa's business sees to that. I might as well use it so bless people. Don't worry. There will be plenty left over for you and your uncle when I'm gone."

"I wasn't thinking about that. You'll still be around for a few more years anyway."

"You never know. None of us are guaranteed tomorrow."

"Yeah, I know, but you're still pretty healthy."

"I guess I am fairly healthy for someone my age, but you just don't know. Anyway, I like blessing people. That girl can put that money to better use than I can. What am I going to do with all that I have? I'll never spend it all."

"How much *do* you have?"

"That's none of your business."

"So Grandpa's shops are doing well?"

"Oh yes, six locations and a reputation for doing good work and not cheating people. There are managers in each location and a general manager over the whole thing. Your grandpa and I haven't had to do much since he retired, but you know he still stopped by the office to check up on things. Those shops will be going strong long after I'm gone, and probably after you're gone. I still get some pretty healthy deposits after all the expenses are made. Patrick set all that up. After I'm gone it will go to you and your uncle. You guys can leave it the way it is or go public, but I'd probably leave it. If it ain't broke..."

"So you don't have to do anything, make any decisions?"

"That's what Anthony does, and he gets paid well to do it. You ever go into business for yourself, you'll understand. You find good people and you pay them well, and they'll take care of you. There's a lot of peace of mind when you have good people working for you and they're happy."

"I'll keep that in mind."

"So, what's the plan? We can't be that far from your house."

"No, it was 11 hours from Salt Lake. I emailed Frank and he's good with me coming in on Monday, so we'll probably spend the night in Reno and finish up tomorrow. We'll arrive tomorrow afternoon, get everything set up in the house, and then we'll have the weekend before I need to go back to work."

"Does that mean we can go to the ocean? I haven't had a day at a beach in quite some time. Patrick used to take me, but..."

"Yeah, we'll go to the beach. Monterey Bay isn't far, plenty of beaches there to choose from. I haven't been in a while. Went with some guys from work a couple months back. There's something else we have to do over the weekend too, maybe Friday evening."

"What would that be?"

"Have you forgotten the baseball schedule?"

"Oh, how could I forget. The Reds are playing the Giants...in San Francisco."

"Yep, and we have tickets, right behind the dugout, for Friday night. Unless you want to watch the game on TV and give the tickets to someone else."

"No need to give them away."

"I figured as much. It's a nice looking ballpark. I'm sure you'll enjoy it."

"You've been there? I thought you weren't into sports."

"Well, I really don't follow it, but a friend from work invited me once and we went to a game early in the season. It can get nippy there, so you'll need a sweater. The city's weird that way. You can be a little bit away from the water and it will be hot as heck, and you go over by the bay and the temperature drops like you wouldn't believe."

"So why stop in Reno? Why not push it a bit farther."

"Because with the stops we've made, I don't feel up to making it all the way home tonight, and there's not much but small towns between Reno and Sacramento. We get plenty of rest there and leave early in the morning, we can be home fairly early tomorrow. That will give us enough time to get everything moved in and return this car and trailer."

"How are you going to get back from home after you drop the car? I can't drive you know."

"It's Enterprise. They'll bring me back home. If we get back after they close, I'll just leave the keys in the drop box and grab an Uber or Lyft."

"What the heck is that?"

"Uber and Lyft are like taxis, but you can order it on your phone. Little cheaper than cabs too. It's people using their own cars."

"Well, this has been a fun trip but I think I'm looking forward to getting there and settling down."

"You should probably take that journal of yours to a publisher. Who knows what interesting things you've written in there."

"Oh, nothing that interesting. Just whatever I'm thinking about. I'm not sure who'd want to read the musings of an old woman."

"Knowing you, it's probably quite interesting."

Myrtle retrieved her journal and continued writing, filling page after page with random thoughts and musings, nothing anyone would find that interesting, she figured, but she always did seem to have a lot on her mind. This time she wrote about Natalie and Cassie, the two young women she had been blessed to meet on this trip. It's funny how that works, she thought. Someone is in need and you do what you can to meet the need, and you end up being blessed almost as much as the person you helped. That's the way she saw it at least.

She had been extremely blessed in her life, had always had more than enough money, at least after the business started taking off, and she never had many material desires, so she was always giving it away. She thought back over the trip and how much she had learned about her grandson. The boy had lived under her roof for four years and she had learned more about him in the last week than in those four years. He didn't seem so caught up with things either, unlike a lot of people his age, or any age for that matter.

She wrote page after page until the sun coming in the window hit her face and her eyelids began to feel like lead. She wondered why she was taking more naps these last couple days and just chalked it up to fatigue from the trip, and then shut her eyes and drifted off, not waking up until the car was stopped in front of a hotel in Reno and Nathan was gently shaking her shoulders.

"How long was I out?"

"Only the last 175 miles."

"Wow. Didn't seem like that long. I'm kind of hungry."

"That's not a problem in this town. All kinds of places. Passed a sports bar on the way, maybe a couple miles down the road. We can go there if you want to watch the game."

"Sure, sounds good."

Twenty minutes later they found themselves sitting in a booth at Bart's Sports Bar and Grill, a new establishment with a spacious dining area that stretched back from the bar in the front, so new in fact that name on the server's badge was Bart.

"You have the same name as the guy who own's the place," Nathan asked as soon as Bart arrived at their table.

"One and the same. Bartholomew T. Pinkerton at your service."

"Wow, not often we stop to eat and get waited on by the owner."

"Well, just opened the place a week ago. Don't have a lot of employees yet. Got a girl coming in, but not for another half an hour. So, what can I help you with?"

"We'd like to see a menu, and is there any chance you could get the Reds/Dodgers game on one of these TVs?"

"Like anything to drink while you're looking over the menu?"

"A Coke for me and iced tea for my grandma here."

"Ok, I'll be back with your drinks, and I'll see about getting the game on."

Nathan looked over the menu and asked his grandmother, "Split a basket of onion rings with me?"

"Huh? Oh, onion rings...sure," she replied, turning her attention away from the TV where the game had just come on.

A minute later a young woman came to their table with their drinks and said, "Hi, I'm Leslie, what can I do for you?"

"Wow," Nate replied. "Bart there said you wouldn't be here for another half hour."

"Well, I got in early and he said I could start early. The cook called off, so he's got to handle that and I get to wait on you. You know what you want yet?"

"We'll take an onion ring basket to start with, and we might need a minute with the menu. Looks like you have a bit more than the average sports bar."

"Yeah, Bart wanted to stand out from the other places, so we offer a full menu. I'll be back in a minute."

When she came back, they were ready to order, Nathan ordering a burger and fries and Myrtle grilled salmon with asparagus.

"Not often you see asparagus on a bar menu," she commented.

"Like I said, Bart wants to be more than a bar," Leslie said.

Leslie left to give the orders to Bart, but returned to the table rather quickly, looking Nathan and Myrtle over thoroughly.

"Say, you guys look familiar from somewhere. Hold on a sec."

She returned with her phone, opened to Facebook, and asked, "This you guys here?"

Nathan took a look at the phone and there was the photo they took with Natalie that morning in Salt Lake City.

"Yeah, that looks like us. Where'd you get that photo?"

"Oh, it's going viral. The girl from the restaurant in Salt Lake posted the story this morning and it's going all over. You guys are famous. And I think it's awesome what you did for her."

"It's was all Grandma here. She's the one who did everything."

"Well, ma'am, it's an honor to meet you," she said, coming around the table to shake Myrtle's hand.

"Oh, it was an easy thing to do. Someone has a need and you just do what you can do. I'm sure if you were in my shoes..."

"Being in your shoes is one thing, but having the means to do that is another. Anyway, you need anything, let me know."

"Nate, what did she mean by going viral?"

"It's when someone posts something online and people keep sharing it. Next thing you know, it's spreading all over the internet. Apparently the girl from Salt Lake put our picture and told everybody what you did. Now people keep sharing it. Surely you've heard of Facebook."

"Yeah, a couple of my friends are on there, but I don't have time for that stuff."

"It can be annoying, and a lot of people spend too much time on there, but it can be a good way to keep in touch with people. So one person posts a story like that, other people like the story and they post it. One post can go all over the country in a day or two if enough people see it and share it. Looks like that's what happened here. Natalie must have a lot of friends and it spread fast."

"Sounds interesting, but you know I don't have the time to try to keep up with every new thing young people are into these days. Well, I'll be. The Reds have actually taken a lead. Let's see if the bullpen can hold one for a change."

Leslie dropped the onion rings off at the table and said that their meals would be up shortly, and they set about the appetizer like they hadn't eaten in days.

"Great, there goes my heartburn again," said Myrtle as she took the last onion ring from the basket a couple moments later.

"These things give you heartburn?"

"They do sometimes. Depends on what's in the breading, but anything fried tends to do that to me these days."

"It does that to me sometimes as well. Milk helps with mine."

"When you get to be my age, it takes a bit more than just milk to get rid of it."

"You could drink a Coke and then belch like crazy until it's gone."

"Your granddad used to do that, but never in public."

"You should try it. It feels good getting rid of it that way."

"Maybe when you're young. My friend Alice has acid reflux and she's always taking these purple pills, and even then she has to watch the fried foods. She even has trouble drinking juice. I guess I've been lucky."

"Here you go," said Leslie as she set down their plates. "Burger and fries and salmon and asparagus. So you guys had breakfast in Salt Lake and you're having dinner here in Reno. Where you headed, if I may ask?"

"San Jose," replied Nathan. "Going to spend the night and head in tomorrow. Probably be home by early afternoon."

"So you live there? You coming back from somewhere, vacation or something?"

"Not exactly. My grandpa died and Grandma here is moving in with me. We left after the funeral."

"Where was that?"

"New Jersey."

"You've been driving from New Jersey with your grandma? Isn't that sweet."

"I don't know if sweet is the word I would use," replied Myrtle, "but he's a good chauffeur...and we've had some fun on the way."

"Well, I'll leave you to your food before it gets cold. Let me know if you need anything."

"Well, Nate, she certainly is a sweet thing, and about your age too if I had to venture a guess," Myrtle said with a wink and a sly grin.

Nathan stifled a few remarks that came to mind and simply replied, "Your fish is going to get cold."

20

They left the hotel early the next morning, both of them waking quite early in anticipation of finishing the trip that day. As they pulled out, Myrtle went straight to her journal and Nathan pulled onto I-80 and began driving west. He turned the volume up and chuckled softly when he heard Simon & Garfunkel singing Homeward Bound.

Myrtle smiled and commented, "It would appear that they're playing our song."

"Yeah, it's been a fun trip, but I'm kind of glad we're almost there. I have to admit something, though."

"What's that?"

"When we set out, I wasn't sure about driving all the way out here. I wanted to just get on the plane and be back the same day. Maybe I thought you would act more like an old lady."

"What do you mean by that?"

"I had a college friend who just took his grandpa down to New York and the trip took forever. Dude had to go to the bathroom every half hour and was a horrible back seat driver. He said he'd never drive the guy anywhere again if it was more than a trip around the block. I wasn't sure how this trip would go. I mean, there's a big differ-ence between 200 miles and 2000."

"So, have I been a pain like your friend's grandpa?"

"Not at all, quite the opposite actually. You surprised me. I didn't think old people were so spontaneous. I've been the one acting old, not you."

"Well, Nate, the minute you start acting old is the minute you start to die. What's the line from that movie you and your grandpa used to watch all the time? Get busy living or get busy dying?"

"Yeah, that's the line. Great movie. You packed his DVDs, didn't you?"

"I'm pretty sure they're in one of the boxes."

"Good, I'm going to have to watch that again. I might have forgotten one or two lines. I could use a refresher."

I-80 west out of Reno is another of those stretches of highway that is good for passengers, especially passengers with a camera and a love of mountain scenery, and Myrtle soon found herself taking photo after photo while tapping her feet to the radio. She was in unusually high spirits. She had no idea what she would do with all the photos she had taken. Did places still print them for you? It seemed like everyone she knew was using digital cameras and nobody ever printed their pictures and put them in albums anymore. Heck, Nathan didn't even use a camera. She still didn't understand the way young people did everything on their phones. They crossed the border into California and shortly after she saw the sign for the Donner Memorial State Park.

"You think we can stop for a bit at that park ahead," she asked.

"Donner Memorial?"

"Yeah, that's the one. This must be the Donner Pass."

"I believe it is. I guess you remember what happened there."

"I'm not *that* old."

"Ha ha. I actually remember that story. One of the few things I remember from history class. Pretty sad."

"Yeah. I'd just like to see the park and maybe use the bathroom while we're there."

They came to the entrance to Donner Memorial State Park and drove through, stopping to read a historical marker and use the restroom near a picnic area. When they got back in the car to leave the park, Nathan commented, "Seems kind of inappropriate to have a picnic area there, you think?"

"Why do you say that? Oh, never mind. That was bad."

"Well, sarcasm is one of the services I offer."

"You might want to be careful where you offer it and how often."

"Oh, I can be careful when needed."

"So, we'll be home this afternoon?"

"Yeah, depending on traffic. We have to pass through Sacramento and then cut south before we get to Napa."

"Napa? Where they make the wine?"

"Yep, but we don't go through there. We head south before we get there and we'll stay away from San Fran and Oakland. We should miss all the bad traffic areas."

"Does traffic get bad near San Francisco?"

"It can, depending on the time of day you pass through there, but we don't have to go near there today. We should make good time getting home."

"Well, the first thing I want to do is take a long hot bath. You do have a bathtub, don't you?"

"Yeah, one of the bathrooms has a tub."

"You have more than one bathroom?"

"Yeah, it's a pretty nice place for just one person. I was going to have a roommate a couple years back, so I got a place with two bathrooms, but that didn't happen."

"Roommate?"

"Yeah, another programmer who was going to work at Tempest, but he ended up taking a position down in L.A."

"I've heard about college students having roommates..."

"It happens sometimes in my field, especially out here where the cost of living is high. A lot of new guys look for roommates until they get on their feet."

"So you have two bathrooms and a couple extra bedrooms and you've been living in that by yourself."

"Pretty much, but I use one of the extra rooms as a computer room. I can work from home sometimes and I play games in there. Hopefully we won't catch too much traffic and you can take a bath while I go to the grocery and return this car."

"You need to go to the grocery?"

"Yeah, I used up most everything before I flew to Jersey. Figured I fix something for a change, after all this eating out we've been doing lately."

"Sure, that sounds like a good idea."

Myrtle pulled her camera back out since they were still in mountainous areas and kept snapping photos out of the window. Nathan was wondering how many photos she had shot during the trip, especially since they got into the western states. She must have a huge memory card in that camera. He remembered getting her that camera almost two years ago for Christmas and how reluctant she was to use it since it didn't take film. It took a while for her to get used to it, but she even managed to learn how to transfer the pictures to a computer. How many were on that computer, he had no idea, but he would take a look at it over the weekend and see about getting some prints made. She loved photo albums, would tell you the story behind every photo in every album she had, an inexhaustible memory.

He would take care of that this evening when he took the car back. It would be a good weekend before going back to work, a baseball game on Friday and church on Sunday, with a trip to the beach somewhere over the weekend. After a week in the car together, he was till looking forward to doing things with her. She had become not only his grandmother but his friend. She was the kind of woman he wanted to marry, he thought, and that thought brought Phoebe to mind. He knew what he needed to do. Grandma had been harping on him all the way about it.

Grandpa described it in what he thought were somewhat crass terms. Nathan remembered the conversation quite well. They were out fishing and Grandpa had chosen the moment to impart whatever wisdom had come to mind. He was always doing that, taking advantage of moments they had alone to give advice. Most of the advice went over Nathan's head, but those conversations would often come back to mind at odd times, or when the lesson was most needed.

Nathan was 16 at the time, and was at that age where girls had gone from being the enemy to being a source of fascination, and his grandfather had figured that he would need some fatherly advice along those lines. Patrick also realized that his grandson shared his own fear of risk and that he would need to get over that. Nathan asked him how he started dating Grandma and Patrick had replied, "Nathan, you have to have a 'what the hell' moment."

"Excuse me," Nathan replied, somewhat taken aback because he rarely heard his grandpa use crass language.

"You heard me. There are times in your life where you face something difficult. You can do two things. You can slink away in fear or you can just say 'what the hell' and go right ahead and attack it. Those are the moments when you accomplish things in your life, the times where you just ignore the risks and charge right ahead. Sometimes you fail, but that's the only way you succeed. It's easy to see an obstacle and decide you don't have what it takes to get past it, but you never really know if you have what it takes until you say 'what the hell' and just go for it."

"Like when you asked Grandma out?"

"That was one of those moments. Your grandmother scared me. She was a real dish back then..."

"A dish?"

"Yeah, a beautiful woman, a knockout. She was all that. You young people would say she was hot, but I don't like that term. She was everything a guy could want; she had beauty, brains, and class. I fell hard. She would walk into a room and I felt like I couldn't breathe and my knees would go weak. I was so sure she wouldn't go for a guy like me. Friends even tried to tell me that she had a thing for me, but I didn't see it. Finally I just figured that if I never asked I would never know and getting shot down was better than never knowing. That was my 'what the hell' moment. I decided to ignore the risk and go for it, and that was the best decision I ever made. If I hadn't taken the chance, where would I be now? Where would you be? And you know what? She still does that to me. She's still quite a dish."

"I guess you're a lucky man," Nathan had said.

"Luck...maybe...but I'll tell you what, Nate. I'm blessed. She could have ended up with any number of guys, a lot of them better than me, but she ended up with me. That's a blessing."

Nathan was amazed at how much of that conversation he recalled now, almost like it was yesterday. He could even remember the feel of the breeze blowing over the lake, the ripple of his grandfather's muscles as he effortlessly rowed the boat to a different spot on the lake, the can after can of Coke that they shared from the cooler in the middle of the boat, and the sheer delight on his grandpa's face whenever a fish would bite. This was a man in is element, a man still in his prime. He was more than a grandfather; he was like a second father to Nathan.

"Earth to Nathan. Hello...anybody home?"

"Uh, yeah, guess my mind was wandering a bit."

"Wandering a bit? No kidding. You were in another zip code."

"I was thinking about Grandpa."

"He's been on my mind a lot too."

"I keep remembering conversations we had. He would be giving me some advice and I wasn't really listening, but now I'm remembering what he said. I should have paid attention then."

"What kind of advice?"

"Same kind of stuff you've been saying lately."

"Ah..."

"He said I needed to have a 'what the hell' moment."

"That sounds like something he would have said. Is there a town coming up by any chance?"

"You have to pee again?"

"No, I want to go bowling."

"Huh?"

"I can offer that service too. Where do you think you got it. Just find an exit with a restroom, ok."

"Yeah, I thought so. You ever been bowling?"

"Your grandpa and I went a couple times, but that was a long time ago. It was probably the only sport he wasn't good at, which I guess is why we didn't go much."

"You remember Tony?"

"Was he the boy who used to come over and play video games with you on the weekends, the black boy?"

"Yeah, that was him. He liked to bowl and he tried to interest me, but I never cared for it. I asked him one time why he liked to bowl and you know what he said? He said that black people loved bowling because the big black ball always knocks down all the white rednecks."

"Ha ha ha...oh Nate, don't make me laugh when I have to pee. This is a rental after all."

"Well, there's an exit up ahead with a McDonald's. You can always count on them for having a clean restroom."

"Whatever happened to Tony? He seemed like a nice boy."

"Oh, you don't know? He was a fairly decent basketball player. Ended up getting a scholarship to Xavier. Played there for four years, got a degree, and now he's still in Cincinnati working for P&G. He's engaged now, getting married in a few months."

"Wow, you guys still keep in touch?"

"Yeah, through Facebook mostly."

They exited and stopped at McDonald's, and by the time Myrtle exited from the restroom Nathan was walking away from the counter with two drinks in hand.

"Here you go," he said, handing her a cup.

"What's this?"

"Thought you'd like some more iced tea."

"I thought we had some in the cooler."

"Oh, we finished what was in the cooler yesterday. I didn't think it would be a good idea to buy more this close to home."

"Well, if I keep drinking this stuff, we'll never make it home."

"You should be good at least to the other side of Sacramento. We're not far from there right now."

She did last to the other side of Sacramento, but just barely, and they found themselves stopping again in Fairfield, Myrtle having put the camera away in favor of her journal, filling several more pages. Nathan had taken up the practice himself, but his grandma seemed to have way more to say than he did. She had filled one book and was starting on another. Nathan noticed the gas tank was getting rather low and filled up while he was waiting on his grandmother to finish using the restroom.

"So, we have to be getting close now," she said as she got back in the car.

"Not much more than an hour from here, so this is the last stop. Home stretch now."

"Wow. I didn't realize we were that close."

"You've had your nose in that journal since the other side of Sacramento. Time flies when you're having fun, I guess."

But time doesn't fly when you're at the end of a long trip. Nathan wondered at this. There were other days where he had gone hundreds of miles and the time and the landscape had flown by. Now that he was back in familiar territory it seemed to drag. He got on 680 to head south and found himself wishing Grandma was talkative, but she was scribbling furiously in her journal again, so Nathan paid attention to the road and tried to plan the next couple of days. He hoped to get the trailer unpacked and the car returned before the end of the day. He would probably need help with the trailer. Hopefully Fred was home. With Fred's help they could get the trailer unpacked and in the house fairly fast. He dialed Fred's number and his neighbor picked up on the second ring.

"Hello."

"Hey Fred."

"Nathan, how's it going?

"Pretty good, you home?"

"We're at the store, should be home in half an hour. Why?"

"Just got on 680, so I should be home in an hour or so. Just wondering if you could give me a hand with some of Grandma's things, a bed and a dresser and some boxes. Shouldn't take more than 20 minutes or so."

"Yeah, sure. Anything to help my celebrity neighbor."

"Celebrity?"

"Yeah, you guys are all over the internet. Your grandma gave some waitress a big check and it went viral."

"She's been doing that lately. She's got a bit of money in the bank and doesn't have a problem being generous with it."

"That's cool. I'll see you when you get here."

When he pulled in, Fred was waiting outside with a dolly and sipping on a bottle of water.

"Hey buddy, how was your trip," he asked as he stuck out his hand.

Nathan took his hand and said, "It was a nice trip really. We took the scenic route."

Myrtle came around the car and Nathan introduced her to Fred.

"Grandma, this is Fred, my neighbor."

"Nice to meet you, Grandma," said Fred.

"You can call me Myrtle."

"Ok, Myrtle, nice to meet you. Ok, Nate, let's have at that trailer."

"Ok. By the way, you think you can follow me to drop this car and trailer off when we're done? You can use my car."

"Sure. Let's get this done."

Nathan showed Myrtle in to the apartment, where she began to run the bath water, and he joined Fred outside where they started to unload the trailer and the car. Half an hour later, everything was in the house and set up. Nathan stood outside the bathroom door and said, "We're going to take the car back and stop at the store. Your things are in the second bedroom on the right."

"Ok, I'll see you when you get back."

They locked up the apartment and Nathan handed Fred the keys to his car.

"Where we going," Fred asked.

"Drop this U-Haul trailer off and the Tahoe goes to Enterprise."

"Ok, I'll just follow you."

"It's the Enterprise on Pearl. You can meet me there and I'll just drop this trailer off on the way."

"Ok, see you there."

After dropping off the trailer, Nathan met Fred at Enterprise and returned the Tahoe. Fred got out and moved to the passenger seat and Nathan got in.

Nathan put his seat belt on and said, "Man, it feels good to drive my own car again, but that Tahoe was kind of nice. Anyway, you and Kate want to come over for dinner? Grandma and I have been eating out so much, I thought I'd fix something tonight."

"Sounds good. I don't think we have any plans. What did you have in mind."

"You know me. I'm going to stop and get some steaks and maybe salmon for Grandma. She got fish the last couple places we stopped. Think she got burned out on steak."

"One does not simply get burned out on steak, Nate."

"I'm with you, but we ate a lot of it on the trip."

"Yeah, whatever. Let me call Kate so she doesn't start fixing something."

A minute later he got off the phone and told Nathan, "Kate had started cooking, but she only had vegetables on. She'll just bring them over to your place."

They came into Nathan's apartment with the steaks and salmon from the store and found Myrtle and Kate sitting in the living room talking amiably.

"I'll go get the grill ready, " Nathan said and headed out to the patio.

Fred rummaged around in the kitchen and then yelled out the door, "Where do you keep your spices?"

"Lower cabinet next to the dishwasher."

Fred prepared the steaks and salmon for grilling and Kate prepared the salad and steamed vegetables, while Myrtle sat in a recliner observing and writing in her journal. Fred looked in the fridge, found nothing but Coke, grabbed two bottles, and joined Nathan on the patio with the meat and grilling utensils.

"Figured you'd want one of these," he said, handing Nathan a bottle of Coke.

"You figured right, thanks," he said as he twisted the top off and took a drink.

"Hoped to find something a little, uh, stronger, in your fridge. Forgot this is as strong as it gets with you."

"Yeah, you know me. Only living Irishman who doesn't drink."

"Not the only one, Nate. You forgot about the ones in AA."

"Yeah, funny. Just never cared for the stuff. Gives me headaches."

"It does that to me too."

"Well, when you drink as much as I've seen you put away before, but with me it's one sip. Alcohol just doesn't agree with me."

"Probably for the best, really. How about your granny? What will she be drinking."

"Grandma has been drinking iced tea every day of her life for as long as I've known her. I've got some Lipton in the cabinet. Just the instant stuff. We can whip up a pitcher when we get in."

"These are some nice looking steaks. Medium on mine, by the way."

"How about Kate? How does she like hers?"

"Well done, but still juicy. She sees any pink she'll scream bloody murder."

"I got you, almost ruined."

"Pretty much. So tell me, why did you decide to bring your grandma back here?"

"Well, she wanted to sell the house and she was talking about moving into a home. Nobody else had extra space, or nobody else wanted to take her in, and I didn't want her to go to a home. I got the room here. It just made sense."

"And she just went along with it?"

"Well, she was hesitant at first...for about five minutes."

"Why in the world did you drive all the way? You could have hired a moving truck and taken a flight a few days later."

"That's what I thought we were going to do, but she said she couldn't fly. Some medical reason or something. Here's the funny part. I was not too happy about it at first, but I wouldn't change a thing now."

"You must have stopped and smelled the roses a bit."

"Yeah, saw a baseball game, hit some parks and museums, and busted a pimp."

"I heard about a huge trafficking ring that got broken up, found the bastard somewhere in Wisconsin. That was you?"

"It was, kind of right place, right time really. Grandma saw this girl looking out the window of an RV, thought something didn't look right, and we called the cops. We only stopped there because she had to pee."

"So this girl owes her freedom to your grandma's bladder. That's something else."

"Yeah, we thought it was pretty cool, but you should have seen her. I had a couple bad dreams after that. That guy had her basically chained up in that RV and was pimping her out across the country. Sick."

"Well, those dudes are right bastards, but...looks like that fish is done. How about the steaks?"

"Ours are done, but Kate's will be another minute."

"Ok, I'll head in and help Kate get the table ready and get the tea made."

A few minutes later they were all seated and the food was on the table, and right when Fred was about to cut into his steak, Nathan interjected with, "Wait a sec Fred. Have to pray before we prey."

"Huh?"

"P r a y before we p r e y."

"Ah, clever. I'll have to remember that."

All heads bowed and Myrtle, once again sensitive to the appetites of those around the table, made the grace quick, a simple prayer of thanks for the food and for the safe travel across the country. When she was finished, Kate said, "So Nate, your grandma tells me you got that promotion at work."

"Looks like I have a good shot. Got an email from Frank a couple days ago."

"That must be exciting."

"I guess so."

"Don't sound so thrilled."

"Oh, I'm happy about it, just apprehensive a bit."

"You'll do ok, buddy. You know that computer stuff inside and out," replied Fred.

"I've also been hearing all about your trip," Kate said.

"Yeah, Nate, sounds epic," Fred replied.

Nathan paused a couple seconds and then said, "Yeah, it was some trip. We got more than we bargained for. When we started out, Grandma said she wanted to see Mt. Rushmore and I decided we would stop in Cincinnati for a baseball game on the way. Everything else was unplanned."

"Nate surprised me with the ball game," Myrtle said between bites of salmon, "and we ended up sitting right next to a former player."

"Not to change the subject too abruptly," said Fred, "but you bought enough books to start a small library. I never took you to be that much of a reader."

"Well, I've always enjoyed a good novel. We met some Indians in South Dakota. Figured I'd learn a bit more about them. They were wonderful people and they have such a sad history. You want to borrow any of those books, you let me know."

"You know what," Fred replied, "I'm going to finish this excellent meal while it's still warm, and when we're done I'm going to go grab a beer and you're going to tell me all about it."

21

The conversation went longer than anyone had planned, continuing two hours after Myrtle went to bed, and eventually Fred and Kate excused themselves and went back to their apartment. Nathan wanted nothing more than to collapse, but instead tiptoed into Myrtle's bedroom and retrieved her camera bag, taking it into his computer room. There was a full memory card in the bag and the one on the camera was nearly full. He made a mental note to pick up some larger memory cards, or dump all of these photos onto an external drive he had and wipe these clean for future use. Maybe one big card would be better. He searched through his desk and found a 16 gb thumb drive, transferred the contents to his external hard drive, and connected the camera to the computer via USB.

He hadn't thought it would take too long to go through the photos, but when he got them all transferred onto his computer he realized how many there were. There were already photos on there and she had taken hundreds since they left New Jersey. He went to the kitchen and grabbed another Coke, put some music on, and set to it. What he thought would be a simple exercise of picking out the good photos turned into a more emotional experience than he had counted on. There were photos taken when his grandfather was still alive, some around the house with him sitting in his favorite recliner, sitting at the kitchen table, sitting on the back porch, always sitting. Of course he was always sitting. These were recent photos, taken right before he went to the hospital, when he didn't have the strength to do much but sit. The next photos were taken at the hospital, and then there were photos from the funeral. He saw himself and his grandmother in several of those and he was getting choked up.

He deleted duplicates and extremely blurry photos, and paused over several as memories came flooding back. The photos from the trip were easy enough. Many were too blurry to keep, but many others were breathtaking. She had quite an eye for the good shot. Once he had sorted them out and figured which ones to keep, he loaded them onto the thumb drive and looked up a drug store that had 24 hour photo processing.

He got the dinner dishes cleaned up, dropped the thumb drive at the drug store and went to a large grocery that was still open late. He bought some food for breakfast and a coffee maker, and headed back home.

Myrtle was a late riser in the morning, no doubt from fatigue and the later time zone. The aroma of bacon and coffee drew her from the bedroom, but it was what she saw next to her breakfast plate that brought a smile to her face. A photo album was open to the first page and there was a pile of prints. She enjoyed this almost more than taking the pictures, and could give a detailed account of each photo.

"Thank you, Nate," was all she said when she was done.

"You know, you have quite an eye for photography."

"Your grandfather always said that, but you know what? That camera makes it easy. Just line it up and snap."

"The newer ones are like that. They do a lot more for you, but you still have a good eye for taking the right shot. A lot of those look like postcards."

"I just wish your grandfather was here to look at them with me."

"When you get cleaned up, we have somewhere to go."

"Where is that?"

"You'll see. I'll be in my computer room when you're ready."

A few minutes later Myrtle emerged ready to go, and they went out and got in the car, after Nathan showed her which car was his.

"So this is your car? Nice. I always liked Subarus."

"Yeah, I kind of like it. It's supposed to have a good safety rating, but I hope I never have to find out."

"So where are we going?"

"A place not far from here, just down on Monterey Rd."

A few turns later they arrived at the San Jose Animal Care Center, and Myrtle smiled when she figured out what he was up to . She said she wanted a pet, but hadn't expected that to happen immediately.

When they entered the building, they were greeted by a young woman who said, "Hi, you must be Nathan. This must be your grandmother," as she stuck out her hand to Myrtle.

"Hello, I'm Myrtle," she replied, shaking the young woman's hand, "Pleased to meet you."

"Nice to meet you too. My name's Jennifer. Nathan told me you were looking to adopt."

"I might have mentioned it on the way out here."

"Are you looking for a cat or a dog?"

"I don't have much experience with cats, so maybe a small dog, something suitable for an apartment."

"Ok, come this way. This first area is where we have the cats, and we keep the dogs down this way."

"What's that area over there," Myrtle asked, pointing to a room off to the side where a small dog was running around.

"Oh, that's where people can meet with animals that are up for adoption to see if they might be a good fit."

"There's a small dog in there and nobody is meeting with it."

"Someone was just looking at that dog a minute ago. Hold on a sec," and then to another man who was walking by, "Hey Ed, what's up with the meeting room? Is Mrs. Dalton still looking at dogs in there. It looks like Cleo is still in there running around."

"Oh, she isn't interested in adopting Cleo. Just haven't had a chance to move him back to his cage," Ed replied.

"Ok, thanks. I'll take care of that."

"He's a cute little fellow," Myrtle said. "Jack Russell?"

"Yes he is. You familiar with the breed?"

"I had one when I was a little girl."

"You want to go in there and meet him?"

Jennifer hadn't had to ask since by the time she got the question out of her mouth, Myrtle was already walking toward the room, looking 20 years younger, and ready to meet Cleo. She went in and the little dog bounded right up to her, sniffer her proffered hand, and began licking her fingers and wagging his tail. She scratched his head and smiled at the instant look of gratitude on the little dog's face. It was obvious that the two of them had hit it off quite well.

"They seem to be getting along well," Jennifer told Nathan.

"You could say that. Where'd he come from?"

"He was a surrender. A couple was moving and they just dropped him off. It's sad really, the way people will just abandon a loving animal when it no longer suits them. We see that all the time around here."

"Yeah, he looks like a great dog. Why would anyone give him up? How old is he?"

"We think he's around five years old. Has all his shots and is completely house broken, and it looks like he's quite fond of your grandma."

By this time Myrtle was sitting down in a chair and Cleo was on her lap, reaching up and licking her chin. Myrtle was giggling and scratching his ears.

"They look fond of one another. I don't think she'll be wanting to look at any other dogs."

"That's good. We've all been hoping he could find a good home. He's such a sweetie. There's just one catch with him, though."

"What's that?"

"He has a friend here. They're pretty much a bonded pair. We'd hate to split the two of them up. I know you only came for one animal, but if you could find it in your heart..."

"So he has another dog he's friends with."

"Not exactly. Hey Ed, bring Cleo's friend in here, will you?"

Ed came shortly carrying a grey tabby cat and he went in and put the cat in the room with Cleo and Myrtle. The little dog saw his friend and immediately jumped down and the two of them met in the middle of the room. The bond was obvious from the start as the cat ran up to Cleo and began rubbing her cheek against his head, first one side and then the other. Then they chased each other around for a minute before sitting down on the floor, the dog submitting himself gladly to the grooming attention of his feline friend.

Myrtle watched all of this with a look of amusement on her face, clearly never having seen a cat and a dog getting along in this manner. "They're rather cute together," was all she could manage to say.

Jennifer and Nathan entered the room and Jennifer said to Myrtle, "Cleo and May are what we call a bonded pair. May was dropped off here back in May so we just called her May. She was in bad shape and Cleo took to her right away, stayed by her side until she was better. They've been inseparable ever since. We'd like to keep them together if at all possible. We can waive the adoption fee for anyone willing to take them both."

"Well, I've never had a cat before..."

"We'll take them both," Nathan interrupted, and then to Myrtle, "They can keep each other company when we have to be out, like on Sunday mornings."

"I suppose that makes sense. They do seem to love each other so much, and if May is half as sweet at Cleo is..."

"Ok then," Jennifer said, "Just come this way and we'll take care of the formalities. I don't guess you brought carriers, did you?"

"Forgot that little detail," Nathan said.

"I'll tell you what. We can loan you a large carrier to get them home and you can just drop it back off here when you get a chance, ok?"

"That'll work. Thanks."

"No problem. You're also going to need a litter box for May. We'll send you with one, some litter, and some cans of her favorite food. I can give you some toys too, and you can get some more at the pet store down the road."

"Wow, you're so helpful."

"Every day one of our babies gets a home is a good day. We really appreciate you taking these two. We just wish we could find homes for all of them."

Nathan took care of the remaining paperwork and they loaded the supplies and the animals into the car for the drive back home, stopping at the pet store for more food, toys, litter, and animal beds that they would hopefully use. When Nathan came out of the pet store and approached the car, he noticed the silly grin hadn't come off his grandma's face since they left the shelter. She was leaning into the back seat talking away to the two animals who looked back at her with bemused expressions on their faces.

They got home and once Nathan had taken everything inside, he opened the carrier and let the animals out to settle into their new home. Myrtle sat down in a recliner and within five minutes both of them were in her lap, Cleo licking her fingers and May kneading her leg and purring. They curled up together on her lap, their little bodies intertwined, and in the security of a new loving home, went fast to sleep. Myrtle sat completely still and just stared down at them with such a look of adoration that Nathan was taken momentarily aback. He wasn't much of an animal person, but he could see the attachment certain people felt for them. Clearly taking Grandma to the shelter had been the right decision.

He busied himself with setting up the litter box in the laundry room, setting up the food bowls in the kitchen, and putting the cat and dog beds against the wall, before he retrieved *Post Captain* from his night stand and settling onto the couch to read. He looked across at his grandmother with the two animals on her lap and gave her a smile. He hadn't seen her this happy since before Grandpa died, and it warmed his heart. She looked over to him and said, "Thank you Nate."

"Oh, it was nothing."

"Not just for today, for everything."

"You're welcome."

"You know, I have a lot in common with these little guys."

"What's that? You're not nearly as hairy as they are."

"Not that. Look at them. They've found a loving home and they're content."

"That's more than just content there. They haven't even been here a few minutes and they're already acting like they own the place."

"There's just one problem."

"What's the problem."

"I have to pee and I don't want to disturb them."

"I might have just the thing for that," Nathan said as he went into the kitchen and popped the top off two cans of food. He barely had time to fill each bowl before they were both there, instinctively knowing which bowl of food was which.

Nathan sat back down in his chair, only to be interrupted by the doorbell. He went to the door to find Fred standing there.

"Come on in."

"I won't be long. Kate left a dish here last night. Wait a sec. When did you get a dog...and a cat too? When did this happen?"

"Grandma said she wanted a pet, so we went down to the shelter and ended up coming back with two. They're buddies and the shelter didn't want to separate them."

"I can see that," Fred said, as he approached Cleo with his hand out, "Hi there buddy."

Fred scratched the dog's ears and asked, "So what are their names?"

"The shelter named the dog Cleo and the cat May, but I might try to come up with something better. What kind of a name is Cleo anyway?"

"Whatever his name is, he's a friendly little fellow. Is the cat friendly?"

"Haven't had time to figure her out. We only got back here with them a few minutes ago."

Myrtle came back and sat down, and it was only a minute before May found her lap and started getting comfortable, prompting Fred to remark, "Well, she certainly seems to like your grandma."

Myrtle reached down to stroke the top of the cat's head and was instantly rewarded with a loud purr. A minute later Cleo had joined the fun and Myrtle had a full lap once again. Nathan snatched up his phone and snapped a couple photos and then spoke once again to Fred.

"Grandma and I have tickets for the ball game tonight. You wouldn't mind checking in on the critters, would you?"

"No problem, buddy. You want me to feed them?"

"I can feed them before we leave, but if you can just check in and make sure they're not tearing the place apart," Nate said as he returned from the kitchen with Kate's dish.

"Yeah sure. Kate's going out with a friend, girls' night out, so I don't have anything better to do anyway. When are you leaving for the game?"

"Oh, I don't know. Depends if Grandma wants to watch batting practice."

"I wouldn't mind that," replied Myrtle.

"Well then, looks like we'll leave here around 4:30."

"Alright. I'll see you then."

"Ok. There's a leftover steak in the fridge. You can help yourself when you come."

For the next two hours, Myrtle sat in the recliner and wrote in her journal while Cleo and May played together around the living room, occasionally jumping on her lap to say hi and then jumping down again. They were clearly best friends and clearly favored Myrtle over Nathan. Sure, Nathan was the one who had fed them and at times they would look at him fondly, but always go back to Myrtle for attention.

This suited Nathan fine and he sat on the couch reading and sipping on a Coke, until Fred showed up at the door shortly before 4:30. Myrtle retreated to the bedroom and came back out wearing her Reds attire that she had worn at the game in Cincinnati. Nathan put food in the animals' bowls, said farewell to Fred, and they were off.

The drive to AT&T Park took longer than he had counted on since he had forgotten it was a week day and he had to negotiate rush hour traffic. Still, he was able to drop his grandma off near the stadium gate, park the car, and then meet her to enter the stadium well before batting practice was scheduled to end. They took their seats in the first row behind the visitor's dugout just as the Giants were wrapping up and the Reds players were taking the field. Nathan soon lost interest in watching batting practice, but Myrtle was paying rapt attention to each hitter and taking photos of the field.

"This is a beautiful ballpark," she exclaimed.

"Told you you'd like it."

"What do you suppose they're pointing at," she asked Nathan, and then he noticed it too. A few of the players seemed to be pointing right at them, and then one of them came right over.

"Pardon me, but you wouldn't be the Callahans would you," the player asked.

"Why yes," Myrtle replied, "How did you know?"

"We've all seen you on the internet, with that waitress in Utah."

"Oh, that was nothing. I just had a chance to help her out."

"Well, I'm impressed. Not many people are that generous."

"It helps that I had the means. It's easier to be generous when you have the extra cash. Anyone would have done it."

"No ma'am, I doubt that anyone would have. Anyway, I'm honored to meet you. Hope you enjoy the game."

"I'm sure I will, even more if you hit a homer, Mr. Votto."

"Just call me Joey, ma'am."

Nathan observed the whole exchange in something of a sense of awe. He wasn't what anyone would call a sports fan, but even he was familiar with the first baseman for the Reds, and if he said he was honored to meet them, well...he would take that as a compliment.

The scene was repeated throughout batting practice as other players came over to tell Myrtle how glad they were to meet her and that they hoped she enjoyed the game. When it got closer to game time and more fans were filing into their seats, the same scene was repeated on several more occasions as other people who had seen her photo and story online recognized her and came over to say hi, some even taking selfies with her.

The attention was overwhelming to say the least, and she commented on it to Nathan.

"Well, that's how the internet works these days. One person shares something and it can spread like wildfire."

"Yeah, you mentioned that, but it just hadn't sunk in."

"Like it or not, you're a bit of a celebrity. A lot of people are impressed with what you did."

"But all I did was give a girl some money."

"You changed her life. That's what I love about you. You're incredible and you don't even know it."

"I'm just an old woman with a lot of money and nothing better to spend it on."

"No, you're more than that. You're not just my grandma. You're my second mom."

"Why, that's the sweetest thing you've said to me in ages. What's got into you?"

"I was thinking about Mom when I woke up, how I left so many things unsaid when she died, and how I'll never get a second chance to tell her all those things. I don't want to make the same mistake again."

"I'm sure your mother knew that you loved her."

"Yeah, maybe she did, but I was only fourteen when she was killed and most fourteen year olds aren't exactly that good at expressing such things to their parents. Half the time I was arguing with her about something. Then when someone is taken from you, you realize all those things you should have said and never did. And then there I was this morning thinking about her and how much I miss her, and how much I'd give to have one more chance to tell her how much I love her."

"You'll get another chance, Nate."

"Yeah, I know that, and I believe it, but it could be a while. Until then, I have to live with the regret, and make sure I don't make the same mistake again."

Very little you say in a ballpark seating area remains completely private, and unbeknownst to Nathan, his words had struck a chord with his left hand neighbor who was on his cell phone surprising his own mother with a call out of the blue to tell her that he loved her. When the man hung up, he turned to Nathan and said, "Thank you young man."

"Huh," Nathan said as he turned to his left, "what are you thanking me for?"

"My mom's in a nursing home. I heard what you said. I just got off the phone with her. I think I made her day."

Nathan looked around and saw other people in his immediate vicinity hanging up their cell phones, some wiping tears from their eyes. Then he looked back to his right and his grandmother was in conversation with another player who had just handed her something.

"Will you look what I just got," she said as she handed Nathan a baseball.

He took the ball and looked closely, seeing the signatures of the entire team with the inscription, "To Myrtle, from your biggest fans."

Myrtle was grinning from ear to ear. All Nathan could say was, "Well, isn't that something."

The game got underway and was something of a surreal experience for Nathan and Myrtle. Players would smile at her and say hello on their way in and out of the dugout. Even some of the Giants players came across between innings to say hello after being told who she was. The game wound along rather quickly, each pitcher being on top of his game, but the Giants had managed to plate a couple runs in the 7th inning and carried the 2-0 lead into the 9th.

"Last chance to try to score some runs," Myrtle said to Nathan. "I'd hate for them to get shut out."

"Come on Reds! You can do it!" she yelled with everything she had.

Given their proximity to the dugout, the first player to come out and approach the plate had heard her, had known who had yelled the exhortation, and gave her a wink on his way to home plate, where he promptly lined the fist pitch into the right center field gap for a double.

"Oh Nate, the tying run is at the plate. There's still a chance."

The next batter up, knowing he was the tying run, tried to do just that, only to strike out on three aggressive swings, much to Myrtle's disapproval. She kept that disapproval to herself, but cheered at the top of her lungs when the shortstop bobbled a ground ball and couldn't make the throw to first in time, putting runners on the corners with one out. The next batter went to the plate and then the on deck batter came out to warm up, giving Myrtle a wink and a big smile as he took his warm up swings.

"Look, Nate, that's Votto on deck, but they've been pitching around him all game. Even if he gets up, he probably won't get a chance to do anything."

No sooner were those words out of her mouth than the count went to 3-0 on the hitter.

"I don't know Grandma. I might not follow baseball much, but if they walk this guy, they'll have to pitch to him. Nowhere to put him with the bases loaded."

And walk him they did, which brought Votto up, with a smile and a nod to Myrtle before he went toward the plate.

Myrtle was on the edge of her seat. She heard but took no notice of the fans around her who were cheering their Giants on to finish the game and get the win.

"Come on Joey! You can do it!"

Nathan was caught up in his grandmother's excitement, but remained silent. Looking at her he thought she looked half her age. She was like a little girl cheering on her favorite player.

The first pitch was on the outside corner for strike one and the next two were out of the strike zone. Then the next pitch was on the inside corner and he fouled it off into the seats. Another pitch out of the strike zone and then three more were fouled off.

"He's really dialed in," she said to Nathan, "He's going to get one he likes and nail it."

The next pitch was indeed to his liking, a fastball about thigh

high on the inner half of the plate, and he sent it soaring high and far to straight away right field, landing with a splash in McCovey Cove. The home fans were silent as he rounded the bases, but one fan was on her feet cheering with all she was worth. She only stopped her cheering when she realized that after the customary high fives with teammates, the batter had retrieved the bat he had just used and was coming toward her seat.

"Here you go ma'am. Hope that will do," Votto said as he handed Myrtle the bat. He then descended into the dugout to leave Myrtle speechless holding the bat.

22

Driving home that evening he witnessed the impact sports could have on someone, how for a few brief moments nothing else in life mattered. He saw the joy on his grandmother's face and heard it in her voice as she recounted the game to him as if he hadn't been there right next to her. Here she was, a couple weeks removed from losing her husband and still in mourning, and a simple game had taken her mind off everything for a while, had been a balm to her in a way he simply didn't get.

That wasn't entirely true. When his parents died he needed a diversion as well, and although he didn't have a love of sports to turn to, he did have his computer and music. He found in music an outlet for his emotions and in gaming something to occupy himself in much the same way his grandparents could watch a game for three hours. For that brief moment, the outside world was kept at bay and all of its concerns could be set aside, and even though they would still have to be dealt with, the brief respite often made that task easier.

So maybe he could understand his grandma's love of sports, although he would never completely share it. He often made fun of sports fans and how seriously they took things. He saw people almost come to blows arguing over their teams and had read stories of people having heart attacks because of how a game had turned out. He would never understand that level of devotion, or insanity more precisely, but with his grandma he saw the ideal. She could turn off the game and move on like switching a switch if her team lost, and she could revel in a win as well, but she always kept it where it needed to be.

They walked in to the apartment to see Fred still there, relaxing on the couch with a beer in one hand and the other hand absent-mindedly stroking the head of the sleeping cat that was on his lap. Myrtle took in this scene and remarked, "The two of you look cozy. I trust they weren't too much trouble."

"Just the opposite. We've had a ball. I wore them out good," he said as he pointed toward the dog sleeping down by his feet. I guess you must be a happy camper. I watched the game. Couldn't believe the ending." Then he noticed the bat Myrtle was still holding and asked, "Got some souvenirs there?"

"Yes I do. The team gave me this," she said as she showed him the autographed ball, "and this bat is the one that hit the home run in the 9th."

Fred read the inscription on the ball and examined the bat, letting out a low whistle. "Wow, isn't that something," he said. "So you a big Reds fan?"

"Yeah, lived in Cincinnati until I went away to college. Never moved back, but never considered rooting for anyone else. You like baseball?"

"It's ok. I'll watch the games every now and then but I don't really follow it that much. I'm not from here originally. Moved out here from Boise about ten years ago. Never followed pro teams growing up."

"Well, this old fan is worn out. I'll see you in the morning, Nate."

"Ok, good night," Nathan replied.

"So, how did your grandma manage to get a signed ball and a home run bat? You know someone on the team?"

"Nothing like that. We had good seats, front row by the dugout, and a couple of the players had seen our photo online. They came over to chat during batting practice. Votto is her favorite player. When he hit the homer I thought she was going to jump out of her seat, and when he came over and gave her the bat...I can't describe it. She looked like a little girl. You should have seen it."

"I can only imagine. My uncle is really into it. Crazy dude broke a TV when Boise State lost a game. I mean he really broke it. A $1000 flat screen and he knocked it right over. Can you believe that?"

"How did he manage to do that?"

"He was sitting there watching the game. They had the lead most of the game and they were driving, had the ball down around the two yard line and were about to punch it in to seal the win. Running back fumbled and the other team ran it back all the way. He picked up his shoe and threw it across the room. Hit the TV and knocked it right off the wall mount and broke it. My aunt won't let him watch big games in the house anymore, makes him go to a sports bar."

"Man, that's messed up. Broke a nice TV over a football game?"

"Yeah. I like to watch a game like the next guy, but I don't get those kind of fans. Your grandma's not like that is she?"

"Oh no. She's reasonable about it. She enjoys it but she doesn't go crazy."

"That's good. Those kind of folks have a screw loose. So why'd you decide to bring her out here anyway?"

"Well, I hadn't given it any thought until we were sitting there in the house after most of the funeral guests had left and she was talking about selling the house and going to a home."

"She was going to go to a nursing home?"

"I think it was one of those assisted living facilities, but nobody in the family liked the idea."

"So how did you end up being the one?"

"Not sure exactly. We were sitting there talking and my Aunt Lilian said, 'Oh no, you can't go to one of those homes' and my uncle agreed with her right away. When I suggested they could take her in, it was all about not enough room with their son back from college, blah, blah, blah. Everyone but me had an excuse. No room, kids moving back in, kids haven't moved out, you know how people are.

So I just popped up and said she could move in with me. I figured we could hire a moving truck, wait a couple days, and then fly out here and get here when the truck did."

"So why didn't you do that? Would have been quicker than driving."

"Yeah. Grandma said she couldn't fly for medical reasons. I didn't ask what medical reasons could keep someone from flying. I think she just doesn't like airplanes, but I didn't want to argue the point."

"Well, Buddy, I'm jealous. I've always wanted to do a cross country trip, but Kate and I could never get the time off at the same time to try something like that. And I don't think she's as keen on the idea as I am. I think it would be a blast."

"It had its moments. You do it with an old person, you have to stop a lot. Every time you turn around it's 'I have to pee' or 'Is there a town coming up?' She was a good travel buddy though. I never would have thought it."

"What did you guys talk about all the way out here?"

"Mostly about family. We both miss Grandpa something awful and we talked about him a lot...and she lectured me a couple times."

"Lectured you? What about?"

"Mostly about coming up on 30 and still being single and what am I going to do about it."

"Come to think of it, what are you doing about it? You haven't mentioned dating. There's got to be somebody you're at least interested in."

"Great, why don't I just wake her up and the two of you can gang up on me?"

"I'm just curious. Young guy like you with a good paying job and a nice pad like this. You'd be a good catch for some lucky girl. So what gives?"

"I don't know. Just not good at talking to women, I guess."

"Yeah, I can see that. Let me give you a little tip. It's not as hard as it seems. Well, it can be at first, but like my dad used to say, use makes master. I guess you never talked to them much growing up, no passing silly notes in class and all that?"

"Girls scared me back then."

"Seems like they still do, if you ask me. You really just have to say 'hell with it' and just go for it. You'll crash and burn a few times, but you learn."

"My grandpa used to say the same thing. He said you have to have a 'what the hell' moment and just go for it."

"Your granddad was right. You finally just figure that you have to take the chance. So, is there one you're interested in?"

"Kind of, at least I think so."

"You think so? Either you're interested or you're not. Who is she?"

"She works with me. We have to work together sometimes."

"Details. I need details. Is she hot?"

"You might say that. It's more than that. She's just so...I don't have the word for it. She's like, old fashioned, really polite, not like other girls."

"So she's not from around here?"

"No, she's from...what's the country's name...Tanzania, but she's been here since she was little. Family came from there a few years ago."

"Oh, you know what they say, Nate. Once you go black..."

"Yeah, I've heard that one before. But you know what's funny? I don't really see her as black. I can't explain it. We have a lot of diversity at work, so I work with a lot of black people, but she's different. Probably the cultural difference."

"Probably, buddy. I worked with a couple African guys at an old job. They were different too. Always polite, said sir and ma'am a lot, but that wasn't really the difference either. It was hard to put a finger on. Just like white guys from Europe are different than white guys from here, I guess. Those guys could drink though. I went to a bar with them one night. Holy cow..."

"I don't think she drinks a drop, really strict family."

"So let me get this straight. She's good looking, well mannered, and comes from a good family. Dude, what are you waiting for, some other guy to beat you to the punch?"

"I hear you. I spent half the trip hearing the same thing from

Grandma. I've been trying to screw up the courage. I go back to work Monday. I don't want to be too awkward. You think I should figure out what to say in advance?"

"Look, once you decide to do it, you'll figure out what to say. If she's at all interested in you, it probably won't matter anyway. Just go for it. Ok, enough lecturing. What are you and Grandma doing the rest of the weekend?"

"We're going to find a church for Sunday, and then probably go to the beach. She's been wanting to go to the beach."

"Kate and I were planning on going up to Muir to see the redwoods, probably grill some burgers and dogs at the picnic area, make a day of it. You guys want to tag along?"

"I'm sure Grandma would love that. She loves to take nature photos. What time you leaving?"

"Oh, probably around 8:00."

"Sure, that will work. We'll see you then."

8:00 am rolled around and Myrtle and Nathan were ready when Fred rang the doorbell.

"Well, you guys look ready to roll. Shall we be off," Fred asked.

Myrtle replied, "Just let me get my camera."

"I cleared everything off the big memory card, so you can snap away to your heart's content," Nathan told her.

"So Nate, you ever been up to Muir," Fred asked.

"I've always wanted to go, but I've never managed."

"You've been here since you got out of college and you've never seen the redwoods?"

"Just never took the time to go up there."

"Man, you do work too much. You need to live a little."

"What are we going to do for lunch," Myrtle asked.

"You like burgers and dogs," Fred asked.

"Who doesn't?"

"Good. There's a picnic area there with grills. I've got everything we need for a good lunch in the trunk."

Myrtle's reaction to seeing the giant redwood trees was as Nathan had figured it would be. Fred and Kate wanted to hike around some and Myrtle had wanted to as well, but her knees were bothering her and she kept stopping to catch her breath, so she and Nathan sat down on a bench to wait.

"Wow, these trees are truly magnificent," Myrtle said while snapping another photo.

"Yeah. Some of them are over 1000 years old. To think I've lived near here for six years and this is the first time I've been here."

"Well, if you had someone to take to places like this..."

"Yeah, yeah, I hear you. I'm working on that."

"Well, at the rate you're going, you'll be as old as these trees by the time it happens."

"Now, aren't you the comedian?"

"Just poking at you. So where are we going to church tomorrow?"

"There's a non denominational one not far from home. I've gone there a couple times. If you don't like it, we'll pick a different one next week."

"Is it like that one we went to in Cincinnati? I liked that one."

"It's pretty similar. Good music and the people are friendly. I haven't been in a while though."

"There's more to it than the music and how friendly the people are."

"I know. We'll see how it is tomorrow and then we can decide whether we want to check out a different one."

They sat in silence for a while, just looking at the trees and marveling at their beauty, Myrtle taking more photos and Nathan staring at them lost in thought. It was this way that Fred and Kate found them over an hour later.

"You got a lot of good pictures there," Fred asked Myrtle as he reached for the camera, and while browsing through the pictures, "Wow, these are pretty good. You sure you were never a photographer?"

"Nope. I just enjoy it. I like nature."

"Well, you have a good eye for it. Nathan showed me the ones you took on the way out here. From the window of a moving car? Impressive."

"Thank you. I got lucky a few times."

After more sight seeing, they made their way to the picnic area where Fred found a grill and prepared a very typical picnic lunch of hamburgers, hot dogs, potato salad, grilled corn on the cob, and a melon. When the food was ready, Fred opened the cooler and retrieved a Coke, a bottle of iced tea, and two beers. He then handed Nathan the Coke and the car keys.

"What's this," Nathan replied.

Fred simply twisted the cap off of his beer and held it up reply, to which Nathan smiled and put the keys in his pocket. They ate their fill, and when Nathan went to the cooler for another Coke, made a note of the number of beers Fred had brought with him, and understood right away why he had the keys for the drive home, a drive they made sooner than they had planned since the day was hot and Myrtle's knees were still bothering her.

"So Grandma," Fred asked Myrtle, "you know any card games?"

"Oh, Nathan and I like to play Rummy, but I know a few others."

"You know Euchre?"

"Haven't played in years, but I know how to play. Not sure if Nate does though."

"He knows how. He's played a few games over at my place. I think we should play some when we get back. The day's still young."

"The day's still young and you're already drunk."

"Maybe, but tomorrow I'll be sober and Nate will still stink at Euchre."

"You paraphrasing Churchill?"

"Huh?"

"Churchill and Lady Astor. You nearly quoted him there."

"The line about still being ugly tomorrow? I knew I had heard it somewhere. Just couldn't remember where."

"Well, we can play a few games. Might even teach you a thing or two about old age and treachery."

They arrived at home and gathered around Nathan's kitchen table, where they played game after game of Euchre, drank large quantities of Coke, iced tea, and beer, the latter all consumed by Fred, until Kate said, "Well guys, it's been fun, but we all have to get up in the morning and I think my dear husband needs to be tucked in. He's not going to be feeling so well in the morning."

"Ok, you need help getting him to your place? It doesn't look like he can walk too well."

"Oh, I think I can manage ok. I have experience."

"Say, Grandma and I are going to head to the beach after church and just chill for the afternoon. You want to join us? Heck, come in the morning and you can join us for church as well."

"Well, I don't know if Fred will be up for church, but we can join you at the beach. What time does the service let out."

"Last time I went there it was over by noon. We'll probably be back here by twenty after or so."

"Ok, Fred and I will see you here around 12:30. We haven't been to the beach in a while. Should be fun."

23

Nathan awoke Sunday morning to the smell of coffee. Myrtle had risen early and was already dressed and sitting at the kitchen table, sipping a cup of coffee and reading her Bible. Nathan put some sausage links on his Foreman grill and went to the shower. Most mornings he could shower and dress in the time it took to cook, and this morning was no exception. He entered the kitchen right as Myrtle was thinking about getting up to check on the meat.

Myrtle took one look at him, whistled, and said, "You going to church or looking for a date?"

"You never seen a guy in a suit before?"

"Haven't seen you wear one in a while. You clean up nice."

"You don't look so bad yourself."

"What time does the service start?"

"We have an hour. Plenty of time to eat breakfast."

Nathan put some bread in the toaster and poured a couple glasses of orange juice, and Myrtle continued reading her Bible. After they ate and they were going to the car, she asked Nathan, "You don't have a Bible?"

"I have two on my iPad."

Myrtle just shook her head slightly, but said nothing, and they got in the car and headed to church. Ten minutes later they walked into Daystar Community Church, went through rounds of introductions on the way to a pew, and sat down for the service. The church had a broad demographic and the service was an attempt to cater to most of the people there. Myrtle looked around and saw several people her age, several young adults, and about every ethnic group imaginable. The service wound its way though music, prayer, and preaching in what was a mostly familiar pattern that she took comfort in; it reminded her of where she and Patrick had gone in New Jersey for the last several years.

At the end of the service, they got up, greeted the pastor and many friendly members who hoped they would come back, and went to the car for the drive back home. When they got in the car, Myrtle said, "I rather liked this one."

"I was hoping you'd say that," Nathan replied, "I didn't really feel like a drawn out search."

"I'd like more older music, but the people seemed friendly and the preacher was challenging, no wishy washy feel good fluff."

"Ok, then that's settled. Now it's time to get our daily dose of vitamin sea."

"Vitamin C? That was a pretty big glass of orange juice I had this morning."

"No, vitamin S E A, not the letter C. Vitamin sea is always good for whatever ails you."

"You're right about that. I haven't been to the beach since the last time your grandfather and I went."

"Wow, how long has that been, a couple years?"

"Probably a year and a half ago. It was after he found out he had cancer, but before it had affected him that much."

He was about to pull into his apartment when his phone buzzed. When he parked, he had a text message from Fred.

Have to take a rain check on the beach trip. Not feeling so good. Maybe next weekend.

"What was the message," Myrtle asked.

"Fred and Kate aren't coming. Fred's not feeling well, probably just hungover."

"I thought he had a few too many last night. He does like his beer."

"Yes, he does. I don't know how people can drink that stuff."

"Your grandpa liked beer, but he never drank more than a couple in a week."

"I never saw him drink it."

"He didn't want to around you. Didn't think it was the best example, you being underage and all. Plus, you remember how the folks at church were about alcohol."

"Yeah, pretty much against it if I remember right."

"That was it. A lot of folks viewed it as a sin. We didn't see it that way, but your grandpa didn't want you to have any conflicted views, or didn't want you bringing it up at church and causing division."

"So he liked to have a beer every now and then, but basically gave it up for the four years I lived with you guys?"

"He didn't give it up entirely, but he didn't have too many during that time."

"He could have explained everything to me. I'm pretty sure I could have made the distinction."

"Oh, I'm sure you could have, but it wasn't a big deal really. He was never addicted to the stuff, but that's not the case with everyone. It's just as good you don't like it. It can cause problems if you're not careful."

"Tell me about it. I know a few guys who can't seem to have a good time without getting lit, then there's Fred who I haven't actually seen really drunk that often. I think he just got carried away last night. Anyway, I'll pack some sandwiches while you get changed. You have a bathing suit?"

"I have one, but I don't know if I'll go in the water. Might as well take it just in case."

When they were in the car Myrtle asked, "Which beach are we going to? There must be a few to choose from around here."

"There's a nice one down in Santa Cruz, little over a half hour drive. I've been there a couple times."

Arriving in Santa Cruz, Nathan drove down close to the beach and dropped Myrtle off close before finding a place to park the car. When he returned, they made their way down close to the water, where they set up their beach chairs and the cooler. Myrtle had her camera and her journal and the first thing she did was recruit a passerby to take a photo of her and Nathan with the water in the background.

"I like to do selfies the old fashioned way," she explained.

"I'm sure they didn't have a name for them in your day."

"Yeah, and we weren't so self absorbed back then to want to call anything a selfie."

"Well, you can sit here if you want, but I'm going to test the water. It's weird around here. Sometimes it can be darn cold and other times it's pleasant."

Nathan returned five minutes later soaked head to toe and shivering slightly.

"Water not so warm," asked his grandmother.

"It's a bit nippy. Try it if you want."

Myrtle went as far as walking in the edge and letting the water wash over her feet for a few minutes before coming right back to her chair.

"You're right, a bit too chilly for me. I still love everything about the ocean, don't you Nate?"

"I suppose so. It's kind of relaxing."

"It's more than that. The sound, the smell, the vastness of it all. It's relaxing and invigorating at the same time. It never gets old."

"I can see that. Say, you hungry? Got ham or turkey, on wheat."

"Sure, I'll take turkey. I assume you have drinks in there as well?"

"How could I forget that," he said as he brought out a bottle of tea and a Coke for himself.

They ate their sandwiches and Myrtle brought out her journal and began to write again. Nathan sat there sipping his Coke and watching the beach. There were a lot of people there that day, and he observed small children building sand castles, older people reading books or taking photos of grandchildren, dogs cavorting in the surf and shaking themselves all over their owners, a couple making out without a care in the world, and all the birds. Bold birds too, swooping right down to anyone with food. Shameless beggars the whole lot, thought Nathan as he watched them snatch food from anyone willing to offer it, and from some not so willing.

His grandmother was people watching as well, between stings of writing in her journal. He was curious to see what she was always writing, but figured it was simply rambling thoughts that might nor might not make any sense to him anyway, so he pushed the thought away. Finishing his Coke, he decided to take another dip in the water, cold as it may be.

He went in the water and waded out until it was about waist deep and just stood there, letting the waves wash over him. This was one of his favorite things to do in the ocean, just try to hold his ground as wave after wave came in and hit him head on, most ducking him under for a couple seconds. As he was coming back in, squatting down so only his head was above water, he saw that Grandma had put her journal down and was people watching once again, staring toward the ocean with a smile on her face. She looked so relaxed sitting there, like all of the cares had been washed away.

She had really been through a lot over the last couple weeks, with losing her husband and traveling all the way across the country to move in with him. He hoped he would be able to give her a good life for however many years she had left. He owed her that much for all she had done for him since his parents' death. As he came out of the water, he saw that her journal was lying in the sand next to her chair. Odd. It must have fallen when she set it down and she didn't feel like getting out of her chair to retrieve it. He had to use the restroom, so he mentioned it as he walked by the chair. When he was returning from the restroom, he noticed that the journal was still lying in the same spot and that she had apparently made no effort to pick it up. He also noticed that she hadn't finished her iced tea that was still in the cup holder in the arm of the beach chair. In fact, she had hardly touched it.

"You going to finish that tea, or should I put it back in the cooler for later," he asked.

No answer.

He walked over by her chair, picked up the journal and noticed some folded up sheets of paper inside the cover, and went to hand it back to her.

"Hey, you dropped this," he said as he reached to hand it to her.

When she didn't acknowledge him or even reach to take it, he looked at her face. She was still smiling, her hands folded in her lap, her lifeless eyes staring out to sea.

He stood there for how many minutes he couldn't recall, part of his mind telling him what had happened and the other part not willing to accept it. Shock became disbelief which gave way to a profound sadness that threatened to overwhelm him, and he still just stood there, trying to process everything. He wasn't sure how long he stood there, but he was startled when he felt a hand on his shoulder and he turned to see the kindly face of an elderly man who asked him gently, "Is she gone?"

"Y y yes," was all he managed to say before the tears came flowing and the elderly stranger just stood there with his arm around his shoulder. When the tears subsided and he managed to gain control, he said, "She's my grandma. Don't know what happened. We were talking...I...I went in the water for a few minutes...came back...and she's gone." He lapsed into another round of sobbing.

The man looked at his wife and nodded, and she called 911. Time was a blur from that moment on. An ambulance came to remove her body, the elderly couple helped him pack his things in his car, and he followed the ambulance to the hospital. By the time he got there, he had composed himself enough to call his uncle back in New Jersey and tell him the news. Sean said he would take care of notifying the funeral home there so they could make the necessary arrangements. A hospital chaplain prayed with Nathan and assured him that everything would be taken care of, Andrew if he wanted to go home someone would call him the next day to discuss arrangements.

As he was walking through the lobby, he was stopped by a nurse.

"You might want to take these with you," the nurse said as she handed Nathan his grandmother's purse and journal.

"Thank you," he managed to reply.

The thirty mile drive home went by in a tear filled haze. He was sad and angry, angry at God for taking her right when she had moved in with him. Did God not know that this was extremely poor timing? He spent the drive expressing this out loud, but eventually the anger gave way to a deep grief and something of a peace came over him. He got back to his apartment and as soon as he walked in, he was greeted by Cleo, obviously happy to see him and also needing to go outside. He came back in and put some food out for the animals and then collapsed onto the couch in complete exhaustion. The anger at God was gone now, but the grief was coming in waves. He didn't remember it hurting this much when Grandpa died, but he had seen that coming and had been able to prepare for the inevitable. Grandma was just there one moment and gone the next, no warning.

He couldn't get her face out of his mind. She was smiling when she died, smiling and staring at the ocean. Wow, she was really blessed. She loved the ocean and she died right there, and died so fast she probably felt nothing at all. Well, she was with her husband again, he thought, and only a couple weeks since she lost him. The dog came back to the couch, and sensing he was not feeling well, licked his hand a couple times and curled up next to him with its head resting on his knee.

"Oh, you're such a sweet creature, aren't you," he said as he stroked the top of the dog's head. "And what kind of a name is Cleo anyway? You need a better name than that. Patrick, that will do. You couldn't be named after a better man. Just then the cat came up and snuggled up next to Patrick, looked up at him, and started purring.

"Oh, I forgot about you. I don't think I could pick a finer name than Myrtle. If you live up to it, you'll be the finest cat anyone ever knew."

Myrtle seemed to respond favorably, because she gave a sigh, laid her head on the dog's back, and went right to sleep.

He looked down and saw his grandma's purse with the journal sticking out. He still felt bad about violating her privacy, but then he remembered the folded up notebook paper inside the front cover. He removed the pages and unfolded them. There was more than one page there, with writing on both sides. He looked at the first page, saw his name, and began to read.

My dearest Nathan,

If you're reading this, one of two things has happened. Either you're a sneaky guy and you're snooping into my journal when I'm not looking, or I have passed on. Since I know you're not the sneaky type, it's probably the latter. I also know that you're probably feeling pretty sad. Well, I am too, just thinking about what you must be going through and how you must be feeling. I don't know how I went, since at the time I'm starting this letter we're just setting out from New Jersey to head to your place. You are a smooth driver, so writing in the car isn't as hard as I thought it would be.

I can't explain why I'm writing this. I'm not sick or anything, but I have been getting tired more often lately and I just have a feeling. I can't explain it. At my age there are things you just know, and I feel that my days may be numbered. In truth, all of our days are numbered, but I can't shake the feeling that my number might come up soon.

I don't know when I'll finish this letter. I hope by the time we get to California. We were at the Reds game today and I'm so grateful to you for the thought. I have a feeling this trip is going to be enjoyable, but let me get on with it. I love you, Nate. I really do. I know that you are a sensitive boy and that you are probably taking my death hard, but you mustn't take it too hard. I'm old and old people die. That's the way of it. And I'm ready to go. That might sound trite, but it's true. I've made my peace with the Lord. Patrick knew the Lord as well, so you can be sure that while you're reading this, your grandpa and I are enjoying one another's company. Sure, have a good cry, but know that I am in good hands.

You can probably tell by the writing that this letter isn't being written all at once. I've not attended to it for a while and now the trip is almost over. I've learned a lot about you over these few days. You're a real softy. You care deeply about others, but you have to do some things for yourself. Get off your butt and ask that girl out. She won't wait around forever for you. If we find out that you haven't, your grandfather and I will come down there and give you what for.

Well, it's been a good trip and I'm still alive. I hope you don't have to find this letter for a long time and by then it will be irrelevant, but if not, I want to thank you so much for everything you've done. Thank you for the little sweet animals, but you have to give them different names, and promise me that when I'm gone you won't give them away. They deserve a good home for the rest of their lives and I know you will provide that.

I know you can succeed in anything you set your mind to, so don't be so worried about your job situation. You are a younger version of your grandfather, maybe without the athletic prowess, but you're still like him. Whether you continue working there or start your own business, I know you will succeed, as long as you surround yourself with good people who are as smart as you are, or smarter.

I think maybe I should wrap this up. I so hate writing at the beach when I could be watching the waves. I do so love the smells and the sounds, and even this cold bottle of tea. You are such a dear grandson, better than I could have hoped to have. You have done so much for me these last few days. It might not seem like much, but it really was. You made me feel young again, and you let me see some parts of the country I have never seen before. Now as you're reading this, I'm enjoying far better scenery, but I am so grateful for these last days with you. You helped me get through the grief. If I had stayed in New Jersey and moved into that facility, I don't know if I would have been able to get over it as well, or in such pleasant company.

So mourn me if you must, but don't let it hold you back. Grab a hold of life. Don't wait for it to come to you. Go out there and take it with both hands and squeeze it for all it's worth. Live in such a way that you won't have any regrets at the end. Don't grow old and ask yourself what if. Don't leave anything on the table. Don't be afraid to take chances. Don't forget to love, even if it hurts, because love does hurt. It will break your heart, put it back together, and break it again. Loved ones will wound you, but you mustn't stop loving them. You must live life to the fullest, love to your fullest, and laugh to your fullest, and you must never forget that I love you and I will see you when you get here.

LOVE,
  Grandma

24

Nathan read the letter over again until the tears blurred his vision and he had to put it down. He woke up right there on the couch at 6:30 in the morning and read it again. So she had known. Somehow she had known she was going to go soon and she didn't want to bring it up. Part of him wished she had brought it up. It would have changed little. Or maybe they would have tried to cram in more. For his part, there were no regrets. He was glad they had taken the drive, glad they had done what they had done and seen what they had seen. Few people were given that blessing, to be able to spend that much time with a loved one at the end.

He knew that intellectually, but he was still kind of mad that she was gone. To do all that he had done and then this happens. Wasn't it enough that he had just lost his grandfather? Quit being selfish, he told himself. She was certainly better off, reunited with her husband and her son, and Nathan was still a young man with his whole life ahead of him. It was time to start living that life, to take it by both hands and squeeze it for all it's worth, as she had stated in her farewell letter.

He looked at the journal and while there were the usual introspective musings, there really wasn't that much written there. She had been concealing those pages in the book and working on the letter the whole way, and he had been none the wiser. It was nothing more than a written version of what she had been telling him, but it seemed to carry more weight. Maybe it was his grief that was giving the words more weight, but he was determined not to let her down.

He pulled himself off the couch, put some sausages on the Foreman grill, and headed to the shower. Coming out of the shower, he got dressed, took the dog outside for his morning necessities, and came back in to eat his breakfast. He looked at his phone and there was a text from his uncle saying that he was going to contact the funeral home in New Jersey and they would coordinate with the hospital in California for transport of the body, but they would have to talk in the next couple days to schedule the service. Luckily, Myrtle had left specific instructions as to what she wanted, so their job would be easy. The house hadn't sold yet, so Nathan could stay there while he was in. He also had an email from work. Frank had heard the news and there was no need to come in today. How had Frank heard? Had the news covered it or something? Probably, since it had happened in a public place.

He took his time with his breakfast, filled an extra glass of orange juice in a travel cup, and decided to drive into the office anyway. Orange juice. His co workers chided him for that. 28 years old and still drinking juice instead of coffee. He simply didn't care for coffee and found that he rarely needed caffeine if he got adequate sleep. He drove around a bit before going to the office, gathering his thoughts and thinking again about what Grandma had said to him and written in the letter. Then he heard, almost as clear as if he were in the car with him, his grandfather's voice saying, "What the hell." That was it.

He walked into the lobby of the building and started heading for the elevator when the guard behind the security desk noticed him and said, "Hi Nathan. Nice to see you back. Heard about your grandma. Sorry about your loss."

"Thanks James. How have you been?"

"Oh, as well as I could be. Got another grandbaby to spoil. Daughter had a girl last week."

"Well, that's great. I guess you have lots of pictures."

He did indeed, and opened them up on his phone to show them proudly.

"Wow, she's a cutie," Nathan replied, "Have fun spoiling her."

"Oh, I will. Wasn't expecting to see you this morning. You sure you're up to working today?"

"I'm not working today. Just came in to take care of a couple things."

"Ok, Nate, don't let me keep you waiting."

Nathan went over and took the elevator up to his floor. Upon exiting the elevator, he saw that most of his co workers looked astonished to see him. People were getting up from desks to offer their condolences, which he graciously accepted. His boss came over to him and said, "You get my message? You don't have to come in today. In fact, I don't expect you to. Take a couple days off."

"I just wanted to stop by and pick up a couple things. I wasn't planning on working today."

"Could have fooled me, the way you're dressed."

"Didn't feel that casual."

"Well, I'm sorry about your loss. I guess you're going to be needing to take more time off to travel back for the funeral."

"Yeah, looks like it. I'll let you know when we have the date set."

"Sure thing. Anyway, I'll see you in a couple days. If you feel up to it, you can work from home for a bit as well."

"Thanks. I might take you up on that."

Nathan walked down the hall, turned left down another hall, past his own desk, and into the area where the artists were working. He ducked into the restroom before anyone saw him and checked himself in the mirror. "Of course you look fine, silly, " he thought to himself. He didn't have butterflies in his stomach. No, there were darn condors flying around in there. He heard his grandfather's voice again in his head and steeled himself for what he had come here to do.

He walked toward a particular work station and found it empty, was about to walk away, when Phoebe Imani came from around the corner, looking surprised to see him standing next to her desk.

"Why, Nathan, I wasn't expecting you to be back at work today. I heard about what happened. I'm so sorry," she said, in a tone that sounded like music to him, so much that at first he didn't catch what she said.

After an awkward pause, he said, "Thank you. I don't think I'll be sticking around to work today."

"You're certainly dressed for work. What did you come in for then?"

"Do you have a piece of paper I can borrow?"

"Sure, got plenty of that here," she said as she handed him paper and a pen.

"Thanks, " he said and he took the paper and wrote a quick note on it and folded it in half.

"So you got all dressed up just to come in here and borrow a sheet of paper from me," she asked with a sly smile.

Man, that smile could light up a pitch black room. Nathan swallowed a lump in his throat and wished the condors in his stomach would stop flying loops and find a perch for a moment.

"Well...I guess I could have gotten the paper from my own desk," he replied awkwardly, and then continuing as he fixed his eyes on the corner of the cubicle wall near her face, "There's this interesting place that just opened up over in Sunnyvale...kind of wanting to check it out."

"Why don't you," Phoebe replied, and thinking to herself, "He looks so nervous he might faint."

"Well...didn't want to go by myself...You want to check it out? I mean, if you want to go there, and I kind of want to, maybe we could go together?"

Phoebe fixed Nathan with an expectant look, waiting on him to finish, which he finally did.

"Do you want to have dinner with me there, or someplace else, or is there somewhere around here you like? I thought that place looked..."

"Sure, silly, if you'll ever give me a chance to say yes."

"You mean...you will? You'll..."

"Yes I will, Nathan. I thought you would never ask."

She wrote hastily on a piece of paper and handed it to him.

"Here's my address," she said, "7:00. I'll be waiting. Don't be late, ok?"

"Uh...yeah...7:00...your address...Yeah, I can do that. See you then."

"See you then, Nathan," she said as she flashed him a stunning smile.

He traversed the length of the office with his feet hardly touching the ground, that smile filling him with a warm glow that was entirely unfamiliar and entirely welcome. The churning in his stomach was gone, replaced by a bubbling mix of happiness, or something beyond happiness, some joyous state as of yet undefined. He went to Frank's desk and found it vacant, so he left the note on the computer keyboard and walked out of the office.

As he exited the elevator in the lobby, James could see immediately that something was different.

"Why Nathan, you look like the cat that swallowed the canary."

"I got a date."

"Well, I didn't think you had it in you. Who's the lady?"

"Phoebe Imani, works over in..."

"I know her," James replied, "Punching above your weight class with her, son."

"Tell me about it. I can't believe she said yes."

"Maybe she was waiting for you. Girl like that. You can't be the first chance she's had. So, where you guys going?"

"That new place that just opened up over in Sunnyvale."

"Man, Nate, they're paying you better than I thought. That place ain't cheap."

"I do ok here, and I've saved a bit."

"Well, good luck tonight."

Nathan went home and ate one of the sandwiches he had packed for the beach the previous day, took the dog outside for a walk around the block, and grabbing a Coke from the fridge, went into his study and sat down at his computer. His intention was to play some games for a while and just shut off his brain, but as he booted up the computer he found that he didn't feel like playing video games. He loved to play games, but he hadn't played any the whole time he had been away and now he felt that he had no desire to play at the moment. Instead he went into the spare bedroom that had been his grandmother's and went through the boxes that were in there. Finding his grandfather's music collection, he selected a few random CDs and put them in the player in the living room. Then picking up the copy of *Post Captain* that he was more than halfway through, he sat down to read.

He got up after finishing the book, shaved his already smooth face, put on a suit, and showed up at Phoebe's door at 6:59. As he was getting out of his car, her door opened and she walked out, looking absolutely stunning in a modest cream colored dress and diamond earrings, with a faint hint of perfume. He just stood there in awe and when she got closer all he could say was, "Wow."

"Just wow," she asked.

"Yeah, wow. You look incredible."

"You don't look so bad yourself. Nice suit."

"Well, shall we be off," he said as he held the car door open for her to get in.

"When's the last time you were on a date," she asked him when they were both in the car.

"Uh...well..."

"I thought so."

"Is it that obvious?"

"When you asked me, you were staring at the corner of my desk. You keep looking past me or at the ground, and you're as nervous as a long tailed cat by a rocking chair."

"Well, I don't have much experience. Who wouldn't be nervous, the way you look. You know what James said?"

"James, the security guard in the lobby?"

"Yeah, he said I was punching above my weight class. I kind of agree with him."

"Well, thank you...I think."

When they arrived at the restaurant, he tried to do everything he thought should be expected of a gentleman, which was everything he could remember seeing his grandfather do with Grandma. He held the door open for her before handing the keys to the valet, held the door going into the restaurant, and pulled her chair out at the table. He was hoping he was doing everything right.

After they looked over the menu and made their choices, they just sat there awkwardly, until Phoebe finally smiled, looked right at Nathan, and said, "You really don't know what to do next, do you?"

"No, I really don't. Have you dated much?"

"Not much really. A couple here and there in high school and once or twice in college. I think guys were intimidated by me. I worked through school and always had my nose in my books. Didn't leave much time for dating. And when I did, most of the guys just wanted one thing, and I wasn't willing to give them that."

"If you could count all the times I almost had a date, it would be quite impressive."

"I figured that. The way you asked me I could tell you hadn't done it much."

"It was that awkward?"

"You could say that again. Good thing I'm a sucker for shy guys. It's kinda cute."

The waiter arrived, took their orders, and then left again. Phoebe looked at Nathan and said, "I'm really sorry about your grandma. She must have been an incredible woman."

"Yes, she was, the best."

"She's kind of famous, you know. What she did went all over the internet. I saw your picture on Facebook with the story."

"That wasn't the only one. There was the Indian reservation in

South Dakota, the girl in Wisconsin, and the bait shop owner in Indiana as well. She was quite generous. She had a lot of money and didn't care to hang on to it."

"It must have been an incredible trip."

"Yes, it was. I didn't want to do it at first. I just wanted to fly out here, but she didn't want to fly, so we just rented the car and took off. I'm glad we did it. She had a ball. Knowing what I know now, even how it ended, I'd do it all over again."

"She was lucky to have a grandson like you."

"Thanks, but I think I was the lucky one."

"So, you were close to your grandparents?"

"Yes, they took me in when my parents died."

"Oh, I'm so sorry. When did that happen?"

"When I was 14. They were killed by a drunk driver. I moved out to New Jersey right after and stayed with my grandparents until I went away to college. I went to school at MIT and then got the job here right after graduation."

"Wow, I didn't know you had lost your parents. Was it difficult?"

"At first it was. I took it hard, but my grandparents were the best. Grandpa was like a second dad. If I can ever be half the man he was..."

"Oh, I think you are."

"You hardly know me."

"I'm observant. You're not like other guys. You really care. I've seen how you are when someone at work loses a loved one. It really gets to you. You try to hide it, but you're not that good at it. You have a big heart. Anyone can see that. Well, anyone who's been observing you."

"You been doing some observing?"

"Guilty as charged."

"I don't know what to say."

"Don't say anything. It looks like our food is coming."

As they ate their food, their conversation slowed down a bit, and eventually Nathan became more relaxed and found himself looking at her more often instead of at the corner of the table or the wall.

"You checking me out, Mr. Callahan?"

"Huh, well..."

"Ever the shy boy. I saw you looking at me."

"I can't help it."

"Earlier today you couldn't look me in the eye. Now you can't take your eyes off me."

"Yeah...well..."

"Out with it," she said with a grin, teasing him.

"I've never seen anyone as pretty as you. I've imagined this ever since I first saw you."

"Now, that's the sweetest thing anyone's ever said to me. You know what? I've been hoping you would ask me out for three months. I thought about dropping hints, but I didn't want to look too forward."

"Wow, if I had known that..."

After getting in the car, Phoebe put her hand on Nathan's arm, sending a wave of electricity through him, and said, "I really had a good time. This place was incredible. Thank you."

"Thank you for saying yes. I couldn't imagine a better evening."

When they got back to her place, Nathan put the car in park and jumped out to open her door. He shut the door after she got out and walked her to her front door, sporting a smile that would shame the Cheshire Cat. She replied with a smile of her own that made his knees weak and said, "Well Mr. Callahan, you might be a shy boy, but you're the perfect gentleman. I'd say you've earned a second date."

"How about tomorrow?"

"What place do you have in mind?"

"Mine. I can cook. Do you like fish? I have these salmon filets I bought because Grandma liked salmon and..."

"That sounds delightful. Can I bring a side dish?"

"Sure, whatever you like. Same time then, 7:00."

"7:00 it is, see you then," she said, flashing him another smile and heading inside.

～

NATHAN ENTERED the lobby the next morning and headed toward the elevator, only to be stopped by James.

"Nate, you don't have to tell me how last night went. It's written all over your face."

"Is it that obvious?"

"Boy, I was born at night, but not last night. You working today?"

"No, just going to pick some things up and work from home this week. Frank said I could ease back into it that way."

"Ok, Nate, and congratulations."

Nathan went straight to Phoebe's desk and from the silence that came over the work area when he entered, he surmised that everyone there knew what had transpired, and he blushed a little as he approached.

Phoebe looked up and said, "Oh, hi Nate. You know one advantage of being black? We don't blush."

This brought even more color to his cheeks, but he managed to say, "I never gave you my address last night, and I never even got your cell number."

"Well, that has to be a first. How did you manage to get a date with a girl before you even got her number?"

This brought subdued laughter from some of the people in the nearby desks and Nathan stood there blushing, knowing that all eyes were on him, as Phoebe handed him a note with her number on it.

"Just text me your address," she said, "I'll see you tonight."

NATHAN WAS JUST COMING in from the deck with the salmon filets, grilled to perfection, when he heard the doorbell. He looked at his watch, 6:55.

He opened the door and there was Phoebe with a couple dishes, dressed in the same clothes she had worn to work.

"Wow, you look nice. You didn't have to get dressed up to come here," he said.

"I didn't have time to change. We worked late and I had to run home for this."

He took the dishes off her hands and carried them to the kitchen and before she could take another step, the animals were both there, Patrick looking up at her expectantly and wagging his tail, and Myrtle rubbing around her legs.

"I think they like you," he said.

"They're adorable. When did you get them?"

"Just the other day. Grandma wanted a pet, so I took her to the shelter to adopt. She fell in love with the dog, but the lady at the shelter talked us into taking both of them. They really are best buddies. You should see them together."

Nathan put food out for them and they both went to their bowls. Phoebe asked him, "What are their names?"

"They had names when we brought them home, but I re named them yesterday when I got home. The dog is Patrick and the cat is Myrtle, named after my grandparents."

Nathan turned on some music and pulled out a kitchen chair for Phoebe to sit down. He already had the table set with the salmon on each plate and he was getting a spoon for the bowl of green vegetation she had brought. He put a spoon in the bowl and asked her what it was.

"We call it sukuma wiki. It's just greens."

"What's the flat bread in the other bowl? Looks like pita."

"We call that chapati. It's just flat bread fried in a pan. You can dip it in your vegetables or eat it dry."

"People ever put butter on it?"

"Can't say I've ever seen anyone do that, but whatever floats your boat."

"I dont' have a lot of choices for drinks. Got Coke, lemonade, orange juice, milk, and apparently a beer that my neighbor left here. I'll have to tell him to come and get that."

"You don't drink beer?"

"Can't stand the stuff, and you?"

"Never tried it, and the way it makes people act, I don't think I want to."

"Can't blame you there. You should see my neighbor when he's had a few."

"You said you had juice? That sounds good."

"This fish is delicious," she said a couple bites later, "How did you fix it?"

"Just on the grill with a bit of lemon juice, salt, and pepper. Nothing complicated. This green stuff..."

"Sukuma."

"Yeah, sukuma. Anyway, it's pretty good too. You fix this today?"

"No, when I got home last night. I was going to invite you over, but you beat me to it."

They finished eating and Nathan put the plates in the dishwasher, and Phoebe ventured toward the couch.

"Mind the fur," Nathan said as she sat down, "Can't seem to keep them off the couch."

"That's ok. I have lint rollers at home. I heard a rumor today that you're in line for a promotion."

"Yeah."

"You don't sound so thrilled."

"Oh, I'm thrilled that they would consider me, but I just don't know."

"What do you mean that you don't know?"

"At first it's all I could think of. Then a couple days into our trip I got a rather strong email from Frank about getting back here fast before they promoted someone else. Then a couple days later he changed his tune and told me to take my time. I think that was after he saw the news from Wisconsin. I got to wondering about how secure my job really was."

"Your job has to be secure. You do incredible work."

"So do you. I got to thinking though. I have a lot of money saved up. I've been there six years and I've never spent that much. Not dating all that time made that easy. Anyway, I have a lot of know how. I'm thinking about starting my own company."

"Whoah, that's a big step."

"I've crunched the numbers. I can live comfortably without income for a couple years. Plenty of time to get a project off the ground, at least to get funding on kickstarter. I've already got some good game ideas. I'd just need to get some good quality people to work with me."

"I don't know, Nate, but if anyone could pull it off, you could."

"Say, you want to see some pictures from the trip," Nathan said as he handed Phoebe the album, "Grandma took all of these."

Nathan sat down on the couch and Phoebe snuggled up next to him with the photo album across both of their laps. She turned the pages slowly and marveled at the photos.

"She took all of these? They're beautiful. This was some trip, Nathan. Who's this," she asked, pointing at a picture of Cassie."

"That's Cassie Ferguson. She was being held against her will by some scumbag trafficker out of L.A. We pulled into this truck stop because Grandma had to pee and she saw this girl peeking out of the window of an RV, looking all scared. We called the cops and she was rescued. Dude that took her's heading for prison."

"Wow, I heard something about that on the news. That was you guys?"

"It was mostly Grandma. She stayed in the car while I was inside and she thought something looked suspicious."

For the next couple hours they looked through the photos and Nathan had a story behind each one, or at least had an idea where they were all taken. He told her about the old Indian he met in South Dakota and about his visit to Wounded Knee and about the people he had met there.

"She just wrote them a check?"

"Yes, you should see the place. It's not kept well. Grandma thought they could use some cash to fix it up a bit. I hope they put it to good use."

"Wow, she was some lady, and that must have been some trip. Your grandma was a lucky woman to have this adventure at the end of her life, and to go out the way she did."

"Yeah, I can think of worse ways to go. You know, she died with a smile on her face, just staring at the ocean."

"That's how I want to go, peacefully and knowing that I'm loved. You really blessed your grandma."

"You know, I think she blessed me more. Man, I'm going to miss her."

Phoebe continued to browse through the photos and continued to be amazed. Nathan was looking at the photos, but was also aware of her head resting on his shoulder and he didn't want this moment to end. He wanted to put his arm around her, wasn't sure how she would respond, and kept pondering such an action. Finally he simply moved his arm over and placed it around her shoulder and she instinctively moved closer. He felt a tenderness he never imagined and he barely heard her when she said, "Nathan, these last two nights have been amazing. Thank you."

"Yeah, me too."

"Huh?"

"Oh, I think so too. More than I expected. We'll have to do this again."

"Definitely, but I need to get going soon. Some of us have to work in the morning."

"Oh, yeah, work."

"When are you coming back?"

"Frank said I could work from home. I'll probably be back in the office after the funeral."

"You have a date set yet?"

"Not yet. My uncle and I still have to nail it down. Got relatives traveling in and all that."

She got up off the couch to get ready to leave and Nathan said, "Don't worry about your dishes. I'll wash them and bring them by tomorrow."

"My, aren't you presumptuous? Same time then, 7:00, and you'd better not eat before you come."

"Sounds good to me."

"I'm coming with you to the funeral. You let me know and I'll take the time off."

"You don't have to."

"Yes I do have to. Your grandma seemed like a great lady, and you could use the support."

"I don't know what to say."

Nathan followed her to the door to say goodnight and she looked him right in the eyes, said, "I know exactly what to say," and leaned in and kissed him before walking out the door.

25

The plane touched down at Newark Liberty International Airport and Nathan and Phoebe got their luggage from baggage claim and went to the rental counter to get a car. A few minutes later they were rolling down the Garden State Parkway heading to Piscataway.

"So this is where you grew up?" Phoebe asked.

"Not right here in Newark. It's about a half hour drive to Piscataway, but I only lived there during high school. Came up here when my parents died and I went to college up in Boston."

"So, Cincinnati, New Jersey, Boston, and now San Jose. Wow. You've lived in some different places."

"Yeah, Boston was kind of neat, lot of good seafood up there. I like where we live, at least for the work, but I kind of miss Cincinnati as well. It's a lot smaller. You can get out of the city and into the country faster. You drive an hour and you're in rural country surrounded by Amish people."

"I've read about the Amish people. I'd love to see them someday."

"There are a lot near here too, over in Pennsylvania. Maybe we can go up there tomorrow. Our return flight's not for a couple days."

"Can we see the Statue of Liberty while we're here too?"

"I'm pretty sure we can squeeze that in before we go back. We're actually not far from there right now, but my uncle's expecting us."

"So we're heading to his house?"

"No, Grandma's house. It's on the market, but it hasn't sold yet, so it's still mostly furnished and we can use it. The only thing we brought out of there was her bedroom stuff."

"I know about the note you left Frank."

"Oh, he shared it, did he?"

"He said he had a note from you, and after what you told me the other day, I put two and two together. I was walking by and overheard him talking with Jordan about it. I thought they would be more upset, losing someone like you."

"I offered to stick around to train my replacement. I'm good at what I do, but finding someone else shouldn't be that hard."

"You're going to need to find good help."

"You're right about that."

"How are you going to go about affording that?"

"Well, I can do a fair amount of work myself and I can work for free for a while. I have a few game ideas and I plan to put a good proposal together on kickstarter for one of them. If enough cash comes in, then I can hire some other programmers."

"You're going to need good artists."

"Hmm, you wouldn't know any would you?"

"I think I can ask around. I might know somebody."

"I will trust your judgment."

"It sounds like a bit of a risk, but kind of exciting. Do you think you can pull it off?"

"Well, not to sound arrogant, but I know I have the know how, at least on the technical end. I don't have any experience with the business end, but my grandfather ran a successful business for years. I observed him and I think some of it rubbed off. I'll have to hire some people who are smarter than I am. Grandpa always said that to succeed in business you need to have people around you who are smarter than you are and you need to listen to them."

"That sounds like good advice."

"I'm sitting next to one at the moment."

"Huh?"

"Someone smarter than me. And a whole lot better looking too."

"Hey, you're not so dumb...and not that bad looking either, for a white guy."

"What do you mean by that?"

"The Lord just didn't leave you in the oven long enough. You're only half baked."

"He did a fine job with you, couldn't have done any better."

"Flattery will get you somewhere."

"That's not how the saying goes."

"I know that. I knew what I was saying."

"Man, Phoebe, you're the best thing that's ever happened to me, and when I think about what all had to happen for us to meet..."

"Life is funny like that."

"I was thinking the other day. Everything in my life lead to this point and if anything had been different, I might have been in a different place. I might not have met you. Some of those things were pretty bad though, but all things considered, I don't think I would change a thing."

"You've had a lot happen. You wouldn't change anything?"

"Not if it meant not meeting you."

She fought back a tear and simply said, "That's sweet of you."

"I love you."

"Did he just say what I think he said?" she thought to herself. She was pretty sure that's what she had heard, and she was pretty sure now that she felt the same. The last few days had been something and she had been thinking that what they had could be long term, but now he had gone and said it. Well, no turning back now.

"I love you too, Nate, I really do."

Nathan was afraid that if he tried to say anything else at the moment his voice would crack, so he just stared ahead at the road and concentrated on his driving. He felt her hand resting on his right leg and she said, "Oh, my dear shy boy. Cat got your tongue?"

"Yeah...man...when I first laid eyes on you...I never imagined...wow."

She knew that for him to say what he had said, as bashful as he could be, had taken a lot. He had changed so much in the last few days. Maybe the change had been in the works for longer than that, probably during the drive west with his grandmother. This was not the co worker she had known for the last couple years. She had been mildly interested in him for a few months, interested enough to turn down six other men who had asked her out, but she hadn't thought he would ever gather up the courage. In truth, she had been about to give up and move on when he had walked in that day and asked her. It had been the most awkward thing she had ever witnessed, and now after getting to know him better, she understood what a big step it was for him, and it endeared him to her that much more.

They made the rest of the drive in silence, her hand resting gently on his knee as he drove, until he turned onto Glenwood Drive and into the driveway. His uncle's car was there and when he got out of the car and came around to open the door for Phoebe, Sean came out of the house.

"Hello Nate, glad to see you made it ok. How was the flight?"

"Nice and smooth. We actually landed a few minutes early."

"And this must be your friend you said so much about," and to Phoebe, "Hi, I'm Sean, Nate's uncle."

"I'm Phoebe, Nate's girlfriend. Nice to meet you," she said as she shook his hand.

Nathan blushed and Sean said to him, "Wow, nephew, you got the better end of that deal."

"You're not the first one to tell me that. I'd have to agree with you there."

"I think I need to go in and use the restroom," Phoebe said, "I'll leave you two to catch up."

"Man, you said you had a couple dates, but you didn't tell me she was this freaking gorgeous," Sean said when Phoebe was out of earshot. "Where's she from by the way?"

"Her family's from Tanzania, but she's been here since she was two, so she's pretty much American."

"Nah, she's too classy. Good catch there."

"Thanks."

"Well, let's get your things in the house and then we can go eat. I didn't cook anything, figured we could go for a steak. Does she eat steak?"

"I don't think there's anything she doesn't eat. She's not as picky as we are."

"That's good. I've already made a reservation for four. We just have to swing by and pick up Lilian."

Nathan and Sean took the luggage in and put Phoebe's bag in one bedroom and Nathan's in his old room. When Phoebe came out of the bathroom, they showed her the room her luggage was in and she decided she would change quickly before they left.

THE NEXT MORNING, Nathan and Phoebe took their place near the front of the church. The service was supposed to start soon and the pews were filling up fast. There were already way more people than had been at Grandpa's funeral and people were still coming in. When it was time to start, the minister came to the pew and said to Nathan and Sean, "People are still filing in. I think we should hold off until everyone gets in. A bus just pulled in."

"A bus," Sean asked.

"Yes, with South Dakota plates. Who did she know from South Dakota?"

"Are they American Indians?" Nathan asked.

The minister looked at the people coming in the back door and said, "They certainly look like it."

"We visited Wounded Knee on the way out. Grandma wrote a check to the Pine Ridge reservation and told them to fix the memorial up a bit. Hold on a sec."

Nathan got up and walked to the back of the church where the people were still coming in, and Phoebe followed him.

"Thank you all for coming," he said to one of the Indians he recognized from the memorial, "You didn't have to come all this way."

"Yes, we did. Your grandma honored us. Now we honor her. She deserves it," said Diane.

"Well, thank you anyway," Nathan said as he gave her a hug.

Looking over he spotted a young black woman hanging by the back door with a couple that appeared to be her parents. When the young woman met Nathan's gaze, she tugged at her parents and they all came forward.

"Hi Cassie," Nathan said, "Are these your parents?"

"Yes," the man replied, "We are very pleased to meet you, and very sad to hear of your grandmother. We owe her a debt of gratitude."

Nathan replied, "We all do. By the way, this is Phoebe. Phoebe, this is Cassie, the young lady we met in Wisconsin."

Cassie shook Phoebe's hand and asked, "Are you Nathan's girlfriend?"

"Yes, I am," she replied, "Are you jealous?"

"Maybe," she replied.

"Nate," Phoebe exclaimed, "There's a dog under that pew, a rather large dog."

Nathan looked to where she was pointing, and there was indeed a large dog stretched out underneath the pew and a familiar looking man sitting in the pew.

"That would be Thad and Oliver," Nathan replied her, "We met him on the trip. He loaned me a fishing pole and I lost it. Maybe he wants it back."

They walked over and Thad stood up when he saw them coming and said, "Nice to see you. Wish it was under better circumstances. I'm really sorry about your grandma. She was a fine lady."

"Yes, she was. By the way, this is Phoebe."

Phoebe shook Thad's hand and then reached underneath the pew to scratch the dog's head and asked, "What's this big guy's name?"

"That's Oliver. I couldn't find a dog sitter on short notice, and I wasn't going to miss this. I have to pay my respects."

"Well, thank you for coming," Nathan said. "Catch me when the service is over. You can come over to the house for the wake."

Nathan and Phoebe started making their way back to the front of the church when another young lady came running up to him.

Nathan saw her and said, "Natalie, isn't it?"

"Yes, Natalie Peterson. I'm so sorry. Your grandma was a special lady. I can't thank her enough."

"Being here is thanks enough. I appreciate it. By the way, Natalie, this is Phoebe."

"Nice to meet you Natalie," said Phoebe.

When they got back to the front pew, Phoebe asked, "Is that the waitress?"

"Yes. Some small restaurant in Salt Lake."

"She's the one who posted your photo online. I saw it before you got back."

They sat in the pew and the service started, pretty much the same service as the one for his grandfather. The same familiar hymns and scripture readings, assurances that the Lord was preparing mansions for all of us and that those who followed him would have one, and that Myrtle was no doubt enjoying her time in the Lord's presence at this very moment.

Nathan once again found his mind wandering, but not as much as it had at his grandfather's funeral. Part of the reason was the woman sitting next to him. How in the world had he pulled that off.? Out of his league was an understatement. His mind didn't wander too far and when the minister finished the eulogy and said that there were others who were going to share a word, Nathan looked up at the minister who gave him an affirmative nod. He walked up to the platform, taking from his pocket a folded sheet of paper with his notes on it. He laid the paper on the podium and addressed the congregation.

"It wasn't that long ago that we sat here and said goodbye to my grandpa. Now we're back here way too soon to say goodbye again to one of the finest women I've ever known. When I agreed to take her in, I didn't know what I was getting myself into. I had no idea what the journey would entail when she said she couldn't fly. I had no idea what would transpire on that trip, the lives she would touch, mine included. I had no idea how much I would grow.

I had no idea about a lot of things. I lived under her roof for four years and I learned more about her, and from her, during that time we spent crossing the country. I learned that you're never too old to learn new things, to have new experiences, and to have the time of your life. I also learned that there is really only one reason that God blesses us, and that is to be a blessing to others. If all you do with what you have is keep it to yourself, it does you no good. We are blessed in order to serve, and if we aren't using what we are given to serve others, we are the ones to be pitied.

Grandma understood that, and she understood far more about a lot of things than I ever realized. In those few days, she taught me that sometimes you just have to do what you have to do, and that being shy is no excuse not to do it. She gave me the courage to do things that I never imagined I would be able to do. She showed me how to live life to the fullest and how...excuse me...She's still teaching me things and maybe she always will. There was more said over all those miles than I can take in right away.

My grandma loved everyone she came into contact with, and she served everyone in whatever way she knew how. She loved her God and she served him with all her heart. If she were here, that is what she would want you all to take away from this, that she got everything she could out of life and that she served her God and her fellow man with everything she had. That is a life well lived, and this is the life we celebrate today.

So there's really nothing else I can say, so I leave you with the closing words of a letter she was writing to me in the event of her death. These words were written only moments before she passed and I could not say it any better than she did. '*So mourn me if you must, but don't let it hold you back. Grab a hold of life. Don't wait for it to come to you. Go out there and take it with both hands and squeeze it for all it's worth. Live in such a way that you won't have any regrets at the end.*

Don't grow old and ask yourself what if. Don't leave anything on the table. Don't be afraid to take chances. Don't forget to love, even if it hurts, because love does hurt. It will break your heart, put it back together, and break it again. Loved ones will wound you, but you mustn't stop loving them. You must live life to the fullest, love to your fullest, and laugh to your fullest, and you must never forget that I love you and I will see you when you get here."

Nathan folded the paper, put it back in his pocket, and sat down. The entire church was silent, and few eyes were dry. The minister had other comments prepared, but all he said was, "Well folks, I find that I have nothing more to add. Let us pray."

He gave a brief prayer, the closing song was sung, and instructions were given for those who would be going to the graveside. As he was joining the other pallbearers to move the casket out to the hearse, he glanced over at cars lining up for the procession and caught sight of three Harleys, with the little flags attached. He smiled to himself and after the casket was in the hearse, the bikers came up and each gave him a massive bear hug.

They went to the graveside, had the usual service there with more hugs and more tears, and went back to their cars. Another man approached him, said he was sorry to hear about his grandmother, and have him a brief hug before going back to his car.

"That man looks familiar," said Phoebe.

"He certainly does. I can't recall his name, but the last time I saw him, he had a baseball bat in his hand."

Back to the house for the wake and the usual abundance of food and drink that was common in Irish families. Eventually Nathan had his fill of social interaction and was sitting in a corner of the room sipping on a Coke. Phoebe had made the rounds and had met everyone, causing many appreciative glances his way, and now she came to sit next to him.

"What you said was amazing. How long did it take you to prepare?"

"Only half the night."

"I'm sure she would be proud of you. You're not the same guy you were before, are you?"

"No, that guy wouldn't have you by his side. That guy is jealous."

"You look like you're worn out."

"Yes, I can only take so much socializing. It drains me."

"So, when everyone's gone, you want to take me to meet some of those Amish people?"

"That sounds good. We can get some food from them and have a picnic, just the two of us."

"Just the two of us. That sounds real good."

"Then tomorrow we can see the statue in the morning and still have plenty of time to catch our flight in the afternoon."

"Oh dear, did I forget to tell you," she said before kissing him," I canceled the return flight. We're driving back."

AFTERWORD

Did you enjoy reading Going Home? If so, would you be so kind as to write an honest review? It would be much appreciated.

Click here to leave a review

AUTHOR'S NOTES

Writing this novel was a journey of sorts for me, maybe not as eventful as Nathan and Myrtle's trip, but still memorable. Nathan is much as I was at the same age, but more successful in his career, so when I speak of his nearly debilitating shyness, I am speaking from experience. I also had to do what needed to be done when I met my "Phoebe" and there were a few people who had to kick my butt a bit to get me to do it.

When I was Nathan's age, I took my grandma on a lengthy road trip, from Kentucky to Colorado and back, because she wanted to visit her son. I learned more about her over the course of those 2400 miles than I had in my entire life. We had wonderful conversations over the miles, and she kicked my butt a couple times. Grandma was a tower of faith and one of the most genuine people you would ever meet. I miss her every day.

I also spent a few years traversing the country hauling freight, so all of the places Nathan and Myrtle stop at are real places I have visited, with the exception of the sports bar late in Chapter 19. I would recommend the others in a heartbeat. The encounters with the Native Americans in Wall and at Wounded Knee are based on real conversations I had while passing through there, but the names have been changed, partly because I can't remember all their names. Sadly, I was not able to make the same lasting impression Myrtle did, but the need is great and I would encourage you to go there if you get the chance and talk to these wonderful people. Your life will never be the same.

The trafficking incident in Wisconsin is loosely based on a similar incident involving a trucker I know. I inserted my characters into his story with very little embellishment. Trafficking is a very real problem in this country. Keep your eyes open. You never know when you might save someone's life.

Thad doesn't own a bait shop in Indiana, but he does have a huge dog and he was in the Marine Corps, and he does have occasional anger issues when playing video games. He's also one of the best friends a guy could have.

ACKNOWLEDGMENTS

No novel is written in a vacuum, and this one was no exception. There are a few people who deserve a thank you, although some of them might not think so. First is my wife, Carren. She is in so many ways my "Phoebe." No man can accomplish anything worthwhile without a good woman behind him. I found myself with more writing time in 2016 due to an auto accident that cut my work hours back, and she stepped up and took up the slack, allowing us to keep the bills paid. It's hard to write without the lights on.

My two best friends in the world, Thad Krahulec and James Partin, who have been rocks of encouragement and have listened to me drone on and on about plot twists and ideas, no doubt to the point of boredom at times. Their positive encouragement took me through first drafts and revisions, and saw me through some periods of self doubt.

And of course this story would not have been possible were it not for my "Myrtle", my late grandmother Susie Owens. She was a never ending source of good advice, faith, encouragement, and steadfastness. So much of what Myrtle told Nathan is taken from conversations I had with her.

Finally, this book would not exist in its current form without the excellent editing services of Carol Tietsworth.

There are countless others who have contributed to this book in one way or another and to attempt to name them all would be an exercise in futility, partly because I'm lousy at remembering names, and even if I could remember them all, the acknowledgements page would be a book in itself.

Edited by Carol Tietsworth

Cover art by Amrita Chowdhury

ABOUT THE AUTHOR

Charles was born in Cincinnati, Ohio and has lived there for the majority of his life, except for a six month stint in Colorado. He currently resides in Cincinnati with his wife and a couple extremely spoiled cats.

Made in the USA
Monee, IL
06 July 2023

38719355R00142